BOOK ONE,
THE BROOM CLOSET STORIES

The Boy Who Couldn't Fly Straight

Archie,

May your life be filled w/ magic!

♡ Jeff

BOOK ONE,
THE BROOM CLOSET STORIES

The Boy Who Couldn't Fly Straight

Jeff Jacobson

NewFreedomPress.com

The Boy Who Couldn't Fly Straight:
A Gay Teen Coming of Age Paranormal Adventure about Witches, Murder, and Gay Teen Love

Book One, The Broom Closet Stories

Jeff Jacobson

NewFreedomPress.com
© 2013, 2017 by Jeff Jacobson

All rights reserved. No part of this book may be reproduced in any form or by any electronic or mechanical means, including information storage and retrieval systems, without written permission from the author, except in the case of a reviewer, who may quote brief passages embodied in critical articles or in a review. Contact the author at jeff@jeffjacobsonworld.com.

This is a work of fiction. Names, characters, places, and incidents are either products of the author's imagination, or if real, are used fictitiously.

Trademarked names appear throughout this book. Rather than use a trademark symbol with every occurrence of a trademarked name, names are used in an editorial fashion, with no intention of infringement of the respective owner's trademark.

ISBN 978-0-9989145-0-3

Contents

    Prologue 3

1 Home Invasion 6

2 A Boy and His Dog 17

3 Cat's Cradle 23

4 Escape 29

5 The Long Drive 34

6 A Homecoming of Sorts 40

7 Answers 43

8 Anger Management Issues 49

9 More Answers 57

10 Witches 62

11 Mexicans 65

12 Midnight Cereal 70

13 Show and Tell 77

14 The Note 82

15 Moving In 87

16 Mandarin 90

17	How Was Your Day? 95
18	The Money Talk 100
19	Carson Park 105
20	The Lunchbox 114
21	Dear Diary 118
22	The Market 123
23	Rubbing It In 128
24	An Echo 134
25	Invitation 141
26	The Accidental Spy 144
27	Dinner Party 149
28	How Do I? 153
29	The Leap 157
30	A Storm Is Coming 167
31	The President 180
32	Alliances 190
33	Just Friends 195
34	The Witch of the House 199
35	Midnight Meeting 205
36	Community in Jeopardy 209

37	The Soccer Field	212
38	Bully, Bully, Bully	217
39	Friendly Decisions	220
40	Malcolm	223
41	Shivering	231
42	The High Dive	234
43	Me Too	241
44	Hen Weixian	245
45	The Warehouse	250
46	Chicken and Egg	256
47	You're Getting Sleepy	260
48	The Best Day Ever	266
49	Home Safety	271
50	The Quick Brown Fox	274

Acknowledgments *282*

About the Author *291*

OTHER BOOKS BY JEFF JACOBSON

The Boy Who Couldn't Fly Home

BOOK ONE,
THE BROOM CLOSET STORIES

The Boy Who Couldn't Fly Straight

Prologue

WEST SEATTLE, LATE OCTOBER — "It's barely ten o'clock!" huffed the girl in the Lolita costume, watching the last of her friends walk away down the street.

"Knock yourself out, Zoey!" Her friend Ross's voice carried to her as the group disappeared around the corner. Hoots and hollers of laughter faded on the cold wind.

She looked up and down the street. A few jack-o'-lanterns still glowed from their porch perches scattered throughout the neighborhood, but most house fronts sat in shadow.

Halloween was over for the year.

Zoey shivered, then sighed. Several fathers handing out candy earlier that evening had stared openly at her before looking away in embarrassment. She wished her friends had agreed to stay out a little longer because she wanted to knock on more doors and watch the men watch her, their lips parted, their faces red.

Stepping past a pile of sodden leaves near a storm drain, she headed over to the neighborhood park to see if any kids were hanging out.

The park was empty.

Using her plastic trick-or-treat bag to wipe away droplets of rain, she sat down on one of the swings, removed a mini Snickers bar from her stash, ripped open the bronze-colored wrapping, and popped the cold square of hard chocolate into her mouth.

Zoey pushed at the dirt with the toe of her Lolita boot, swinging back and forth in a lazy arc. The chains supporting her swing creaked and groaned. In the distance a ferryboat traversing Puget Sound blared its horn, the sound forlorn as it traveled over the water.

Zoey set her bag of candy on the ground, gripped the chains on either side of her, and leaned back, looking up at the bare branches above her head as they rustled in the wind. A slight drizzle spotted her cheeks with moisture. Soon she would be freezing cold and wet. She knew she should go home, but she didn't want the night to be over just yet.

"All dressed up and no place to go?" said a soft female voice near her ear.

Zoey started, nearly losing her grip on the chains, and her teeth clamped down in fright, missing the melting lump of Snickers and biting down hard on her tongue. She barely noticed the taste of blood in her mouth as her head jerked to the side.

A tall, pretty woman who looked to be in her mid-thirties sat on the swing next to her, smiling and flipping her red-orange hair off her shoulders. Her pale skin reminded Zoey of her mother's Peaches-n-Cream Facial Night Milk. She wore a light-colored cowl-neck sweater, and a nearby streetlight cast her eyes in emerald green.

"Wha- what? How did you ...?" Zoey tried to say as she pulled herself up into a sitting position and looked at the woman, her words rushed and breathless.

"How did I get here? Without you seeing? Never you mind." The woman smiled, then reached over and placed her hand on Zoey's black-stockinged leg. "Let's say we have ourselves an adventure!" Her face glowed with the promise of excitement.

Zoey looked at the grand Craftsman homes surrounding the small neighborhood park. All the porch lights were off now. No trick-or-treaters roamed the streets. Not even a late-night dog walker could be seen.

"But I ... I have to ... my parents," she said, already more than a little confused. The smell of wet wood filled her nostrils. The woman's hand was warm on her knee, and Zoey thought the twin green lights of her eyes to be the loveliest thing she had ever seen.

"Oh pooh!" said the woman in the hushed tone of a friendly librarian. "Come on. It'll be fun!"

"But my parents …" said Zoey again, though she wasn't really sure if she said it out loud or only thought the words inside her head. She found herself standing up from the swing and turning with the woman toward the thick woods behind the park, which the grown-ups in the area called "The Green Space" but all the kids referred to as "The Forest."

The tall woman waited near the entrance to The Forest with her hand extended, fingers wiggling in invitation. Zoey walked toward her, stumbling slightly in her new high-heeled boots, thoughts of appreciative glances from older men already forgotten. She glanced over her shoulder one last time at the cozy street with its charming homes, wondering if she were making the right choice, not seeing how the tall woman's eyes flashed with something like hunger.

Zoey placed her fourteen-year-old hand into the palm of the lovely woman, whose skin was warm and soft. Fingers encircled, they passed beneath the conifers dwarfing the entrance into The Forest, the woman's long-legged gait slowing to accommodate Zoey's young wobble.

If you had been standing nearby, you would have heard a whooshing sound as late-night gusts rattled the tree branches overheard. You would have tasted the sea brine, drifting off of the nearby Sound, on your tongue and in your nose. You would have seen the three-quartered moon slip from behind the clouds to silver the surrounding sky before going back into hiding.

But you would not have worried.

This neighborhood had always been a safe place.

CHAPTER 1

Home Invasion

SIERRA NEVADA FOOTHILLS, LATE AUGUST — Charlie Creevey sat in the back seat of Mrs. McMeniman's minivan as she drove along the state road toward his house. His friend, Mike McMeniman, sat next to him. Mike was trying to get his mom to change the music.

"But, Mikey! I love this song. It's so hip-hoppy. I thought you did too!"

"Yeah, Mom, but not every single day on the way home from school! Plus it's embarrassing. Moms aren't supposed to like what their kids listen to. And don't say 'hip-hoppy.'"

"Whaddya think, Charlie? Should I change it or leave it?"

Charlie looked up at Mrs. McMeniman's face in the rearview mirror. He knew she didn't expect an answer. It was just her way of trying to include him in conversation. For nearly four years now, she and his own mother had been trading off driving the boys to and from school. Charlie was well aware of the fact that Mike's mom had long given up expecting him to be social.

He smiled back at her and shrugged his shoulders.

"Charlie, do you know how easy you are? You know how to compromise, something that your friend Michael over there doesn't. That, combined with your blond curls and your hazel eyes, wowee! You'll make some girl very happy one day."

Charlie ducked his head and pretended to look out the window at the passing scenery, wishing he could hide the deep red burn, probably bordering on nuclear, that was invading his cheeks as his shyness spread over him.

Not soon enough, the minivan pulled off the county road and stopped at the head of the lane leading to Charlie's house.

"You sure you don't want me to drive you to the front door?" Mrs. McMeniman asked. It was the same question every time.

"Mom," said Mike, answering for Charlie, "why do you always have to ask him that? You know he likes to walk."

"Thanks for the ride!" Charlie yelled over his shoulder as he slid open the minivan door and stepped onto the dirt. The cool air from inside the van disappeared as he was hit with the intensity of the late afternoon heat.

"Dude, can I call you if I get stuck on geometry?" Mike asked through his open window.

"Yeah. Give me a call," he said, already having slid the car door closed, already walking down the long lane.

He heard the tires spin in the gravel behind him, then the heavy base of the car stereo fading away. And then, nothing.

Or at least, no one's voices. He could hear the dry-paper squeak of the afternoon cicadas, the rustle of brown grasses as a welcome breeze blew across the fruit orchards that sat between the road and his house. Faraway birdsong followed the breeze.

Charlie liked it when it was quiet, when there was no one around. He wasn't put on the spot to have an opinion; he wasn't expected to do or say anything specifically. And most importantly, he did not have to suffer his shyness and blushing in the presence of anyone else.

He looked around at the trees, full of apples and pears needing picking, at the brown hills rolling off in the distance, at the hot sky without a single cloud marring its wide stretch of blue.

This is my home, he thought. This is where I live.

This thought was followed by his own admonishment: Well, no, duh, Sherlock, where else would you live?

And so, a familiar battle began in his head, the one where he chastised himself for his thoughts, his actions, his lack of thoughts and lack of actions, and all he could do was sigh and walk down the long lane, flanked by black walnut trees, to his house.

The walk took about two minutes, and by the time he reached the house, his T-shirt was already stuck to his body in several places, including where his book bag sat against his back, and drops of sweat beaded along his forehead. Summer had been long and hot this year; it would probably be mid-September before the weather began to cool down.

He looked at the house, a rickety but well-cared-for, two-story Victorian with a wide covered porch. There were vegetable and fruit gardens running along the north and east sides, two old rocking chairs on the porch, and a big welcome sign above the door.

Sometimes he laughed when he looked at the sign. His mother, whose hands had burnished the lettering, was nearly as untalkative as he was. He thought the sign should read: "Two Quiet People Inside — Go Away!" He stood still for a moment, letting the breeze cool his neck. Then he waited.

Like clockwork, his mother came around the side of the house, one thin and freckly arm raised to brush the hair, which was a light blonde-red color, from her eyes. In one hand she held a bottle of water out to him. She wore her standard summer uniform: baggy blue shorts, and a ratty T-shirt (today's choice read: "Clarkston Library Renewal Committee: Books Are Life").

"Hi, kiddo."

"Hi, Mom."

"Whew, it's hot. Let's get to it so we can get out of the sun."

Charlie took a long drink from the water bottle, then handed it back to her.

She was already in motion, heading back toward the orchards, speaking to him over her shoulder.

"Just a few things today. Some birds have gotten through the strawberry netting, and if we don't get to the pears and apples, they'll all go to rot."

Charlie sighed. His idea of "just a few things" was always less than hers.

But he didn't mind. He actually liked working with her. She never asked him useless questions and seemed to enjoy the silence and the outdoor smells as much as he did. Despite the heat, it was a nice break from school and everyone talking all day.

In less than an hour they finished their work, replacing the netting and picking enough fruit for pies, sauces, and trades. Plus an afternoon snack. The trees had provided pleasant enough shade.

"Okay, Charlie, why don't you get to your homework while I start dinner?"

He nodded, knowing it wasn't a suggestion as much as the way it would be.

Two hours later, Charlie sat at the dining room table finishing his geometry assignment while his mother cleaned up the dinner plates. When summer gave way to autumn, he would begin to do his homework upstairs in his room. But for now, they both avoided the heat trapped on the upper floor of the old house for as long as they could. When it was really bad, they would even sleep on the porch outside or stretched out on the floor in the living room.

"Wow, it's hot," his mother said for the fourth or fifth time that day, pausing at the kitchen sink to wipe her forehead with the back of her hand.

"I know. When is this heat spell supposed to break?" Charlie asked, looking up from his books and pulling the front of his shirt away from his chest.

"I have no idea, but not soon enough," she said.

"I can't believe school started a full week before Labor Day. It seems so early."

"Who can figure out the ways of the school board," his mother replied with a smile, which quickly turned into a frown. "Sit up straight, Charlie. Slouching like that won't help you do your homework and will only give you a bad back later in life."

Charlie sat up, then watched his mother put away the leftover green beans and the chicken from tonight's dinner. The beans were from their own vegetable patch, and the chicken came from the neighbor's coop, bartered with their tomatoes and corn and some late-summer apricots.

For as long as he could remember, he and his mother had worked their land, just over four acres, tending to the fruit and the vegetables, the mulching and tilling, the planting of seeds. He never used to like the work, though he had done it without much complaint. Recently, however, something had changed. He had begun to enjoy it more, to feel some pride, maybe the same pride he imagined his mother felt, in the harvest they produced.

Tonight, as they ate the food from their own gardens like they had done a million times before, he thought that it had tasted especially fresh.

His mother liked to remind him that they weren't like those New Age types living in their expensive Craftsman homes over in Lark Springs, paying too much for everything to be organic. She had gardened her whole life and thought it was funny that only now people were riding the "new" green movement.

"I'll tell you what 'organic' is," she had said to him more than once as they hauled soil between the vegetable beds. "It's doing things the way they used to do, with hard work and constant vigilance. I don't know why these people think they've discovered something new. You should read the articles they write these days."

His mother not only gardened, she also knew how to keep their old Toyota truck running all year long, repair fences, can fruits and vegetables, lay tile (which she had done in both their upstairs and downstairs bathrooms), trap gophers, make unguents to cure skin rashes and bee stings, and according to some of the women up the lane, make "the best pies and cakes this side of I-don't-know-where."

When people complimented her, she tended to look away or to brush off their words. "Oh, Sue, come on, your apple pie is delicious," she would tut-tut.

As he watched her now, Charlie wondered where she had learned everything. It seemed silly, but he had never really thought about it before. Instead, he took it all for granted. Who had taught her how to fix engines, to fish for trout in the stream, to lay bathroom tiles? She was only thirty-three years old. His own friends' parents, some of whom were nearly twice her age, couldn't do half the stuff that she could. She had taught him a lot of what she could do, but where did she learn it? Even though she was on the board at the library, he doubted all the knowledge came from books.

Snippets of conversations ran through his mind:

"Elizabeth, how did your berries survive this summer? Seems like bugs got to everyone else's."

"Lizzy, that crust of yours. Really. It's the best ever."

"That lotion you made? You'd think Laurel had never even been sunburned!"

Why hadn't he ever wondered about it all before? He supposed he was just used to it. She was constantly in motion, fixing things, fussing over others. He had heard her say more than once to neighbors that she had grown up on a farm in Iowa. Yet when he had asked her over the years about her family, she would say that her parents were killed in a car accident when she was young, that she had been raised by distant relatives, and that she didn't want to talk about it. As for Charlie's father, her pat response was, "The only nice thing about that man was that he brought me you. End of story."

His mother was a person of few words. When she said "end of story," she meant it. Regardless of how much he persisted, he could never get any more information from her about his father. He had long ago given up trying. Instead, he had invented a kind-hearted fisherman with a beard who worked up in Alaska. As he had grown older he had stopped thinking so much about his fictitious father, but every so often he had let his mind wander, trying to guess what his "fisherman dad" might be doing now.

Charlie supposed he had inherited the same tight-lipped habits from his mother, though for her it seemed to come from a natural distrust of anyone other than herself and her son, while for Charlie it was because talking to people, especially adults, could bring on such intense attacks of shyness that he did his best to avoid it all together. Mother and son spent most of their time together without much conversation, which suited them both just fine.

"Son, what are you doing? Don't you have work to do?"

Charlie was startled to see his mother looking at him, dishtowel in hand.

"Oh, um, just thinking. I'm almost done. Besides, it's still birthday week." He pushed a curl out of his eyes only to have it fall back again. It was too hot to keep trying.

Charlie had turned fifteen the previous Thursday, nearly a week into his sophomore year at Clarkston High School, and already his classes were getting challenging. He liked the challenge, liked seeing how quickly and accurately he could learn new things, then apply them to his homework. But the amount of work was proving much greater than it had his freshman year.

His mother had surprised him with two birthday gifts. One was a small stone pendant on a leather necklace. He had never worn anything like it before.

"I thought it would look nice on you. It's supposed to bring good luck," she had shrugged, and Charlie could have sworn she looked a little embarrassed when she said it. "Just keep it on, okay? Who knows? It might work."

His mother was the least superstitious person he knew. She never even went to church like most of the other mothers in town. But he had shrugged and put it on anyway. He liked how it felt around his neck.

The other gift was even more of a surprise.

"For one week, you get to watch as much TV as you want, after you've finished your homework."

He would have been less surprised if she said she had bought him an elephant.

He had pestered her off and on for years about wanting to watch something, anything, after school. True, he liked quiet, but all the other kids at school constantly talked about their favorite TV shows. He didn't want to feel so left out all the time.

True to form, she was always very strict about how much he could watch. That usually only meant on weekends, and that was only after the chores were done. Since there were always a lot of chores to do, it didn't leave much time.

"Besides, we have plenty to do around here to keep us entertained, Charlie."

When he had asked if they could get a DVR so he could at least record shows, she had scoffed at him.

"Spend that kind of money on a device just to make our brains stupid? I don't think so."

He had almost asked her why she had relented, why she had given him this kind of birthday gift. But he had kept his mouth closed. He wasn't used to leniency from her and was worried that if he questioned it she would take it away.

He pondered how to find the value for the hypotenuse of a triangle, figured it out, finished the rest of his geometry, and then closed his books and flipped on the old TV with the remote.

"... not sure as to exactly when it happened," an anchorwoman wearing lots of makeup was saying, "but Sheriff Roger Willard will issue a statement later today. Right now it is estimated that it took place some time late last night.

"Once again, if you are just tuning in, local Forkville High School senior Ted Jones was found badly beaten earlier this morning near the weigh station on State Route 23. The sheriff's department is investigating evidence as to whether or not this could have been a hate crime. Jones had just come out as gay to his football coach and teammates late last week."

A yearbook photo of a young black man in a letterman's jacket appeared on the screen. Forkville was just two towns over from Clarkston, where Charlie and his mother lived.

"We go to Forkville High School with Sky Span correspondent Sharon Thomas. Sharon?"

"Thanks, Gina. Sheriff Willard is at Forkville High right now meeting with the principal and key faculty members, including varsity football coach Hank Bourgette. At this point, no statement from the school has been issued. We will let you know as soon as we have the statement."

"Sharon, can you tell us what the sheriff's department has said so far?"

"Only that an early morning jogger found Jones lying near a dumpster on Route 23. The young man was unconscious, but breathing. After the jogger called 9-1-1, paramedics rushed Jones to Clarkston County Hospital where he is currently in critical condition.

"Witnesses found various anti-gay messages spray-painted on a dumpster near where the jogger found Jones. The sheriff's office has not confirmed if the messages were left by those who attacked the young man or even how long they had been there."

"Thank you, Sharon. And will the ..."

The television screen went black. Charlie blinked, then saw his mother standing next to him, her arm stretched toward the TV, remote in hand.

"Of all the things to have happened. And in Forkville, nonetheless," she said, harrumphing as she set the remote down on the table and went back into the kitchen saying, "Finish your homework" over her shoulder.

Charlie forgot to remind his mother that it was birthday week and that he could still watch TV.

Instead he sat very still, shocked in a way he didn't understand.

What had his mother meant when she had said, "Of all the things to have happened." Was she referring to the high school football player who came out as gay? Or to the people who might have beaten him up for it?

There was something else besides the shock, something deeper. Something that Charlie did his best to push aside even though it seemed to be getting more and more difficult to do these days. The news story, and his mother's reaction, had caught him off guard, and so for a few moments renegade thoughts and mental pictures coursed through his head, unchecked.

Was Ted Jones really gay?

Could a football player really be gay?

Were you gay if you sometimes only thought about boys but never did anything about it?

Were you gay if you'd never done anything with anybody, boy or girl, so how could you know?

Images:

Of Brian McGregor and Roddy Espinoza, upperclassman athletes at school. All the girls had crushes on them. Brian's thick shoulders and strong face, Roddy's dimpled smile and dark skin. Charlie felt his cheeks flushed with heat as mental snapshots of the two boys flooded his mind.

Of boys on his soccer team when he was little, of how Charlie wanted to be near some of them, wanted to sit next to them, to touch their messy hair, to hear their voices.

Of scenes in movies or TV shows where a boy or a man was teased for being "too girlie," "too femmy," or simply "a faggot."

Of Ted Jones's high school yearbook photo, his hopeful smile, wearing a letterman's jacket, not looking like someone who could or should be beaten up and left on the side of the road.

Charlie shook his head and looked around desperately for something to distract him.

Homework! He had some Spanish sentences to compose as well as a biology lab write-up to do. It was still hot downstairs, so upstairs would be sweltering. He might as well stay put and finish it all right where he was. His bedroom would be an oven right now.

Aware that the last wisps of troubling thoughts were leaving his head, he was surprised to hear a strange sound coming from the kitchen. He looked up to find his mother staring out the window over the sink with the big green salad bowl in her hands, the blank look on her face much like the look he must have had only moments before.

She seemed to be mumbling something.

"Mom, you okay?"

"What?" she asked, startled, looking over at him as if she had forgotten he was there. "Oh, I'm fine. Get back to work, I just ... no!"

His mother's final word was a scream. Her hands flew to her face, dropping the heavy glass bowl. Her uncharacteristic yell made Charlie jump in his chair, and he watched as the bowl hit the kitchen counter, then tumbled to the floor and shattered, sending small pieces of glass everywhere. One of them must have hit her sandaled foot, for a tiny drop of blood appeared above her ankle and formed a red track as it slid toward her heel.

"Mom? What … what happened? What are you doing?" He slid his chair back and came over to help her clean up the mess.

"Oh, Charlie, jeez, it's nothing, really, just clumsy I guess. Watch your feet, honey. There's glass everywhere. I … no-no-no-no-no-no-no!" she yelled again from her squatting position, head jerking in the direction of the living room.

Charlie turned just in time to see the living room window explode in a shower of glass. Tiny shards caught the light of the setting sun as if someone had thrown a bag of diamonds into the air.

The muzzle and forepaws of a huge dog flew through the broken window toward them. Charlie watched as the rest of its body came through the frame and landed on the floor amidst the broken glass.

"No, you can't, you can't!" his mother screamed.

The dog sat on its haunches staring at the two of them.

CHAPTER 2

A Boy and His Dog

"GET OUT OF HERE! You can't be here!" his mother continued screaming.

Frozen in place, Charlie stared at the dog. He simply couldn't make sense of anything, of the way his mother seemed to know that something was about to happen, how the window exploded, that a huge German shepherd sat on their living room floor surrounded by broken glass and was now staring at them.

And then a most unexpected impossible thing happened.

In the silence following his mother's screams, the dog opened its maw and spoke.

"Give me the boy, Elizabeth," it said in a deep gargled voice. "Give me the boy, and no one will get hurt."

Charlie felt what must be his sanity liquefy in his brain and drain down the back of his neck. He could feel his grasp on anything resembling reality loosen. He simply could not fathom that a dog was talking to his mother.

He felt himself yanked off his feet and dragged backwards into the kitchen.

"No!" his mother yelled, hands gripping his shoulders. "You cannot be here. Get out!"

Charlie's bare feet slid over the floor, scraping across the green shards of the broken salad bowl. There was so much glass.

His mother shoved him behind her. The kitchen counter slammed into his back knocking him out of his stupor. He wrapped his arms around her thin frame and peered out from behind her T-shirt, the smell of fabric softener and her sweat strong in his nose.

The dog rose from its sitting position and walked a few steps toward them.

"Elizabeth," it said, its ragged dog voice filled with chiding. "Come now, you are not in charge here anymore. You never were. Now just give me the boy before I have to do something drastic."

Charlie began to shake. He could smell the musk from the dog as it approached. It stepped onto the linoleum of the kitchen floor. The animal was now just five feet away. It stopped and looked at his mother, its gray eyes flat, its tongue lolling out the side of its mouth, its teeth yellow and sharp.

How could this be happening?

"Do not take another step!" his mother said, the threat in her voice unmistakable.

"Or what? You'll bake something? You'll come at me with a rolling pin? Please, Elizabeth, we both know you're nothing more than a kitchen witch these days. You …"

His mother jerked into action. Extending her arms to either side of her body, she brought them together and slapped her hands against each other creating a loud clap. A flash of white light rippled through the air like a heat wave shooting from her hands toward the dog, while Charlie clung to her hips and peered from her side.

As soon as the rippled light hit the animal, it skidded backwards across the floor to the far wall of the dining room, its paws scrambling for traction, first on the linoleum, and then on the carpet. It struck the wall with a thud and a yelp.

The light vanished, and Charlie's mother slumped back against him, her bird-thin spine rising and falling as she tried to catch her breath, her shoulders blocking Charlie's view.

When Charlie peeked around his mother at the wall, the dog was gone. In its place was a tall blond man, dressed in a loose white shirt and dark pants, a small cut on his chin bleeding red.

Where had the dog run to? Where did the man come from? How did ...

"Goddamn it, woman, I warned you. You didn't have to do it this way. But if you insist," the man said in a soft, and softly dangerous, voice.

He walked toward them again, glass crunching under his tall black boots.

His mother reached behind Charlie and opened one of the kitchen drawers, not taking her eyes off of the man's face.

"Oh what, Elizabeth? Looking for a seed packet? Or maybe a Chinese takeout menu? What could you possibly have in there that could help?" He sounded like a character in a movie, someone arrogant and snide, someone who looked down on everyone around him.

Charlie didn't know what to do. His mother's body was pressed tightly against him trapping him against the counter. The drawer's corner had banged against his right hip when she yanked it open. He could hear the contents sliding around as her hand fumbled about. She never took her eyes off the man.

Her hand came forward, and Charlie saw that she held a small brown stone pendant attached to a black leather strap. It looked like a duplicate of the pendant she gave him for his birthday.

His mother thrust the pendant in front of her and began to mumble something. Charlie couldn't make out the words. A soft orange glow appeared. Instead of flashing forward like the wave from his mother's hands had done, it grew warmly around them the way a candle flame slowly brightens the air around it. It drifted back over his mother's arm, over her head. Charlie felt a soft warmth wash over him as the light spread down over his body extending all the way to the floor. It was as if he had walked under a heat lamp.

"Wha- ... what is happening?" he whispered into his mother's shirt. Where did these lights come from? How could a dog talk? What was the man doing?

"I'd laugh if you weren't pissing me off so much, Elizabeth. Now it's time to take a lesson from my class. Ready for some schooling?"

he said, his lips curling back in a feral smile. His face was lean and proud, sullied with cruelty.

The man pulled his right arm back. Charlie watched as it shot forward in a strong, solid punch. The fist stopped just short of his mother's face, blocked by the barrier of the orange light.

But his mother's head jerked backwards as if she had been struck. The orange light faded for moment before resuming its glow.

The man gritted his teeth and snarled at them, a sound from deep in his throat that shook Charlie with its nearness and inhuman quality.

He punched at Charlie's mother again, this time a jab at her chest. She grunted, and the light flickered. Her body recoiled against Charlie.

"I can do this all night, my dear," the man said, taking a deep breath. "I've got you cornered in your ugly little kitchen. There's nowhere for you to go now, is there? You're trapped. Is that what you want? For me to do this all night?"

His mother didn't answer. She lifted her face from her chest and stared at the man. The right side of her profile showed a sharp cheekbone, lips parted and quivering, a flared nostril, a hazel eye burning with defiance.

The man laughed again, then swiveled his hips. His fist shot upwards in a powerful uppercut, his punch stopped by the orange glow just short of her chin. But her head flew backwards again, smacking hard on the top of Charlie's scalp, a deep grunt escaping from her mouth.

"Give …" the man said as his fist made contact with the light.

"Me …" he said again, standing above her, this time bringing his left arm forward into an extended jab near his mother's shoulder.

"The …" he dropped his right arm with a boxer's speed, punching at the protective light, right in the center of his mother's gut. She made a breathy oomph sound and bent over. Charlie sucked in his stomach as his entire upper body was now exposed to the man and his fists.

"Boy!" the man yelled, taking advantage of her bent-over position to slam his fist upwards into the dim glow striking her directly in the chin and lifting her up off her feet.

"Ungh!" she groaned, her legs giving out when she landed. Charlie grabbed her waist at the last minute, keeping her from falling to the floor.

"Mom!" Charlie wailed.

"Want me to keep doing this, boy?" The man turned his gray eyes on Charlie. "Want me to take your mother out? I'll kill her, you know. I will. You could make this a lot easier on her by coming to me. Do it now, boy, and I'll stop." His voice sounded inviting, gentler, as if what he offered was simply a really good idea.

The violence of the assaults on his mother had deadened him. He wanted to run, to hide, even though there was nowhere to go. But the words the man uttered pulled at him, yanked him back into the kitchen and the situation. He stopped thinking about the impossibility of a talking dog transforming into a man, of his mother's strange ability to make waves of light from her clapping hands, of the orange glow. He saw the fists, saw the look of cruelty and murder in the man's face.

Charlie had never witnessed someone so enraged that he would kill another human being. Nonetheless, he knew beyond a shadow of a doubt that the man would stop at nothing and would probably enjoy beating his mother to death. The orange light was so dim Charlie could barely feel its warmth anymore. Somehow it had protected his mother from the punches even though she was hurt. But he knew that the glow would soon fade away to nothing.

The thought caused electric wiggling sensations all across Charlie's flesh. Without knowing what he was doing, he grabbed at the pendant around his neck, the partner to the one that his mother had retrieved from the kitchen drawer.

The mind-numbing terror vanished from his chest, replaced by a deep and unfamiliar fury. How dare this Dog Man break into their home and attack his mother? How dare he threaten their life out here in the countryside?

The fury seemed to descend upon him from his scalp while at the same time rise up from the floor into the bottoms of his feet. The two forces raced toward each other, meeting at the epicenter of his chest.

Charlie's left arm, seeming to act of its own accord, shot outward while his right arm held his mother against him to keep her from falling to the floor. The man reared back, preparing to deliver the next, possibly fatal, blow. The orange glow was completely gone now, and Charlie knew his mother couldn't survive another hit.

The fury narrowed and focused in his chest. Without knowing quite how, he let it rise into his voice.

"No!" he bellowed, and more orange light began to pour forth, this time from the pendant in his own hand.

Dog Man's fist struck his orange light. This time his mother's body did not shudder. Somehow the pendant's light held firm.

"No!" he yelled again, his voice stronger. The light barrier broadened and pushed outward, forcing the man backwards a step as if Charlie had shoved him in the chest.

He knew he couldn't stop now. He had to finish this.

Rage arose, red and fierce, taking over his mind, filling him with a potency he had never known before. He could tell that it was on the verge of exploding from him.

"No!" Charlie screamed. His voice echoed with a metallic sound, amplifying around the room and ricocheting off the walls. He felt the heat in his chest pour forth. The light from the pendant narrowed into a thin beam and shot at the man, who had barely regained his footing.

The beam of light lifted the man clear off the ground and tossed him high in the air, slamming his back up against the ceiling. He barely missed the overhead lamp that hung over the small table where Charlie's unfinished homework sat. Puffs of dust and plaster particles sprinkled down like snow. Charlie and his mother slid down onto the floor together, their legs jellied and weak, eyes locked on the face of the man, now unconscious, glued to the ceiling above them.

CHAPTER 3

Cat's Cradle

CHARLIE DIDN'T KNOW HOW long he sat slumped against the counter on the kitchen floor. His mother was no longer beside him. He could hear her footsteps upstairs as she rummaged through closets and crossed again and again over the runner in the narrow second-floor hallway.

The red-hot rage had left his chest. He felt empty. Empty of energy, empty of thought. He stared at the thousands of pieces of glass scattered about the floor. The harsh light from the dining room's lamp turned each one into a spark of fire. If he moved his head back and forth, the sparks moved. Like the lights on a Christmas tree. Like the light above his head ...

He wouldn't let himself look up though he couldn't quite remember why. There was something there he didn't want to see. He kept his eyes on the glass and the tiny light sparkling within each piece.

"The light that shines within," he said out loud. The refrain from a pop song was stuck in his head. It felt good to look at the glass and to let the words of the song float through his mind. Nothing else to do. Nothing really, but ...

"Charlie!" his mother called from the doorway into the kitchen. He flinched and bumped his head against the rim of the counter. "I said, 'Get up!' I need your help!"

He looked at her. Most of her hair had come loose from the rubber band tie she always wore. There were stains (sweat? blood?) on her

T-shirt. One of her cheeks was swollen and waxy. She had two of his large duffel bags, one slung over her shoulder and the other in her left hand. In her right hand she held a small stepladder.

"Charlie! Get up!" she yelled. His legs began moving, and he stood up slowly, feeling woozy.

Don't look at the ceiling, don't look at the ceiling … he said to himself, still not remembering why he shouldn't. There was something …

His mother dropped the bags on the floor and scooted the stepladder over near the dining room table. She began to climb up the steps, a look of hard determination in her eyes. He had seen that same look when she set traps for gophers in the garden.

He watched her climb and looked up. A man was pressed against the ceiling.

How could a man be pressed against the ceiling as if he were stuck there? As if the room had flipped and he were lying on the ground? But if he were lying on the ground, then Charlie must be …

A foggy image pushed through the back of his mind. A large German shepherd sitting on the kitchen floor, glass exploding, punches.

"Wait!" he yelled.

His mother stopped halfway up the stepladder. Her arm was stretched out toward the man's face. In her hand was something small and clear.

"Wait, he'll, he'll …" Charlie couldn't finish the sentence. Without warning, he burst into tears. His body began to shake as if it were the middle of winter and he were standing outside in the snow wearing summer clothes.

"It's okay, Charlie," his mother said, her voice soft. "It's okay." Then she resumed her task.

Through his tears he watched as she held the small thing just below Dog Man's chin, then brushed it against his face. It was a container made of glass or plastic. Charlie saw a tiny bead of red blood brush against the lip of the container and slide down into it.

"Gotcha," said his mother, using her gopher-trapping voice. She climbed back down the stepladder, set the container on the table, then squatted on the kitchen floor, rummaging through one of the duffel bags.

"Mom," Charlie whined.

"Now where is that thing? It was just here a minute ago." The freckles on her pale forearms stood out under the harsh kitchen lighting.

"Mom!" Charlie said again more loudly. His chest was rising and falling so fast he wondered if he was going to have a heart attack.

She kept searching through the bag.

"Mom!"

His mother's head jerked up from where she sat squatting on the kitchen floor.

"What? Charlie, I'm right here. You don't have to yell." She spoke quietly. As if they were arguing about tomato vines. As if things were normal.

"Mom! What ... what is ... what is all this? Wha- ... what happened? I don't ..."

"Charlie, listen to me. There isn't time for this, okay? There just isn't time. I need you to stay put while I finish some things, and then we'll go."

"Go? Go where? Go where?" He yelled again. He didn't know why he was yelling. He wasn't thinking about her answers or what they meant. He just grabbed on to her words and shouted them because it was the easiest thing to do.

She ignored him, and his shouting faded as he got lost in watching her movements, forgetting what his questions had been.

"Ah-ha!" his mother said as she removed from the bag one of the balls of twine they used to tie back bean stalks.

"Now," she said to herself. "Let's see if I remember how to do this ..."

She walked over to the kitchen counter and rummaged through the same drawer where she had found the pendant. Pulling out a pair of scissors, she walked back to the duffel bags. The kitchen light flashed along the steel of the scissors' blades. Part of Charlie was terrified that his mother was going to climb back up the stepladder and stab Dog Man in the gut. Another newer part of him wanted her to before the man could wake up and hurt them again.

Instead, she picked up the ball of twine and cut about a three-foot length. She set the scissors down, then began wrapping the twine around her fingers.

"I think if I just …" she muttered to herself. He watched as she formed shapes around her hands. It looked like a complex version of cat's cradle.

"Oh, shoot, I forgot to grab the … Charlie, hand me that little vial."

He looked at her. He couldn't understand what she said. Did he even know what the word "vile" meant? Wasn't it something bad, something evil, something with a rotten smell?

"The glass vial on the table! Over there!" she said, motioning with her hands now bound together in twine.

He saw the small container with the blood in it. He didn't want to touch it. But he was afraid his mother would yell again. He walked over, picked it up, and tried to put it in her hands.

"No, Charlie, I'm sorry. I didn't do this right. You'll have to pour the, the uh, blood, out onto my hands."

He began to cry again, only this time with snot coming out of his nose. He felt ashamed. He couldn't stop his shoulders from shaking.

"It's okay, honey, it's okay, you can do it," she said, her lips forming into a smile even while her eyes looked desperate. "Just tip it over a little bit. Come on now. Everything's going to be all right." Charlie could hear the growing urgency in her voice.

His hands shook, and his chest kept heaving while he blubbered, but he managed to tilt the vial so that its open mouth faced downwards. The blood started to move slowly. He thought of a ketchup bottle as he watched the smear of red slide along the side of the small glass container. His stomach lurched, and for a split second he thought he was going to throw up.

"That's right, that's it." He hated her fake soothing right then, hated what she was making him do. He wanted to yell, he wanted to hit her. He wanted to run outside.

"Just a little more," she said. A groan came from somewhere above them, and Charlie looked up. Dog Man's lips moved, as if he were trying to say something.

"Charlie! Don't look at him! Look at me! Charlie!" his mother yelled, hard and sharp.

His eyes snapped back to her. Now she was all business.

"Do not look away. Look at me and just do as I say. That's all you have to do. Nod if you understand!"

He nodded. Looking at her was the sanest thing for him to do. He knew her face, knew the lines along her mouth, the pale red hair and the wide brown eyes. She had always been skinny, and even though people had teased her, he liked her thinness, liked how he could see the bones in her cheeks. Even today, with the yellow bruises forming, he liked her face, how normal and close it was to him. It was familiar, and it gave him something to focus on.

"Good," she continued. "Now tip that vial over again."

He hadn't realized that he had brought it upright. He tipped it over, and once again the blood slid toward the opening of the container. He could hear raspy breathing but didn't know if it was his or his mother's. Or maybe …

"Just listen to my voice, Charlie, that's it. Focus on my voice."

He focused on her voice, which seemed like a much better idea than thinking too much about what he was doing.

A small drop of blood, barely bigger than a pinprick, swelled onto the lip of the vial.

His mother brought her hands up so that a small section of the twine touched the blood. Charlie watched as the red bead sank into the twine, as if the binding material were thirsty.

"A quicker picker-upper," Charlie said. He didn't know why he had said it.

"What? Oh, oh yes, that's right, a quicker picker-upper," his mother said, and laughed a little. "That's good Charlie, yes, that's right. Now just give me a moment, okay? I have to concentrate."

The lines deepened on her forehead. She moved her mouth, but Charlie couldn't make out the words, just an odd windy sound. The word "susurration" came to mind. He remembered it from a seventh-grade vocabulary quiz four years ago. He kept his eyes locked on his mother's face, her lips moving quickly, her eyes staring hard at her hands.

"Damn it," she muttered. He wasn't sure if he had ever heard her cuss before. He found it oddly thrilling.

"Damn it," he said back.

"Charlie, don't use that word. It's not polite."

Her lips began moving again. This time the words seemed thicker, multilayered, as if someone standing just behind her were whispering the same sounds. He shivered.

She did this for another minute or so and then stopped.

"Okay, okay. I think that might do it. I think ..." she said, smiling. Then she looked up, and her face became stern again. "Gosh, I don't know. I'm not sure."

She moved her fingers, releasing them from the twine.

"Well, I don't know. But here goes," she said. She lowered her hands below her waist, then tossed them up into the air. The twine sailed upwards and hit Dog Man, squarely in the middle of his chest.

His mother yelled something that sounded like "Moogy woogy!"

The bunch of twine stuck to the man's chest instead of falling back down. Charlie heard a whipping sound as the twine stretched out and grew longer and thicker, turning into heavy rope, wrapping itself around the man's belly, his arms and legs, even his feet.

"Oh goody!" his mother clapped, laughing like a little girl at a piñata party. "It worked!"

With that, there was a cracking sound, and the man's barely breathing body broke loose from the ceiling and came crashing down toward them. His mother grabbed Charlie around the waist as she dove out of the way. Together they fell to the kitchen floor. The strong scent of damp lumber filled the kitchen.

They screamed together for quite some time.

CHAPTER 4

Escape

THE BLACK NIGHT SPED past them as his mother ground the gears of their old Toyota truck and they careened along the mountain road. The windows were rolled down. The breeze felt good on Charlie's face, which was still swollen from crying.

He looked over at his mother. There was more of that same steel set of determination in her jaw and chin. Thin strips of hair whipped around her face. Occasionally she would let go of the steering wheel with one hand to tuck the strands behind her ear, which never stayed in place very long.

The road curved out of sight ahead of them. His mother yanked at the gearshift on the floor, pushing them down into a lower gear.

Just a few months back she had begun to explain driving to him, how in a manual transmission vehicle like the Toyota truck, the driver needed to be aware of how much power was needed. He was fifteen years old and would be getting his driver's permit soon.

"Are you going up a hill?" she had asked. "If so, you'll need a lower gear for more power. Are you driving on a flat surface and needing lots of speed, like on a freeway? Then you'll need a higher gear."

It had made sense to him back then. She had even let him drive a bit along the dirt road leading to their house. Only with her in the cab, of course. It had been bumpy. He hadn't known how to manage the clutch and gas pedals at the same time, let alone the brakes. They had lurched and stopped, lurched and stopped, five times before she had said that the engine needed a break. She had seemed pleased with his progress though.

Tonight, none of it made sense. He couldn't remember what anything meant. The whole idea of knowing what you needed in order to maneuver around the road up ahead, a road you couldn't even see, seemed impossible to Charlie. How could you do that? How could you know what you would need around the corner?

How could you know anything, when a dog crashes through your living room window and starts talking …

He tried to erase the image from his mind by looking down at his mother's hand. It just seemed to know when to grab the gearshift. It was dark, so he couldn't see her feet, but he knew they were moving down below, pressing and releasing pedals, pumping on them like an old church organ. She could do things, his mother. She could fix fences and repair cars, make unguents …

"Mom," he said.

She kept looking straight ahead, watching the road, eyes fixed and hard.

"Mom?" He tried to keep the sound of a whine from his throat.

"What, honey?"

"Mom, what, what was that? What ha- … what happened back there?"

"Not now, Charlie. I have to concentrate. We …"

"Please, Mom? I need to know!"

"Charlie, I have to get us out of here. We'll talk about this later."

"But you said that back at home! You already said 'not now!' When will it be now? When?" He started crying again. He sounded like a belligerent child who just kept complaining and crying. He knew they were in danger, and he knew his mother was doing her best. He was trying to hold on to reality even though reality seemed to be at best a moving target. His mother obviously had answers, and if she would only give him some, maybe he could hang on for a little bit longer.

He heard himself scream, "If you don't tell me what the hell is going on, I'll open the goddamn door and jump out!"

The truck skidded across the gravel on the road's shoulder before coming to a stop. The only sound was the wind through the windows, and the strange echo of Charlie's voice floating through the air. He had never yelled like that in front of his mother before, and he had definitely never said "goddamn" in her presence. He worried suddenly that she was going to ground him.

When he turned to face her, his worry changed to fright. Her eyes were pinpoints, her lips were pulled back, exposing pink gums and clenched teeth. She didn't look like she was going to ground him anymore. She looked like she was going to eat him alive, right there on the side of the road, on a warm evening in late August, in the foothills of Northern California. All in one big gulp. And no one would ever know.

"You want me to tell you what's going on?" she said, her voice low and frightening. "You want me to let you know about all this, Charlie? Is that it? Do you really want to know?"

"Ye- … yes," he stuttered, his voice having lost its conviction.

"Well then, I'll tell you. I'll tell you some things, Charlie. So listen up. I have been protecting you for quite some time now, and apparently I have failed at my job. When you needed protection the most, they came and found us, they broke in to our home as simply as if they just turned the goddamn door knob and walked in! As if they were invited over for potluck!"

She was yelling now. Spittle flew from her mouth and hit him in the chin. He was too transfixed to wipe it off.

"I thought I had what it takes. All this time I told myself that it was working, that I could leave Seattle and hide out with you in the foothills of the Sierras," she said, gesturing out the window as if he had forgotten where they were.

Seattle? What did Seattle have to do with anything?

"But no! They found us. They came and found us, and now I don't know what to do. All my good planning out the window, like that!" She screamed. The fury and fear on her breath had a smell to it, like burning grass.

She stopped, inhaling deeply. Charlie breathed in too. In spite of the rage spewing forth from this normally quiet controlled woman, her words were giving him something to hold on to. He didn't want her to stop.

"But, Mom … who? Who are they? Who are these people?"

"You want to know who they are, Charlie? I'll tell you!" she yelled.

He had never seen his mother so angry before, so out of control. It was odd, and oddly thrilling, even if everything about this night already filled him with terror.

"Those stupid, stupid people, out there," she gestured out the window again, "Those everyday people who worry about their mortgages and their promotions, how much foundation they can put on their faces to hide their pimples, what kind of laundry detergent to use. They tell their children things, they lie, they tell them to eat all the food on their plates or they'll starve, to finish their homework or they'll grow up and be poor, that if they stay out late they'll get eaten by the boogeyman! As if they know anything about anything!"

She breathed in, her throat making a high-pitched choking sound. Charlie watched as her eyes creased shut, saw her rage melt, saw sadness wash over her face the way rainstorms washed over their orchards from the east.

"They don't know, Charlie, those stupid, ignorant parents out there. They just don't."

He was getting confused. She kept talking about they and them. Were they the stupid people, or the ones who had come and found them in their house tonight?

"They just don't know," she repeated. Then she turned her head and dropped it onto the steering wheel. She began to sob.

He wanted to comfort her, to rub her back and say, "There, there," the way she had to him a million times. But he was afraid that if he did, she would stop talking. That, and the fact that they seemed well beyond comfort tonight, kept him from doing or saying anything.

She sat up, took a breath, and then looked out the window. "Charlie, those parents out there tell their kids all sorts of things about the dark just to get them to do what they're supposed to do. But they don't believe any of it."

She looked over her shoulder, out over the bed of the truck. Chills spilled over Charlie's scalp and neck. Was something back there? Was something coming at them? Right now?

"Charlie," she leaned in to him, her face close and startling, "things really do go bump in the night. There are things out there that make the boogeyman look like, like, like Saturday morning cartoons!"

His stomach flipped. He wanted to roll up the windows and beg her to keep driving, just so that whatever might be out there couldn't catch them.

"There are things out there that, that … oh God, that kill, Charlie. And you just can't protect yourself, or your children, from them. You just can't!"

She slammed her hands down hard on the truck's dashboard, and even though he watched her do it, he still jumped at the sound it made.

She took a deep breath.

"Come on, Liz. Come on! Keep moving, keep …" She was muttering to herself.

Then she turned to him. And she looked like his mother again, or at least a close facsimile of his mother.

"I won't say any more, Charlie. So don't ask me. I'm sorry that you're involved in this mess. I know you think you should know more. You'll just have to be satisfied with what I've told you already, which is probably too much.

"But believe you me, I am trying to get us out of here. So no more talking. I have to drive. Please buckle your seatbelt. And stop using such profane language. Even at a time like this, we can still be civil."

He checked his seatbelt, which was not unbuckled, then nodded. Now didn't seem to be the right time to point out that she had used some not-so-civil language herself several times today.

Charlie rested his head against the window while his mother started the engine, then checked over her shoulder to see if the road was empty. She flipped on her turn indicator, which made no sense to Charlie, then pulled out onto the road and headed north.

CHAPTER 5

The Long Drive

ON THE TWO-DAY DRIVE to Seattle, he barely thought about what his mother had told him. He wondered why he didn't try to piece everything together. After all, it was just his silent mother and the endless stretch of freeway. Not that he could have figured everything out. Occasional images flashed through his mind: broken glass, his mother's head jerking back, yellow glowing light. But each time they progressed to a huge German shepherd talking to them or a strange man glued to the ceiling in their kitchen, he drove the images from his mind.

He mostly slept, his head against the window. He was comfortable at night because they always kept blankets in the back of the car and the heater worked. But the daytime was hot. There was no air-conditioner in the Toyota, and even with the windows down, the truck's cab grew miserable by midmorning.

At one point, his mother wiped the sweaty curls from his brow. He usually flinched away when she did that because he hated his hair and how it stood up in places instead of lying flat against his scalp like everyone else's.

"Remember how Ramey at the Fabric Mart used to say she'd pay gobs of money to have your hair? 'All those blond curls, it's not fair that you have them and I don't!'" She laughed, mimicking Ramey's gurgling old-lady voice.

This time he didn't pull away from her touch. It felt so normal, so regular, that for just one moment he could pretend they were out running errands together and not escaping from talking dogs, headed who knew where.

* * *

Other than the long stretch of road and the sleeping, there were really only two incidents that stood out to him.

The first came when they were somewhere in southern Oregon. His mother pulled off of Interstate 5 in the early morning saying that she couldn't drive anymore. She was too tired and didn't want to fall asleep at the wheel and get them killed. She pulled into the parking lot of a motel and paid for a room with two double beds. She used a passport as ID and pulled bills from a wad of cash, the likes of which he had never seen before. He had trouble picturing his mother as someone with lots of cash and a passport, let alone someone who accepts the price given by a motel front desk clerk. She usually haggled for everything. But he was too tired to ask her about the money. He simply let her steer him toward their room and didn't even resist when she pulled off his shoes after he had thrown himself flat on his bed.

It was bright and shiny in their room when he awoke the next day.

"Hey, kiddo, you up?" his mother asked him. She sat on a vinyl chair near the window, shades drawn, her legs crossed, dressed in a clean T-shirt and shorts. As the sleepiness left his eyes, he saw that the yellow bruise on her cheekbone had purpled, and there were dark spots along her bare left arm, like stones across a small creek.

"Why don't you hop in the shower, then you and I can get some pancakes at the diner across the way?" Her voice was cheerful. She was trying to act as if all of this were normal, as if they always stayed in roadside motels and ate at diners.

The hot water felt good. He had wanted to stay in the shower a good long time, letting the pressure of the water beat at him and melt away the images crowding his head for attention. But she had knocked on the door and told him to hurry up.

Leaving the bathroom, he saw that she had laid clean clothes out for him like it was his first day of kindergarten.

"Hope you're fine with what I chose," she chirped.

It wasn't until they walked into the diner, his mother wearing a strange pair of sunglasses which made her look like a movie star avoiding paparazzi, that he realized how hungry he was.

They sat at the counter on sticky round stools and ate plates of eggs and pancakes. For once she said nothing about the amount of butter and syrup he used; she ate nearly as much as he did.

When the waitress refilled their coffee cups, she paused and looked at his mother's face.

"You, uh, you all right dear?"

"We're fine. Yes, we're fine. Thank you," his mother said, ducking her head.

"Say, I might be able to help a bit. You know, help?" the waitress replied. She looked to be about fifty, and her hair was a bright pink color. Her name tag read, "Darlean."

His mother looked up from the rim of her coffee mug. She stared at the woman for a long time.

"Oh. Um … how?"

"Meet me out in the parking lot in about ten minutes," she whispered. "Which one's yours?"

"The blue Toyota pickup, California plates."

* * *

They went outside, the sun already hot, and watched as Darlean walked out from the side of the building yelling over her shoulder, "Well, she'll have to cover for a moment, Monty. For Christ's sake!"

She walked over to them. The front of her apron was spotted with coffee.

"Honey, do you …?"

"It was just so awful," his mother started in, her voice nothing like it had been. She started to cry.

"Oh, honey, come here," Darlean cooed, grabbing at his mother. She wrapped her arms around her and held her tightly, while his mother fell apart.

Charlie stared at them.

Since when did his mother hug strangers?

When she came up for air, both of the women looked over at him.

"He doesn't know," his mother said.

Darlean nodded. "Let's do this in the cab of your truck."

Then she turned to him and said, "You wait right there, okay?" as if he were a toddler.

The two women climbed inside the truck. They rummaged around for a bit. He couldn't tell what they were doing. Then they turned their heads toward the front of the truck, closed their eyes, and began to move their lips. Were they praying? Charlie's mother had never prayed before. She refused to go to church but had always told Charlie he could go if he wanted to.

He felt the hairs prickle along the back of his neck. And it seemed like he could hear the whisper of what they were saying. Just like back home when his mother had been whispering while on the stepladder, it seemed like there were more people talking, maybe behind him or surrounding the cab. He looked over his shoulder, suddenly sure he would see a small crowd standing near him. No one was there.

The doors to the cab opened up and they both got out, Darlean smoothing down her apron.

"That should help some, honey. You okay to keep driving?"

"Yes, yes. Thank you so much. Thank you. How can I …?"

Darlean waved her hands in front of her. "Don't even think about it, Liz. We all gotta stick together in this world, don't we?"

Then she looked him square in the eye and said, "You take good care of yourself, boy. Take really, really good care of yourself, okay?"

He nodded, not knowing what he was agreeing to.

* * *

The second incident occurred south of Portland. His mother asked him if he was hungry, then pulled off the freeway exit without waiting for a response.

"Fruit stands," she said, reading a hand-painted roadside sign, "God, that sounds good."

The stand itself was more of a Quonset hut resting in a graveled lot a couple hundred yards from the interstate. A few crates of peaches, apples, and berries sat near the entrance.

His mother's enthusiasm dwindled, replaced by her true gardening spirit.

"Half the fruit's too early. The rest will be mushy this late in the season."

Inside were racks of postcards, dried fruit, chocolate bars, video games. There was a whole cold section with ice cream, beer, and energy drinks.

Charlie took advantage of their odd traveling situation to choose whatever he wanted: an apple, a prepackaged turkey sandwich, and a large bottle of soda. His mother said nothing about the amount of sugar in the bottle or the fact that they both knew how to make better drinks at home.

She chose a small carton of blueberries, a bottle of water, and the same kind of sandwich. They walked to the checkout stand together. An old man sat at the register, eyes round as owls behind the thick lenses of his glasses. Tufts of gray hair stood up from his head like a kewpie doll, and the buttons of his light-blue work shirt were opened against the day's heat.

"Is that all for you?" he asked them as his mother fished for money in her purse.

Before she could answer, the man made a grunting noise and bent over. He sat up, holding the biggest hunting knife Charlie had ever seen.

"You! Get out of my store. Get out of here before I gut you!" he yelled. Both of them stood frozen to their spot. Charlie heard his mother's quiet intake of breath.

"What? But we're not, we're not doing anything to ..." she stammered.

"Take your kind and get out of here!" He screamed, standing up to his full height of four feet nine inches, waving the knife like a fly swatter.

His mother grabbed Charlie, pulling him to the doorway, the unpurchased food still in their hands. The carton of blueberries spilled in front of them as they ran, and they slipped on the fruit several times before making it out to the parking lot.

"Go on, shoo!" the man yelled at them, as if they were gnats.

His mother was crying before they got to the truck. Her ankles were smeared in blue. Charlie hopped in the cab without cleaning off his shoes, guessing that she wouldn't be mad this time about dirtying the floor mats.

His mother was still crying as they drove away. He held his breath until they reached the freeway, looking over his shoulder to make sure there was no knife-wielding old man running at them, no German shepherd leaping through the air into the truck bed.

Once they were on the road again, he decided not to ask his mother what had just happened. Her pursed lips meant that she wouldn't tell him anyway. Instead, he bit into his turkey sandwich while the man's words ran through his head.

Take your kind and get out of here.

What did the man mean? What, exactly, was their kind?

Frustrated with his confusion, he added the incident to his growing list of Weird Things That Keep Happening. He finished his entire sandwich in four bites, then fell soundly asleep.

CHAPTER 6

A Homecoming of Sorts

CHARLIE AWOKE TO FIND them driving on an urban road flanked by industrial machinery and warehouses. A mile ahead of them, the road changed into a huge bridge that arced up and over some sort of river or man-made waterway. The bridge appeared to run straight into a hill covered in trees and houses. To the far right sparkled a large body of water, lit blue and gold from the setting sun. Beyond the warehouses, orange stork-like cranes and multicolored shipping crates surrounded several mammoth cargo ships. A tangle of freeway on- and off-ramps branched away from the bridge, and in the distance Charlie could make out clusters of skyscrapers.

He watched as they passed a Washington State Lottery sign promising eighty million dollars in a digital readout and asking the question, "What would you do?"

His mother took an exit off the bridge following a sign reading, "Admiral Way." The ramp curved to the right where the road banked upwards into a long slope running the length of the tree-lined hill. A digital sign tracked their speed at thirty-five in a thirty-mile-per-hour zone.

"They'll always catch you here going too fast, especially when you're coming down this hill," his mother said to him, suddenly the tour guide.

"Right up here you get a great view of the cityscape."

She was talking as if she had been here before. He had no idea where they were.

The road curved to the left and leveled out. They passed well-tended older-looking homes and were soon waiting at the stoplight of a small thriving business district.

His mother grew more and more excited, commenting on different things she saw.

"The Emerald Market? What's that doing there?"

"Oh my god, the Admiral Theater is still here, running their cheap movies! I'm so glad they didn't tear it down. And over there is where I used to get my shoes shined."

His mother used to live here? When had that happened? Charlie wondered.

They drove through what seemed like a main intersection, took a right and drove several blocks, followed by a left, and another left. The houses and their lots grew larger and prettier. Those on the right-hand side sat on a bluff high above a body of water. He wondered if it was the same one they had passed when driving over the bridge.

Then his mother pulled the truck up along the side of the road. Charlie looked out his window and saw a two-tiered iron fence enclosing a large lot filled with hedges, flowering bushes, and massive trees. He could barely make out the white house through the foliage, but it appeared to be at least two stories tall. Between the trees he spotted several dormer windows at the top of the second story. The property stretched away from the road to a point extending out over the bluff. To its left, masses of blackberry bushes tumbled down the steep hill to the homes below, which must be sitting on or near the beach. Beyond the blackberry bushes sat an empty lot covered in grass and guarded by several more tall trees.

Rich people live here, he thought to himself.

"Well, honey, we're here," his mom said, then patted his knee. She smiled at him, and he saw her lips quivering the way lips do when someone tries to hide nerves. "Let's get out."

Charlie heard a door open somewhere behind the fence as his mother got out of the truck. She stepped up onto the sidewalk, and he was surprised to see that she looked like a young girl, hands behind her back, the lifelong effects of hard work and reticence momentarily washed away. He half expected her to be holding a bouquet of flowers shyly in her hands.

A woman in her late thirties or early forties with long dark hair, dressed in a full-length maroon skirt and a light-colored sleeveless blouse, opened the front gate to the house and stepped out. She was beautiful. Her eyes were deep and wide, her mouth full, and she didn't so much stand on the sidewalk as command it. Her arms stayed at her sides, and she stared at Charlie's mother with a clouded distant look.

A man with dark wavy hair, slightly older than the woman, dressed in khaki pants and a blue short-sleeved shirt, pushed passed the woman, his thick mustache flexing upwards as his face broke into a grin.

"Elizabeth. I can't believe it. It's you!" he said and came toward his mother with open arms.

"Randall!" His mother let out an uncharacteristic squeal as she raced to the man, falling into his hug. He picked his mother up and swung her around like a child.

The woman looked over at Charlie, and something in her face changed. Her eyes softened, and her mouth parted into a smile.

"Hi, Beverly," his mother said after detangling herself from the man, who stepped back several feet and kept smiling. She took small steps toward the woman at the gate.

"Lizzy," said the woman, and her legs began to move toward his mother.

Both women were crying even before they reached each other. Charlie watched as they stood, hugging on the sidewalk, fingers running over backs and arms and faces, as if reading Braille, shoulders shaking.

The man with the mustache winked at Charlie. "Reunions, huh?" he said, and then walked over to introduce himself.

CHAPTER 7

Answers

THE FOUR OF THEM SAT out on a small cedar deck off of the kitchen. They had the uninterrupted view of the water Charlie had seen earlier. Several tree-covered islands appeared to float above the water in the distance, and beyond them large mountain peaks bordered the horizon. Charlie watched the late afternoon light turn the waves to jewels. Two ferryboats traversed the waters in opposite directions leaving trails of white foam in their wakes. The air was warm enough to be pleasant but cool from the salty breeze.

Beverly and Randall had brought juice and beer out onto the round glass deck table, and his mother cut fruit and laid out crackers and cheese on a platter.

"Oh, I've missed this view," his mother said. "It's so fresh, it's …"

"It's been here this whole time, you know," said Beverly, her smile not quite touching her eyes.

"Bev, let it go, okay?" said Randall. "There's a lot to talk about."

The women looked off in opposite directions.

"Charlie, you may or may not know this, but I'm your uncle. Beverly, my wife, is your aunt, your mother's older sister. I understand you may need a bit of an explanation, but I say we start with something to drink, some food, and a little time to get acquainted." There were deep dimples near the ends of his mustache, and his eyes twinkled. His wavy hair was trimmed short, and his fingers fidgeted with the collar of his short-sleeved button-down shirt. Charlie guessed he would be much more comfortable in a T-shirt and jeans.

"Charlie, I am very pleased to finally see you in person," said Beverly. Her voice was slow and deep. He wondered if she sang as nicely as she talked.

"Pleased to meet you too," he said. It was the first time he had spoken since they had gotten here. All three adults stared at him, and he felt his face redden. He tipped his head down into his glass of orange juice and swallowed a large gulp.

They all beamed at him the way parents do when someone compliments their children.

"Um," said Charlie. As usual, he was having trouble finding words in front of strangers. But he didn't know why they were here or what was going on, and he wanted to know if the ban on asking questions had been lifted. Maybe these new people would be more forthcoming than his mother.

"Um," he said again. "Where are we? What uh, … yeah, where are we?"

"Oh," Randall said. "You don't know?"

"Nah, I think I slept the last coupla hours. We're in Seattle, right?"

"That's right. You're in West Seattle, in the Admiral District. Which is the north part. The north part of West Seattle." He chuckled.

"Rand, come on, that's confusing," his wife said, slapping at his arm. He laughed again and shrugged his shoulders.

Beverly turned to him. "Charlie, this is the house your mother and I grew up in, the house our father grew up in before us. Randall and I live here now. Your mother …" she started to stay, then stopped.

"I used to live here too, a long time ago," his mom said. "Before I left the area."

The tension between the adults, especially the two women, was palpable. Charlie decided that it wasn't a good time to point out that his mother had always said she had grown up on a farm in Iowa. He could ask her about that later.

Charlie wondered what being here had to do with what had happened back at home. Maybe his mother wasn't going to tell anybody, including her sister and brother-in-law.

"Um, Mom?" He turned to her. "Why are we here? I mean, it's nice, really nice and all," he added, then blushed again, knowing he sounded rude.

His mom looked out over the water. The light from the setting sun reflected off a single tear sliding down her cheek.

She opened her mouth to speak, only to shut it again, shaking her head.

"Charlie," his aunt said. "You two were in very serious danger. Eliza- ... your mother drove up here to make sure that you both would be safe. It's safe here. It has always been safe here," she added, ignoring the look her husband gave her.

"That's right, Charlie. You ... you saw what happened. Back at home," his mother said, her voice husky. "I told you that I thought I could protect you there, but I was ... I was wrong." More tears fell, and she stopped talking. He felt sad for her, but also angry. Why was it so hard to tell him what was going on? Couldn't she just spill it and get it over with?

"Can I say something here?" Randall asked. Both women looked at him, then nodded.

"Charlie, your mother and your aunt are, well, their family has lived in this area for a long time. A very long time. Many generations. And even before that ..."

Charlie heard a snuffling noise and felt something wet on his hand. He looked down and saw the muzzle of a large black dog looking up at him, wagging its tail, a long pink tongue hanging from its mouth.

Before he even realized what he was doing, he heard himself yelling, "No! Get ... get away!" He jerked his hand away from the dog. He tried to stand up, banging his legs on the table.

"No, son, no, it's okay, it's okay," he heard his mother say, her words trying to be gentle.

The dog cowered and backed away from the table, its head held low.

Images of the German shepherd's talking muzzle filled Charlie's brain. Even though a small voice in his head told him that this was a different dog, he still couldn't help himself from reacting.

He pushed his chair back to stand up, but it caught on a plank on the wooden deck. He hopped up and over the chair as it fell behind him, his feet barely escaping the armrest. He stood, shaking, pressed up against the sliding glass door leading into the living room. The dog slunk to the far corner of the deck, whimpering.

"Charlie, Charlie, buddy, it's okay, really. That dog is good. Amos is good," Randall said.

It took quite some time for his shaking to subside. He knew his face was still as red as a tomato in August. He had seen the look of surprise and hurt on the dog's face as it had backed away from him and had watched the expressions of pity on the three adults near him, which only made it worse. He hated acting stupid around adults, who then always seemed to want to bend over backwards to let him know that everything was going to be all right. Did he really look that weak and scared all of the time? He wanted to be brave for his mother. He wanted to let these new people know that he wasn't some scared little kid.

Half an hour later, they were sitting in the living room. Amos sat at Charlie's feet. Once the dog had calmed down, Randall had called him in from the deck. He was a black lab mix with thick fur and a sweet face. Anyone could tell he was a good, harmless dog.

Ashamed of himself, Charlie held his hand out to Amos, who slowly shuffled up to him, head bent, tail between his legs. Charlie let his hands burrow deep into the dog's fur. Amos groaned with pleasure, then stretched out next to him and stayed put.

"Good boy. That's a good, good boy," Charlie murmured, smiling as Amos's tail thumped against the carpet.

"… thought the binding would keep him pinned to the ceiling," his mother was saying to Beverly and Randall, who alternated between looking at her with rapt attention and stealing concerned glances his way.

"But it didn't. We, uh, we hightailed it out of there with our few bags and drove away."

"You did the right thing, Lizzy," said Beverly. Her approving voice seemed to soothe his mother somewhat. She had been looking at her older sister with wariness and eagerness ever since they had arrived.

"But who was that guy, Mom? How did he do … do that to you? How? How did you, uh, you know, do that stuff with the, uh …" he let go of Amos's fur and held his hands in front of him, trying to demonstrate the wave that had pushed the German shepherd away.

The two sisters looked at each other, then away, then back at each other again. Randall exhaled his breath, then shook his head. None of them said anything.

"Who was that waitress, and what were you doing in the car together? Why did that guy wave that knife at us today? What, what is all this?" Charlie waved his arms at them. "Can't somebody tell me something? Anything?"

His mother winced at his raised voice. Neither his aunt nor his uncle seemed affected.

Beverly spoke first. "Charlie, I'd be happy to answer your questions. Any questions you have. But we'll have to take it slowly. The things we have to tell you will be hard to imagine, or accept, okay? And they'll probably raise more questions than give you the answers you want."

He nodded, and then listened as Beverly began to talk.

"Let me see how I can put this," she started.

Apparently Beverly and Elizabeth came from a long line of people who had abilities that most people didn't have. There were people like them all over the world. Most of them were quiet, good people who kept to themselves, living in small towns and suburbs, keeping who they were a secret from the larger world.

But a few of their kind used their special abilities for personal gain. And a smaller group of those folks did dark bad things.

"They're really bad people," Randall chimed in, nodding.

"Yup, bad, bad people," his mother added.

"Just bad, that's all," Beverly affirmed

If they said "bad people" one more time, Charlie thought he would scream. They were talking to him like he was stupid. But he wanted them to keep talking, so he swallowed his frustration and dug his hands deeper into Amos's fur, which seemed to calm him some.

"You mean like the guy in our kitchen, Mom?" He knew, of course, that the answer was yes. But he wanted more details.

"Yeah, he's one of the worst, Charlie. He, uh, he works for another person. A woman named Grace, whose sole purpose in life seems to be to …" she paused, shaking her head and squeezing her fingers together.

"To do very bad things," Beverly finished.

"Elizabeth," she went on. "I'm afraid this part of the story has to come from you, because I don't know what it is or how to tell it."

His mother's eyes hardened, and she looked out the windows at the sky, which was dark now, as if she could find what she needed to say out among the trees and hedges bordering the grass or out beyond to where the islands sat perched on the dark water like birds nestling in for the night.

"Look, Bev, I'll tell him as much as I'm willing. But I doubt we'll reach any new agreements on all that crap about Dad. Charlie deserves information, not a catfight, okay?"

"I couldn't agree more," Randall said, nodding to his wife.

"Okay, okay, but don't look at me like I'm the problem, all right? I didn't flee sixteen years ago, leaving no note, leaving no word …" her voice broke, and for the first time Charlie saw that beneath the woman's stern façade lay confusion, and even deeper, hurt.

"Sorry, Lizzy," she said to her sister. "I'm, uh, I'm just … I'll try harder, okay?" She looked at her husband, then back at Charlie's mother.

"You know, it's okay, Bev. I get it. You don't understand all of this. You may not believe me, but I'm really, really sorry. I made some mistakes. And that has been made extremely obvious to me these past few days."

His aunt opened her mouth to respond, then decided better. Nodding, she encouraged her sister to continue.

CHAPTER 8

Anger Management Issues

HIS MOTHER, A PERSON HE HAD known his entire life as a woman of few words, with a humble history of farming and parents from the Midwest who'd died in a car accident when she was young, who had lived with relatives until she could go off to college, began to talk. And the story she told was different from anything he had ever heard before. Maybe because it was late and he was tired, or maybe because they had spent the last two days in a car, or maybe because he hadn't recovered most of his mind after what had happened back home in their kitchen—whatever the reason—he found himself listening with rapt attention, believing everything she said. As she talked, he saw that Beverly and Randall also listened.

"People like us have lived in small groups all over the world. In earlier times, when communities sprang up with the advent of farming and controlled agriculture, our people had to keep to themselves, for the most part avoiding townsfolk. If they lived in extremely rural areas, it was much easier to hide from them. Over and over again, we had to find out the hard way that we don't mix very well with regular people.

"Not like today," she said, looking around her as if Beverly and Randall's comfortable living room represented all that was modern, "where people can live in basic obscurity. That and the fact that science and reason helped to wipe a large part of the superstition off the face of the earth, the superstition that has always been dangerous to us.

"Our neighbors just don't suspect us the way they used to, do they?" His mom turned to Beverly. The two sisters smiled and shook their heads as if this were an old family joke, as if they were saying, "Isn't the world silly sometimes?"

Charlie grew restless. He didn't like hearing his mother talk like this, like she was a lecturer delivering a history lesson or a librarian giving a talk on the ancient peoples of Europe. Who was she talking about, anyway? And why did she sound so weird?

A part of him knew, didn't he? A part of him must have guessed after seeing what had happened in the kitchen back home, after seeing glowing pendants, waves of light, and talking dogs. But it couldn't be, it just couldn't. None of it made any sense at all, how could …

But what kind of people are you? Charlie wanted to shout. His mother seemed to be avoiding answering this question. And it made him mad. But he kept his mouth shut, hoping that someone would explain things better, soon.

She looked at her older sister. "Why don't you tell the part about Dad, Bev? When he became leader?"

Beverly took a breath, then began to speak. "In 1975, before your mother was born and when I was still a young girl, our father became leader of our community here in Seattle. It was a good time, a peaceful time, and people joined from other parts of the state as well as from Oregon and British Columbia. It was not a huge community by any means, like some of the older ones found in Europe."

"Or even South America," his mom added.

"But it was large enough, approximately twenty families. Dad took over when he was a young man. It was an exciting time for all these families came together, found great fellowship with each other, supported each other. For centuries, most of our kind, that is, the generations before us, had lived by themselves. Many were quite lonely and isolated. Even worse, some didn't know their heritage, didn't know where they came from, didn't even know that they had any special skills or abilities."

Charlie tried to picture in his mind what she was talking about, but all he could envision were a bunch of people wearing animal skins sitting around in huts in the woods.

"The gift can leak out here and there," his mother said, "but with no one to really teach you who you are, how to control it, well, it can be very frightening."

What are they talking about?

Beverly went on. "The peaceful times came to an end only a few years later, when the community began to argue about how best to carry on. Some, emboldened by the new sense of freedom and integration, wanted even more exposure to the greater world. They were tired of hiding out, of having to keep their children from playing too much with other kids. Our father, Demetrius *(my grandfather,* Charlie thought), was one of these people. He pushed for more of a mainstream approach to the way they lived their lives.

"But you see, Charlie, most of the older ones wouldn't have it. Unlike the younger families, the older ones had lived in times of secrecy, of fear. They knew the cost of exposure. Personally. They had grown up steeped in stories of burnings, of families being run from their homes and children taken away from their parents in the middle of the night, of drownings."

His mom continued. "By now, these old stories had begun to fade away. People didn't believe them anymore. Or at least they didn't want to. Many thought that a mainstream integrated approach would help everyone."

Charlie's head swam as to tried to follow their conversation that was part history lesson, part social studies, part family lore. The women explained that a schism formed in the community. The people led by his grandfather, the headstrong young Demetrius, pushed for more openness, more exposure, while others fought to stay under the radar. They worried that the community had grown too large, become too visible, and wanted to break off into smaller groups for safety's sake.

"Dad should have just let the people do what they wanted to do. He could have kept growing his own ideas with the people who agreed with him and let the others break off," his mother said.

"But he grew too hungry for power," added Beverly. "He wanted the community to expand. He felt that the only way to integrate into society was to have large enough numbers for protection."

"Don't forget," said Randall, speaking for the first time in a long while. "This was an exciting and volatile period in North America. All those race riots had been going on for just over a decade. The women's movement had gained momentum. The possibility of equal rights wasn't just a dream anymore. Change was happening on a much larger scale, all over the place, than just with your mother and aunt's community."

Charlie tried to remember what he had learned in school about racial integration and equal rights, but it all seemed too fuzzy. That was stuff from textbooks, stuff that seemed far away. How could it all relate to why he was sitting in this unfamiliar house today?

"Dad's desire for change," said Beverly, "combined with his ambition, kept him from being able to see the writing on the wall. Whether his ideas were right and he just didn't have enough support or whether he was too radical was hard to tell. But the division that his leadership created was too much for the community."

"I remember all those people coming over to our house and holding meetings."

"You mean fighting?" his mother interrupted. "That's what you told me it was like. Everyone yelling about 'now!' or 'not now!'"

Beverly nodded. "Yeah, there was a lot of that. And then things got really unstable. The Zimmermans picked up and moved to Mexico, the Sawadas went to Canada, lots of families decided that Dad was just too crazy."

She stopped talking for a moment, lost in her own thoughts of friends and acquaintances who had left town. Then she continued.

"The community stayed together in name only, with much of the trust and ideas of expansion lost. Demetrius—Dad—was too proud. He would not step down as leader, and he would not consider that he had been wrong. He held on to the notion that expansion and exposure were what would help them survive over the long haul. Only a small group of his stalwart followers remained in Seattle.

"This was the time your mother was born, Charlie. I barely remember when things had been calm, the 'good days' as they used to call it," said Beverly. "Your mother never knew those times at all."

Charlie looked at his mother, wondering if she would find fault with what her sister said, but she just nodded, then spoke.

"I didn't understand any of it, really. I was too young. I went to school, I learned about my skills—what I could do. I had friends, some of whom were from our community, but a few, well one girl, really, was not. She was a, well, she was …"

"Like me," said Randall. "I am just what you think of as a typical human being with none of the skills or abilities that your mother and aunt have."

"Oh," said Charlie, looking at his uncle. He still didn't know what kind of people his mother and aunt were. Or he refused to accept what they were hinting at. They would have to come out and say it instead of continuing to dance around it. But he liked the story, so he didn't say anything. It helped to hear them talk. Their voices were soothing somehow. It was unfamiliar here, but safe, too, and Charlie didn't want to disrupt the quiet and what seemed like a temporary truce between his mother and Beverly by asking too many questions. As long as they kept talking, he would keep his mouth closed and listen.

His mother continued. "I knew that my dad was always working. Not at home much. Our mother, Margaret—we haven't even talked about her yet—anyway, she stayed at home and took care of me. She was, uh," Elizabeth looked at her fingers as she drummed them on the table, "a quiet woman, lovely really, teaching us lots of stuff but always giving in to what Dad wanted. She never took a stand."

"How could she?" Beverly interrupted. "She didn't know the half of it. She had her hands full with two daughters, a household to run, and a husband who was never around to help."

"But how could she not have known, Beverly? Please! She would have had to look the other way for so long that her neck would have broken!"

"Elizabeth, you know as well as I do that she was crazy for Dad. Whatever he said was law. She was too besotted with him to ever see his darker side."

"Yeah? Well look at the cost of her besottedness, will you?" his mother said, her words wet with sarcasm, "Look at what her willful ignorance cost us. Cost us all!"

"Hey, hey, I thought you two called a truce," said Randall, hands out, looking from woman to woman.

"No, no, she's right," Beverly said, visibly swallowing, as if her throat could hold back the words she wanted to say. "Whether or not we agree on why she did what she did, the truth is she … was blind to what was going on, and it did cost us all—a great deal."

His mother looked at her sister. "You agree then? That the cost was high?"

"How could I not? Of course I do, Liz. Jesus! Dad sneaking off at all hours of the night, plotting with his cronies, our community crumbling around us, nobody knowing what they were doing …"

"We knew what they were doing …"

Beverly cut her off, "… leaving the door wide open for someone, for her to come traipsing in and, and, infiltrate everything. Learning our secrets, gaining our trust."

Charlie wondered who Beverly was talking about. He watched as she paused, running her hands through her hair. The light caught it, bringing out the darker strands, but Charlie also saw some deep red underneath. Maybe that was the only part of her that was anything like his mother. They didn't resemble each other at all. Where his mother was red-headed, thin, with freckles and pale skin, Beverly was dark-haired and robust. He remembered a word from his English vocabulary quiz: *formidable*.

"You have to believe me, Elizabeth. I did not know what Dad was doing. I had my head too far buried in the sand, trying to be the good older daughter, making sure you were okay, trying to keep the peace. In a weird way, I think Dad was trying to groom me for leadership."

"Of course Dad was grooming you for leadership, Bev. You were his chosen one, his perfect …"

"Don't start that shit with me!"

A loud crash came from behind Charlie, causing him to jump. He looked over his shoulder to see a vase from the mantel above the fireplace lying broken on the floor. Charlie watched as Amos hopped to his feet and ran into the kitchen with his tail between his legs.

His mother gasped.

"Beverly," Randall said, his voice firm. "Take it easy, honey."

Beverly stood up. "Damn it! I ... I'm sorry."

She looked at Charlie. "I'm really sorry. I, uh, it's a sensitive topic, and I ..."

"I'll clean up that vase, if you two can stay civil with each other. No more breaking things," Randall said, trying to make a joke. But his smile faded when he looked over at Charlie.

Charlie was breathing heavily. All of his nerves felt like stereo speakers with the volume turned on high. He didn't want to be here anymore, where his mother became someone he didn't know and vases broke when people got angry. He wanted to go out and just get in the Toyota with his mother and drive back home. He knew that wouldn't be happening tonight, but he didn't want any of this. None of it. He wanted to be home, in his own bed, homework finished on the kitchen table. He would get up the next day and eat cereal in one of the blue ceramic bowls, have some toast if he had time, then walk down the lane to the main road, where Michael and Mrs. McMeniman would pick him up in their minivan, listening to hip hop on the radio while she put on her mascara and asked the boys which girls they thought were the cutest. Usually he found that conversation too embarrassing for words. But tonight, he would have given anything for Mrs. McMeniman to be behind the wheel, he and Michael laughing in the backseat, heading to school, and Spanish and geometry, lunch and history, biology. He would get home and help his mother in the orchards, getting things ready for autumn, then do his homework at the kitchen table.

He looked at his mother, who was staring at the wall, and his aunt, who was helping Randall find the pieces of glass that had skidded across the floor. More broken glass.

He had a feeling those simple days of homework and school were long behind him. He could almost see them, bright spots of color in the distance, fading as the strange train-like vehicle he was riding plummeted down its tracks while he held on tightly, having no idea of its final destination.

CHAPTER 9

More Answers

FOR THE THIRD TIME THAT DAY, the four of them sat down together, this time at the dining room table. It was almost ten o'clock. Charlie tried to stifle a yawn.

After the vase's crash and the abrupt ending to their earlier conversation, Beverly and Randall started puttering around in the kitchen, pulling things out for dinner. He and his mother took their things from the truck and brought them upstairs.

The house was bigger than he had imagined. The wide staircase in the entryway led to an upstairs with four large bedrooms, three of which had their own bathrooms. His mother put his things in one of the bedrooms. It had a soft carpet, a large bed, a desk near the window, and a small couch. Light from the streetlamp just outside the front gate filtered in through the gauzy curtains, deepening the warm honey color of the carpet and turning the walls a dark blue.

His mother took one of the other rooms, which seemed to only have a foldout sofa.

"I'll be fine in here," she said to him when he tried to give her the room with the bigger bed. "This used to be my room when I was a girl."

He pulled his things out of his duffel bag. It wasn't filled with much. His mom had thrown in some shorts and a few T-shirts, as well as an extra pair of sneakers.

In the time before dinner, Charlie sat at the window seat looking out through the front hedge at some of the other houses on the street. It was hard to picture his mother growing up in a such a nice home in a neighborhood like this. Where had she gone to school? What had her life been like? Why was she always so careful with money if she had grown up here?

Randall called him down to dinner. "If it was up to me, I'd've ordered a pizza," he said, smiling.

"But you know how those two can get." He winked at Charlie, then nodded at the two sisters, who were carrying platters of food into the dining room. They seemed to be abiding by some unspoken truth to cease arguing while they prepared dinner. In the midst of all of his confusion, Charlie found that he was growing to like his uncle's kind face and smiling eyes.

"Well, why order pizza when we can make something so much better ourselves?" Beverly asked as she opened a bottle of white wine and set it on the table.

Charlie had heard his mother say the exact same thing at least a million times, especially whenever he begged her to stop for fast food when they were out running errands. He had always assumed it was because they didn't have much money and that she was extremely frugal. He doubted that Beverly lacked for cash, yet she had the same exact response.

"My thoughts exactly," his mother replied, as if on cue.

"Okay, new house rules," Randall began as the four of them sat down to a platter of cold roast chicken, sides of summer asparagus, corn on the cob, and fresh tomato and watermelon salad with a light apple-flavored dressing. As different as this environment was, the food looked remarkably like something his mother would have made.

"Randall, there aren't rules. You don't get to …" Beverly said.

"New house rules," Randall repeated, raising his voice. "Rule number one: this is to inform Charlie about … all of this. I had to learn about everything in my twenties. Need I remind you how difficult it was for me?"

The color drained from his wife's face. She looked at her plate, duly chastised.

"I'm not trying to rub it in, Beverly. But I know what it's like to be on the receiving end of this stuff more than you do, and more than you do, Lizzy," he said, raising his chin and looking down at Charlie's mother the way a gemologist might look at a flawed diamond.

"This isn't about settling old scores. It's not about making your point, and it's not about sibling rivalry or whatever you want to call it.

"Unfortunately, it's now inevitable," he went on. "Charlie has to find out. But don't forget: you are asking him to completely change the way he sees things, how things really operate, at least from your quadrant of the world. It's not that easy to do. I demand that you two show him, and his brain, more respect in this process."

There was silence in the dining room as the man's strong words settled down among them. Charlie was surprised by Randall's tone of voice but at the same time felt himself relax a little. Maybe nothing else would break. That would be nice.

"Rule number two: if I feel that things are starting to heat up, I will stop it immediately, and you two will zip it. No more vases crashing to the floor, no more yelling, nothing. We are trying to help Charlie out here." He paused and looked at each of the sisters in turn. "Just remember rule number one and you'll do fine.

"Rule number three ..."

"All right, Rand, how many rules ..." his mother interrupted, rolling her eyes.

"Rule number three, the final rule: if at any time I decide the conversation is going off track, I will hush the two of you up and take over explaining things."

"But you don't know enough ..." complained his mother.

"I know plenty! In a way, I know more than you or your people ever will because I had to accept the reality of who you are and what you can do as a completely clueless person. I had to piece things together that you both had understood your entire lives since you were wee ones.

"It damn near broke me. As you both know, it nearly cost me my sanity, let alone my marriage," Randall said, looking at his wife. Beverly stayed very quiet next to him, hands in her lap, accepting his words even if she wasn't excited about them.

"All this strife that you talk about, all this breakdown of your community, yes, that is awful. I admit it. But to feel that you're losing your mind … you have no idea. I will not allow that to happen to this young man here, my nephew, this boy who …"

Randall stopped. He looked at Charlie, his eyes shining, mouth quivering as he tried to smile at him.

Charlie held his breath. Was Randall going to start crying? That would be so embarrassing. But … maybe a little nice too. Only just a little. Charlie mostly hoped he would keep it together.

"This boy who was thrust into something that until two days ago he knew nothing about. He deserves as much care and respect as we can muster. And that still might not be enough for him to transition into this new way of looking at things.

"Therefore, if, and only if, you two can agree to these rules: number one, Charlie first; number two, I will stop you if things get too heated; and number three, if need be I will tell the rest of the story myself. If you two can agree to these rules," he paused, and looked both women in the eye, "and stick to them, for God's sake, then we will continue. If not, Charlie and I will go for a long walk, and you two can rip each other's hair out."

There was another long pause.

"Okay. Agreed," sighed his mother.

"Me too. Are you finished?" Beverly asked her husband, her voice neutral.

"Quite."

"You sound more like a lawyer than an airplane pilot, Rand," said his mother. "Did you change jobs since I left?"

"You have to keep on these people, and they still don't cut you any slack," Randall said to Charlie, winking. "Yes, dear, I'm finished."

"Good. Because I have something to say. First to you, Elizabeth. And that is, I am sorry. I am truly sorry. You deserve a better homecoming than what I have given you today. It's just that … well … no excuses. I am sorry. It was rude and thoughtless of me to get so angry."

She nodded her head, as if passing the apology off to her sister. His mother looked back at her, then accepted her apology silently by nodding her own head in return.

Charlie was not used to so many words, to adults arguing and then forgiving each other so quickly. His head swam with the speed of it all.

"Secondly," continued Beverly, "I want to say that I am sorry to you, Charlie. I got a little lost there. I truly forget, or as Randall so aptly pointed out, will never know, what it's like to have to grasp all of this in one fell swoop."

If Charlie wasn't used to adults fighting and making up with each other, he certainly wasn't used to being talked to like an adult by anyone other than his mother. Most adults in his life talked down to him the way they talked down to most kids his age. He had long since gotten used to it but had also developed the habit of tuning out a lot of what they said. Other than the salient points during lectures in class, that is, so he could do well on tests.

To have an adult so clearly address him with respect and a sense of, what? Equality? He wasn't sure what else to call it. It was new and weird.

"Um, oh sure, that's okay," he said, feeling his cheeks burn.

"Thank you, Charlie." Randall saved him. "You have been more than understanding of us crazy old adults here. Now, can we just dig in and enjoy some food, and then some easy informative conversation? Huh?"

The food was delicious, fresh, and familiar. His mother asked about their Seattle fruit harvest that year, about their gardens, and filled them in on how the vegetables and orchards were doing back home in Clarkston. His aunt and uncle seemed to enjoy the conversation. The topics were things Charlie understood, and he was able to relax while the words bounced back and forth across the lush setting of the candlelit dining room with the half moon hanging midway in the night sky just beyond the windows.

CHAPTER 10

Witches

WITH THE DISHES CLEARED and the dessert, a warm peach cobbler, divided onto plates among the four of them, the three adults prepared to dive back in to the conversation. Duly reminded of the three rules, it was Charlie's mother who started it back up again.

"For many reasons, mostly because I disagreed with what our father had been doing, I left Seattle when I was sixteen. I guess you could say I ran away from home. I took with me some ... um ... some protections so that no one would know where I was going.

"People like us have methods for finding out where someone is. But there are ways to block that, which I did. I used those ways to get out of Seattle. I left the state and hid out in Oregon for a while. It was while I was there that I found out I was pregnant."

Charlie nearly dropped his fork. Pregnant? It didn't take a rocket scientist to figure out that she meant she was pregnant with him. But who was the father? Probably not the kind-hearted Alaskan fisherman. He was embarrassed to realize that he still held some stock in his childhood fantasy.

Did she have a boyfriend in Seattle? Was it someone she met in Oregon? Why had she always been so secretive about his father?

"I was sad from leaving home, worried about how Beverly," and here she nodded to her sister, "and my mother Margaret would do with me gone. I knew they would worry, but I just couldn't stick around anymore.

"When I learned I was pregnant with you, I headed south, down to California. I didn't know anyone down there, which is what I wanted. I followed maps and the advice of people I met along the way in order to find somewhere secluded. A place hidden away."

"But why? Why didn't you come home?" Beverly stopped, trying to find her words. "We could have helped with the pregnancy. Did you know you were going to keep the baby?"

"Yes."

"But … how were you sure?"

"I was sure. That's all I'm going to say on that matter."

Charlie recognized his mother's tone of voice, the finality of it. He wanted to tell Beverly that it didn't matter how much she asked. His mom would hold her ground.

"Anyway, to make a long story short, I drove into Clarkston and never left. I had brought some money with me, money that I stole from Mom …"

"Liz, honey, that was your money too. There was never an issue about that," her sister replied, sadness making the sides of her eyes draw downwards.

His mother shook her head, a look of defiance hardening her face. Charlie was used to that look; he had seen it all his life. But now, it made him wonder if she used that look to hide things, like guilt: guilt, about the money she took, about leaving her family with no word of where she was going or why, about hiding her pregnancy. These thoughts must have always been there all that time that he was growing up. Maybe they nagged at her during the day even while the two of them worked together in the garden, or while she baked fruit pies, or fished in the stream behind their house. Maybe they haunted her at night. It was hard to believe that she had kept all of this to herself for so long.

She turned to him. "I took some of that money and bought the house. The rest I hid away so that you could have it one day when you grew up.

"After I had you, I got a job at the library and settled us into our new life, doing my best not to look back. You were born and raised in Clarkston, a true child of the foothills. I wanted a quiet, easy, safe life for you. I …" she paused, looking at him, then at his aunt and uncle. "I thought I could give that to him." She looked at him again. "To you, son."

They sat in silence for a while, each lost in his or her own thoughts.

Finally Randall spoke. "Charlie, do you understand what kind of people your mother and Beverly are? What Demetrius and Margaret were?"

"Um, well, I guess so. Er, I mean, not really, but …"

Charlie was frustrated. Were they going to make him say what they were? Why all this talk with no one coming out and saying it?

And then, a funny thing happened (which was just one more thing to add to his list of Weird Things That Keep Happening):

All four people spoke at once. Or nearly almost. Charlie said the words in his own mind.

It was as if every single person in that dining room was tired of beating around the bush, that the fatigue was breaking through their habits of secrecy, as if finally everyone was thinking, All right, already, out with it!

Beverly: "Charlie, we're trying to say that we're …"

Mom: "Son, we come from a long line of …"

Randall: "Well, your mother and aunt are both …"

Charlie (in his mind): Are you telling me that you are …

"Witches."

"Witches."

"Witches."

Witches?

CHAPTER 11

Mexicans

EMILIO QUINTANILLA, HEAD SERVER at the Amber Inn's Moonlight Grill, stood near the host station surveying the state of the dining room. The brunch crowd had finally dispersed. Julito was busy breaking down the buffet table, whistling to himself like always. Jaime was vacuuming the carpet and laying out fresh linens. Emilio never fully relaxed until the final signs of the brunch buffet were gone, and he and his crew could set up the dining room for the hotel's formal supper.

Just as he was about to double-check the reservations list, he heard the elevator chime from across the lobby. An unexpected shiver ran down his back.

The first thing Emilio saw stepping out from the elevator was a suede shoe, impossibly white, beneath the cuff of what looked like expensive jeans. Following the jeans came a navy-blue tailored jacket and a light-blue rock concert T-shirt. Finally a dark-haired man, looking like a Hollywood movie star, stepped through the doors and stood a mere twenty feet away, smiling at him.

Instead of acting like a normal hotel guest, the man turned halfway around and moonwalked across the lobby, moving to the hotel's piped-in jazzy Latin music. Emilio watched as the man stopped midway on the carpet and did a very impressive Running Man, ending in a double spin, then a laugh.

"Be right there, my friend," said the man with his award-winning

65

smile and five o'clock shadow. Emilio stood transfixed, his hand still holding the night's reservations list. The restaurant occasionally had to deal with drunken patrons or arguing business teams, but Emilio had never seen a disco-dancing hotel guest before.

The man slid over to the half-length mirror on the wall and ran his hand through his disheveled hair. Then he pulled the sleeves of his sports jacket up toward his elbows, revealing muscled and darkly Mediterranean forearms.

"Damn, but those are sexy, aren't they?" The man said as he inspected them. Emilio, who'd never thought much of a man's forearm before, found himself nodding.

"Cha cha cha cha cha," the man sang along with the music as he turned and walked toward the host station, one white-sueded foot in front of the other. "Cha rico, la la la la la, la la."

Just before reaching the entrance to the restaurant, the man dropped to the floor and did the splits, one leg in front and one leg straight behind, hands pressed into the carpet, then sprang back up to a standing position while the song reached its crescendo.

"Bring it. You know what I'm saying, hermano? Bring it on!" the man declared, wiggling his neck side to side in a faux-Egyptian head wiggle. He winked at Emilio, who had lost his professional expression and now stood with his mouth open, staring at the stranger in front of him.

For an awkward moment Emilio, whose mind ran with images of dance contests and new clothes he wanted to buy, couldn't think of a single word to say.

Then he shook his head, yanking himself from his stupor. "How can I help you, sir?"

"Dude, you look like you should be in a jazz trio, you know that? Or a mariachi band. I'm Tony. Tony Ambrosio. Though that's not my real name, you know what I'm saying?"

Emilio didn't, in fact, know what the man was saying but found himself nodding once again.

"I'd like to show you and your colleagues something over there," the man said, pointing to the near-empty salad bar. "If I may," he added, with a grin and a wink of such dazzle that Emilio was sure the man was going to hand him a winning lottery ticket or the keys to a well-populated oceanside town.

He shook his head again. Where were these strange thoughts of dance contests and political ambitions coming from?

"*¡Jaime! ¡Julito! ¡Vengan aquí!*" Emilio shouted louder than he needed to, then led the man over to the salad bar, where the heat from the now-extinguished Sterno cans on the nearby sideboard still warmed the air.

The other two servers walked over to Emilio and stood next to him. They were burly men, aproned, and they crossed their arms over their chests as they regarded the stranger.

The man reached into his lapel pocket and pulled out two identical stones, brown-gray and smooth, then displayed them in his open palms. He looked around as if to make sure no one else was watching.

Satisfied, he spoke. "Would you two mind grabbing these?" he asked, indicating the stones with his chin.

Jaime and Julito exchanged a look, then reached forward and each took a stone from the man's manicured hands.

"Go like this," Tony said, making a fist and shaking it next to his left ear.

"What's this about, amigo?" Emilio asked, his shiver returning. He did not like where the conversation was heading, though if pressed for details, he wouldn't have been able to explain why.

Tony's Madison Avenue smile amped up in wattage, and he tilted his head to the side. His eyes sparkled, and it was entirely possible that the brown of his irises liquified, spreading wide, captivating the men.

"Oh, come on, just humor me, okay?" Tony said, sounding part petulant teenager, part entitled bon vivant.

Both men holding the stones brought their hands to their ears and mimicked Tony's shaking motion.

Twin pops like gunshots sounded in the air, and immediately the waiters' eyes bugged out. Julito dropped the stone and grabbed at his throat, making a gurgling sound. Jaime jumped back as if shoved, crashing into the side of the metal omelet station. Both men were dead before they hit the floor.

"What the …?!" Emilio shouted, too frozen in place to do anything else.

"Yeah, I know. It rocks, doesn't it?" Tony declared, narrowing his eyes. He raised his hand, fingers curled into a claw shape, and thrust it at Emilio, stopping mere inches from his neck. He flicked his fingers open and muttered a single word under his breath.

Emilio's head jerked back while thin jets of blood sprayed from several open contusions along his neck. Tony shuffled to his right, saying, "Dude! Watch it! These are new shoes, okay?"

Emilio sank to his knees as he pressed his hands against his neck, unable to stop the flow of blood. In seconds he tipped backward, his upper body landing on the carpeted floor with a soft thud.

"Look at me, killing Mexican waiters!" Tony said, laughing and spreading his arms wide. "How am I even possible?"

Then he paused, looking about as if addressing an audience. "Maybe I'm supposed to say 'Latinos'? It's hard to be politically correct these days."

Emilio, whose life was fading from him as swiftly as water through his fingers, lay still in a face-up position, his legs bent awkwardly beneath him, watching as Tony shrugged, bent over, picked up the stones from the carpet, placed them back in his jacket, then bowed to him and his dead coworkers. If he hadn't been distracted by the horrible fact that he was about to die, Emilio would have smelled a trace of something damp, like wet kindling, in the air.

A cell phone rang. Sighing, Tony removed it from his jeans pocket and held it to his ear.

"Will you knock it off?" a woman's voice barked on the other end loud enough for Emilio to hear. "She wants to talk to us."

"All right, all right, but can you blame a guy for having a little fun?" Tony whined.

"Just get back here, okay? Pronto."

Tony slid the phone back in his pocket, then turned and looked down at Emilio.

"Funkalicious," he said while raising his arms and clasping his hands behind his neck. Then he made several lewd pelvic thrusts toward Emilio.

"Psychological!"

CHAPTER 12

Midnight Cereal

CHARLIE WAS DREAMING. IN THE DREAM, he was trying to make a sandwich for two small children. He had found them wandering in a place that was a cross between a large forest and an amusement park. They had insisted that they weren't lost, but he figured he should probably get them something to eat anyway. Weren't kids always hungry? The problem was that as he worked at the table making the sandwiches, the kids kept running away, and the ingredients for the sandwiches kept disappearing when he would go find the kids and bring them back. Sometimes they were two little girls. Other times they were a boy and a girl. He was pretty sure they were siblings.

Amos was there, and Charlie convinced the dog to watch the kids. It helped a bit, but now that he had the chance to make the sandwiches, he looked down and all of the bread was gone.

"Oh, come on!" he said, slamming his hands down on the counter.

He opened his eyes, confused. He was sitting straight up in an unfamiliar bed, in a room he didn't recognize. It was a strange feeling. He was pretty sure he was supposed to know where he was.

He blinked his eyes, barely able to make out the display on the bedside table clock: 3:36 a.m. There was a long gauzy curtain drifting toward him from the sill of the window, which was open and letting in cool night air.

And then he remembered. He was at Beverly and Randall's house. His aunt and uncle. They were nice people. His mother had brought them here. She was sleeping in the room down the hall. There was a big dog named Amos. A good dog.

Images fluttered in his mind of a growling muzzle, blood, a man punching his mother; of twine, the sound of broken bones as a body hit the ceiling. His heart leaped in his chest, and he felt sweat break out on his forehead.

Was it all true? How could it be? All that stuff that the three adults had been saying? How could any of it be true?

But he had seen it all with his own eyes. Why was he doubting it? Even before the three of them had gotten to the end of their explanation, he had known, hadn't he?

But ... no way. No way! Witches?

His mother, Ms. Worried-About-The-Bean-Vines, Ms. I-Don't-Want-To-Talk-To-The-Townspeople, Ms. ...

Wide awake now, his blood pumping hard in the veins of his neck, he felt his doubts recede. Why would she have made up the story? Why would she drive them out of Clarkston, all the way to Seattle, away from the home and the land he knew she loved as much as she loved him? Why would Beverly and Randall lie along with her? And if they were all lying to him, as a part of some conspiracy pact or something, then why tell this lie? Why not make up something more believable?

But wait. Witches? Please. Witches didn't exist. They were just characters in stupid little kids' stories.

And even if they did exist, his mother? Hocus-pocus? She canned tomatoes, for God's sake!

He remembered his thoughts of two nights ago about how good she was at everything.(Could it really have been only two nights ago? It seemed like more than a year now.) But that wasn't witchy stuff, was it? She was a good mechanic, and a farmer and gardener, is all. People could do that stuff. Big deal. She was just better at it than most. Because they didn't have much money, she had had to learn how to do it all herself. Wasn't she always talking about how rich people were lazy, that they paid people to do things they should learn how to do themselves?

Then he remembered his mother saying that she had stolen money, family money that Beverly insisted was hers to take. So, wait! Did she say all that stuff about rich people because she was one of them? Or had been and wanted to hide from them? Or maybe even to distract people so they wouldn't think she had any money?

Charlie rubbed his eyes with his hands. What the heck was he supposed to believe?

In his mind's eye, he saw the wave of rippled light flash from his mother's hands and push the dog back up against the wall. He hadn't imagined that, had he? No, he didn't think so. And what about that orange glow from her pendant?

Then he remembered the pressure he had felt as he had held his own pendant in his hands. It had been like anger, hot and pressing on his forehead, but it was different too. It had seemed to come at him from all over. Or at least through his feet and head. He had never felt anything like it.

That orange light, the second time. Had it come from him? Or from the pendant? Had he somehow made it? Made that guy fly up to the ceiling?

But how could that be true? It would mean, that would mean ... that he was a ...

That was the stupidest thing he had ever thought.

"You'd know if you were a witch," he said out loud. "Really. You'd know."

Wouldn't you?

He leaned back against the headboard and sighed, his thoughts crowding at him like a herd of hungry sheep, pushing and pressing with their loud insistent bleating.

He stayed that way for some time, running ideas back and forth, wanting to refute the growing evidence that the world was not as it had seemed.

The sound of a door opening and closing in the hallway grabbed his attention. He looked over at the clock again. Someone else was up at this hour? Footsteps shuffled across the rug, and then he heard what must have been the creak of the staircase as someone walked down to the first floor.

As if on cue, his stomach rumbled. It wasn't uncommon for him to awaken in the middle of the night and go downstairs for a bowl of cereal. Could he do that here? Would it be okay?

The hunger in his stomach and the thoughts keeping him from falling asleep won out. He slipped into a pair of shorts, opened the door to the hallway (so different from their own home, so much nicer with shining wood, plush carpet, tall ceilings), and walked down the stairs into the kitchen.

Beverly sat on a stool at the kitchen counter in her bathrobe, her long straight hair only slightly mussed from sleep, an empty coffee mug in front of her. The only light was the blue flame from the stove, heating water in the kettle. She looked at him as he walked in, and then smiled.

"Couldn't sleep either, huh?"

"Uh, no. Is it, uh …"

"Of course it's all right. It's not every day a woman gets to meet such an outstanding young man and learn that he's her nephew. I'd appreciate the company."

She reached over and turned on the light above the stove.

He ducked his chin, not knowing how to respond to her praise.

"Hungry?"

"Uh, I guess."

"Can I make you an omelet? Some pasta? How about …"

"Oh, gee, uh … do you guys have any cereal?"

She smiled, then pulled out a few boxes from the cupboards as well as a tall glass container of granola.

The kettle whistled just as he poured the milk in his bowl. They sat at the counter together, Beverly letting the tea leaves steep in her mug, Charlie crunching away at his cereal.

"Charlie, obviously I don't know you very well. But do you mind if I ask how you're doing? I don't want to pry, but I'm very curious what all of this is like for you."

He thought about it for a while, not sure how to answer the question. He felt less shy right now than he had several hours earlier with three adults staring at him as the tension of their conversation permeated everything. It was quiet now, and Beverly seemed softer, less ready to pounce on everything. Her eyes were so large and thoughtful that it made it easier for him to want to talk. A rare thing.

"I don't know. It's weird, you know? I saw that stuff, I really did. But, it's like, it's like, I don't believe it. It seems ridiculous. Witches?" He stopped, then shook his head slightly. "I don't mean to, uh, you know, offend you or anything."

"No offense taken."

"It's just so hard to believe. I keep trying to remember stuff, but then forget stuff too, you know? It all keeps sort of sliding out of my head. Like that guy, the one who came in, who came in and …"

"That must have been pretty awful."

He nodded.

"You know, your mom called us after you left your house to ask if the two of you could come up here. She explained briefly what happened. I think she said you were in Oregon at the time. But she didn't really say how you two got away from that man."

Charlie looked down at the last bits of cereal floating in the bowl. There were several bubbles in the milk, and all he really wanted to do was to pop them with his spoon. It was a game he sometimes played, to see how many bubbles he could pop without creating any new ones as he dipped his spoon in the milk. It never really worked well, but it was something he had tried to do for a long time.

"If you don't want to talk about it …" his aunt said.

"Well, um, I don't really know. Mom and I were in the kitchen, and he was punching her all over. But she had this thing, like a rock or something, and it made this glow, this light, you know?"

It all sounded so ridiculous. He knew what he had seen, but when he said it out loud, it seemed crazy.

"Yes. I know what that is."

"Oh." Her direct answer gave him confidence, making him feel less stupid. "And, well, even though it was there, he was hitting her, hard, and she was …" He showed his aunt by jerking his head back, and bending over as if getting punched in the gut.

"Oh, God. Oh, God," she said, her hands fluttering up to the sides of her face.

"That orange light was kind of, well, going out, you know? Fading? And he wouldn't stop. He kept saying …" Then Charlie thought about it for a moment. He had forgotten just what the dog, and then the man, had been saying.

How strange. This whole time, these two days away from home, all the way in the car up until now, it was as if he had driven the words from his mind.

"Aunt Beverly?" It was the first time he had said her name. It felt awkward coming from his mouth, like a new Spanish word his teacher had given the class.

"What, honey?" she said.

His chest felt hollow, and he was horrified to feel his eyes burning. Oh, God. Don't start crying, please. Not here. That would be so embarrassing.

He took in a deep breath and held on to the counter with his hands so that his aunt wouldn't see them shaking.

"Why did the man tell my mom to give me to him? Why did he do that? Why did he … come for me?"

There, he had said it. He got the question out of his mouth without crying. But he refused to look in his aunt's eyes, knowing that if he did, it would make it a lot harder not to burst into tears like a little baby.

"We don't know. Your mother doesn't know, or at least if she does, she hasn't said why. It doesn't seem to make any sense. Usually they … usually those people keep to themselves. I'm going to have to ask around and see if we can't figure out what's going on.

"Charlie, I want you to know you're safe now. There are many of us here. And nothing can break into this house. I know you may not believe me, but your mother … your mother let her own skills weaken over the years. She told me so. That means that her ability to protect you faded to almost nothing. I don't mean to say anything bad about her. It's just that it's like a muscle. If you don't use it, it gets weak."

Beverly looked out the window, her eyes narrowing. In that moment she didn't seem like the soft welcoming aunt in a bathrobe with her cup of tea. She was something steely, something dangerous.

"I use my muscles. They are very strong."

CHAPTER 13

Show and Tell

CHARLIE SURPRISED HIMSELF with what he said next, in part because his aunt looked dangerous as she stared out the window, as if at any given moment she would stand up and yell, "Bring it on!" to whatever might be lurking in the dark. And in part it was because he was finally having another reaction to all of this, one that had been overshadowed by the shock and the terror of it all: curiosity.

"Um, could you, like, show me something?"

Beverly turned to him as if she had forgotten that he was still sitting next to her. Her eyes lost their hard stare.

"What? What do you …?" And then her mouth spread into a slow smile. "Oh, you mean like a demonstration?"

He nodded, his desire to see some proof overshadowing his embarrassment.

"Well …" she said, drawing out the word.

Her voice reminded him of his freshman year algebra teacher, Mr. Peyton. He was a really funny guy, always making the students laugh. But he was tough too. He threw more pop quizzes at his students than any teacher Charlie had had before. However, on rare occasions, when there had been several quizzes in one week and the class had been doing well on homework, someone would beg him to tell stories of when he had fought forest fires in Montana. If they could get him talking, they knew they would be spared more tests. Plus, Mr. Peyton's stories were filled with eccentric characters and funny endings.

He would precede each story by saying, "Well ..." and then would look over his shoulder as if at any minute the school administration would burst in through the door and arrest him for not doing his job. Once the students heard him say that one word, they knew they had won out, and the classroom would erupt in applause and shouts.

"I shouldn't just show it off," his aunt said, the smile on her face telling him that she didn't really care what the rules said. Charlie knew he had her then. He half expected her to look over her shoulder à la Mr. Peyton. Instead, she stood up from the counter and walked over to the doors leading out to the deck. She reached up and drew the shades.

Then she said, "Come here," and walked into the living room.

Charlie stood up, feeling a little worried that he had asked for too much. What was she going to do? Turn him into a frog?

She sat down on one of the couches. He took a seat on the matching couch opposite her.

"Now, Charlie," she said, her voice low, "normally I wouldn't do this. But because you've been thrust into this so quickly, and especially since it's been against your will, I figure you have the right to know. However, we're going to start small, okay? Nothing big and scary."

He nodded, though he wondered to himself what "big and scary" would look like.

He watched as she picked up an opaque glass votive from the coffee table. Inside the votive was a small round candle, the white kind his mother sometimes used.

She held it in her open palm, then moved her lips slightly. The wick sputtered, and soon the candle burned, casting a gentle glow over her hands and arms.

"Cool!" Charlie said out loud.

"Shh," Beverly whispered, though her voice came out in a quiet laugh. "We don't want to wake the others."

"Sorry," he said, his voice hushed.

"Not too creepy?"

"Not too creepy. Keep going!" For the first time in days he felt excitement bubble inside of him. Beverly had just made a candle wick light by itself. He wouldn't have believed it if he hadn't seen it himself. She hadn't pushed a hidden button somewhere or struck a match when he wasn't looking. She just looked at the candle, whispered a few words, and …

She laughed. Then her lips moved again, and the votive lifted up and floated several inches above her palm.

"Whoa!" Charlie exclaimed, barely able to keep his voice quiet.

"Pretty nifty, huh?"

"Totally!"

"A little more?" she asked.

"Yeah, yeah."

She nodded, and the votive candle scuttled forward through the air as if pushed. Passing over the coffee table, it went directly to the brick fireplace, then landed on the hearth.

Nothing happened for a moment. He turned his head to see if she planned to do more. She smiled and gestured with her chin. He looked back in time to see the flame on the candle elongate, extending forward in a thin arc. The fire licked at the kindling and rolled-up newspaper laid in the fireplace before shrinking back into the candle. A second later the newspaper caught fire and spread two feet along the length of the fireplace, then began to catch on the small stack of logs. The wood spit and crackled, and soon the fireplace was filled with a cheerful blaze.

"Totally cool!" Charlie whispered, looking at her. He was not afraid at all, only wanting to know how she had done it. And if he were being completely honest with himself, he wanted to know if he could do it too. Was that too much to ask, he wondered?

He turned his head in time to see the glass votive return back through the air and land on the coffee table.

Beverly smiled at the flames sputtering in the fireplace. Then she looked out through the doorway that opened into the living room, and the smile left her face. She lifted her finger to her lips in a shushing gesture.

Charlie looked over at the doorway, and a moment later his mother walked into the room.

"A fire?" she said. "In the summer?"

"It's Seattle. And besides, we wanted some ambiance," Beverly answered, her voice cool.

"You two couldn't sleep either, huh?" Elizabeth asked. Her voice sounded casual, but Charlie saw the suspicion in his mother's face as her eyes darted back and forth between her sister and her son. "Mind if I fix myself some tea?"

*   *   *

As Charlie rinsed his bowl in the sink, his mother opened drawers and pulled out spoons and cups. She clearly knew her way around the kitchen.

"Honey," she said to him. "I'd like to have a chat with Beverly. Why don't you go back up to bed? Some more sleep would do you good."

He knew that there was no choice in the matter. It was his mother's way of telling him what to do. He looked over at his aunt, who now sat on one of the breakfast barstools, the expression on her face neutral, unreadable.

As he walked back up the stairs, he could hear the soft murmur of their conversation but could not make out the words. Amos padded out from Charlie's bedroom and greeted him at the top of the stairs. His black fur was soft, and his hindquarters shook as his tail wagged back and forth.

"Hey, boy, whatcha doin'?" Charlie petted the dog's back. He walked into the bedroom, the dog following.

Charlie's mind swam with what he had just seen, how the flame had arisen on the wick with no match, how the candle had floated, how the fire had started in the fireplace. It wasn't scary or violent. Strange, yes, but totally and utterly cool. He wanted to know if he could do it.

He picked up one of his shoes, held it in his palm and said, "Ooga booga." He half expected the shoe to soar across the room or to turn bright red. Of course nothing happened. He laughed to himself, tossed the shoe in the corner, then crawled into bed and pulled the sheets up to his chin. Amos settled down on the carpet between the bed and the doorway, letting out a long dog-like sigh.

CHAPTER 14

The Note

CHARLIE AWOKE TO SUNLIGHT shining on his face. This time he had no trouble remembering where he was. He had slept deeply, and his mind felt clearer than it had since they had left California. He glanced at the bedside clock, then sat straight up.

Oh, God! It was already nine thirty. He couldn't believe it. He never slept this late. He and his mother would have already been outside this early on a weekend morning, hauling mulch, pruning trees, tying back wire fencing.

Wait! Was it the weekend? What day was it? He couldn't even remember. He walked into the bathroom and turned on the light.

His face was puffy from sleep, and his hair even worse than normal. He was embarrassed by how wild he looked. If anyone at his school had seen him like this, they would say he looked like "a dirty country kid." He hopped in the shower, hoping to wash away some of the mess.

In the tub he found small bottles of shampoo and liquid bath soap. He smelled them and was transported back to his own house. This was the same kind of stuff his mother made: lavender and lemongrass soap, chamomile shampoo. She infused the soaps and oils with herbs from their gardens. Charlie had seen some fenced-in beds from the deck in Beverly and Randall's backyard but hadn't had the chance to investigate them yet. He wondered if they grew their own herbs too.

After a quick shower, he found his toothbrush and toothpaste in the small toiletry kit his mother had packed for him and brushed his teeth, all the while hoping his hair would calm down after it dried. He put on clean clothes and walked downstairs, smelling bacon and coffee, hearing music coming from the kitchen.

Randall stood at the stove, cracking eggs into a bowl and pulling spices down from an upper shelf.

"Hi," Charlie said.

"Wah!" Randall jumped and spun around, nearly knocking the glass bowl of cracked eggs to the floor.

"Shit, Charlie, you scared me!"

Charlie felt his cheeks burn as blood rushed into his face. "Oh, I … I'm sorry. I was, uh …"

But Randall just laughed. "Jeez, I guess I'm a little jumpy today. And don't tell your aunt I said 'shit,'" he added, wagging a wooden spatula at him.

"Sorry I slept in so late. I usually get up at …"

"It's okay, it's okay, no worries, my man. Hey, I'll go get your aunt. She's in the garden."

"Um, is my mom awake?" he asked as he looked around the kitchen and the dining room.

The smile left Randall's face. "I'll go get your aunt. Just a minute, buddy. Pour yourself some juice, okay?" He walked over to the deck door and slid it open. "Beverly," he yelled outside. "Charlie's awake. Come on up!"

* * *

Ten minutes later, his uncle placed plates of scrambled eggs with avocados and leftover asparagus on the table alongside a platter of bacon and some warmed muffins.

"Dig in!" Randall practically yelling as he looked at Beverly and Charlie. His voice seemed too loud in the quiet dining room.

Charlie took a bite. The eggs were spicy and good. He washed them down with juice before adding bacon and a banana muffin to his plate.

"This is good, thanks," he said between bites. But he couldn't help wondering where his mother was. He knew it would be impossible for her to still be asleep.

Randall was shoveling food into his mouth faster than Charlie could believe. His aunt, who had come into the kitchen and washed the dirt from her hands a few minutes after Randall called for her, didn't touch her breakfast; she just stirred the coffee in her mug with a spoon, looked at Charlie, and then looked away. The rims of her eyes were red. He figured she hadn't slept very well.

Finally she spoke. "Charlie, your mother left you a note. She wanted you to read it," she said, handing him a small piece of white paper folded in half. She didn't look Charlie in the eyes. Instead, she stared down at the table with her hand extended.

Dear Charlie, the note began, in his mother's spare handwriting.

"What is this?" He looked up at Beverly.

"Keep reading. Okay, Charlie? Then we'll talk," said Randall, his mouth not full of food anymore, his voice thin and funny-sounding.

Charlie felt his stomach clench. For a second he thought about putting the letter down and diving back into his breakfast. Instead he took a deep breath and read:

Dear Charlie, I am so sorry for dragging you into all of this. I know it wasn't your choice. I wish I could have spared you all of it.

More importantly, I wish I could have done better to protect you and keep you safe. I tried my best, but I only understand now how badly I have failed. Beverly and the others here in Seattle are much more capable than I am. They are strong, and you will be safe here.

I am sorry to leave you like this. But I cannot be here. I just can't. And you must be protected. If you can't find it in your heart to forgive me for going back home and leaving you, I understand. But I need to do what is best for you. I look forward to the day when I can see you again, when all of this has calmed down.

Please know that I love you.

Your Mother

A crow cawed outside the open double doors leading to the deck. Charlie jumped, then looked up to see his aunt and uncle staring at him.

He felt strange, the way he did the nanosecond after bumping his elbow hard, just before the pain shot up his arm: numb, shocked, ready for the agony to flood his nerve endings.

"She left?" He expected his aunt to give him more of an explanation than what the note had said. Instead, she turned away, but not before Charlie saw a fat tear spill over her eyelid and begin sliding down her cheek.

"Yeah, buddy. She did," his uncle said. "I'm sorry."

Charlie looked at his aunt and his uncle, then back at the note, trying to make sense of the words.

His mother wouldn't just leave. She wasn't that kind of person.

He stood up, finding that his legs were a lot sturdier than he expected them to be, and walked out of the kitchen down the hallway and to the entryway. He opened the front door, walked down the steps and along the brick path leading to the front gate. Unlatching the gate, he stepped out onto the sidewalk and held his hand up to block the sunlight from his eyes.

The Toyota wasn't where his mom had left it the day before. He scanned farther down the street one way, then the other.

Nothing.

But …

But … she wouldn't just leave him. That wasn't what she would do.

He looked up and down the street again, half-expecting the truck, their truck, to have reappeared as if it had just been invisible, as if some magic words and hand-waving had all been a way to play a funny joke on him.

He stood still, trying, and failing, to get enough oxygen into his lungs.

"Charlie?" he heard someone say behind him.

He turned to see Randall standing at the front gate, the wavy lines creased into his forehead looking old, like cave paintings, like the Egyptian hieroglyphs they had studied in seventh grade world history.

"You all right there, son?"

"Yeah, I'm just ..." His voice caught in his throat, cracking, splitting into something hot and embarrassing. Before he knew it, tears began to pour down his face. Humiliated, angry, confused, he ran past his uncle, through the gate, up the steps and through the front door, ignoring Beverly, who stood stock still in the entryway looking like a statue of a woman in gardening shorts, up the stairs, and into the bedroom where he had slept the night before, slamming the door shut behind him.

He threw himself onto the bed, wishing that they hadn't seen him cry, wishing that he could hit his mother, wishing that he could hug her. Instead, he clutched the pillow hard to his face to drown out the noise and wept.

Had it been a few weeks ago, or even a few days ago, he wouldn't have believed it if someone told him that his mother would just drop him off at a stranger's house and leave. He would have written that person off as crazy. She was probably the most devoted mother he knew.

But now he just cried into the pillow, knowing without a doubt that what her note said was true: that she had left him, that he was stuck here, that he was for the first time in his life completely and utterly alone.

CHAPTER 15

Moving In

CHARLIE WALKED TOWARD THE KITCHEN, where he could hear his aunt and uncle talking. He felt foolish for running out of the room the way he had; he had stayed in his bedroom for nearly an hour, not knowing how to face them again, not knowing what to say. Finally he just got up, wiped his face, and walked downstairs, figuring that putting it off wasn't making things any easier.

"Hi," he said as he walked into the room.

"Charlie, are you okay?" Randall asked, standing up straight and running his fingers along one side of his mustache. Beverly remained seated on one of the tall barstools.

"Yeah, I guess so. Sorry about leaving here so fast, before."

"Oh, buddy, it's nothing. Sorry to have to give you that news."

Charlie sat down on one of the stools and looked at his aunt and uncle. They looked older than they had the day before. There were dark circles under their eyes. Beverly wasn't wearing any makeup today, and her skin was slightly splotchy.

"Charlie, can I be honest with you?" she said, her voice huskier than it had been.

He nodded.

"Look, your uncle and I have never been in a situation like this before. We're probably going about it all the wrong way. But we just want you to feel welcome here. Your mother left you here with us. I'm still not really sure why, but I'm sure she has her reasons."

"Didn't she talk to you last night? Didn't she tell you what she was going to do?" he asked, trying to sound polite but aware that his words held a tone of accusation in them.

"We did talk. But she didn't tell me much. She just asked me, in several different ways, if she thought you would be safe here, if she thought that I, that the community and I, could protect you from harm. I reassured her that we could. And would. She asked if you both could stay here for a while until the danger died down."

Beverly stopped talking for a moment, and the look on her face changed from an expression of neutrality to a combination of pleading and anger.

"I told her that you two were welcome here for as long as you wanted. I was very clear with her. I thought she meant for the both of you to stay. I thought …" and she stopped again, unable to find the words.

"Charlie," Randall said. "For whatever reason, your mother thought it best to leave you here with us. Alone. We don't know why she chose to leave. She has … she has very strong opinions about things. I'm sure you know that. But I'm also sure you know that she loves you very much and only wants what is right for you."

He looked over at his wife, who continued. "Randall and I would be delighted if you'd live here with us. We have a big enough house for all of us. You'd have your own bedroom and bathroom, and we'll see about getting you into the school system. We're friends with the principal of a local academy we think is pretty good.

"It may not be what you want right now, but seeing as the circumstances are what they are, we feel it would be best if you stayed here. In Seattle. Would you agree to live with us?"

Charlie had thought about it upstairs and had come to the realization that he was probably in Seattle to stay. At least for a while.

He nodded, then dropped his head.

"Well, that's good news," said his uncle.

"There's only one problem," Charlie said, not exactly sure how to explain it.

"What, buddy?"

"I don't, my mom didn't ... we didn't really pack for me to stay. Away from home. I don't have clothes for school, but I don't have any money to buy any."

Randall let out a loud hoot of laughter, but his wife put her hand on his arm. He bit his lip and turned away, pretending to look out the window.

"Charlie, a word on that. Your mother left some money in an envelope. And we have some too, so ..."

"I could get a job. I did a bunch of stuff in Clarkston. I know how to garden and can mow lawns, babysit, fix cars," he said in a rush, feeling ashamed that he had so little and wanting them to know that he was hard-working.

"That's great, Charlie. But you're probably going to be pretty busy with school and getting settled in here. You know, getting used to the place. So how about for the time being we don't worry about the money? Your uncle and I don't have kids, so we'd like to help you out there, if you'd let us."

"Okay. But I could pay you back."

"Thanks, Charlie, for letting us know that. I'm sure your word is good. We'll talk about that later," his aunt said, her firm smile a signal that the topic of money was closed for now.

And so it happened that just two days after leaving California, he was now a resident of 7634 Washington Street in West Seattle, living with relatives he had only just met. It was by far the biggest change he had ever made in his life. He was scared that he wouldn't fit in, that he would look like an idiot at his new school, that he wouldn't understand the way people lived up here. But another part of him was ready. If this was how it was going to be, then so be it. Everything was new here, and he wanted to check it all out, to go out and explore and see what this place was like. He wanted to learn as much as he could so that the next time a talking dog attacked him or the people he loved he would be ready. He only hoped that all the changes would keep him busy enough so that he wouldn't have to think about the sad simple fact that his own mother had dumped him off with strangers and left him, without even telling him why.

CHAPTER 16

Mandarin

"*TONGXUEMEN HAO,*" said Chen Laoshi as she sat down on the edge of her desk.

"*Laoshi hao,*" the students responded.

Charlie glanced sideways at his classmates without turning his head, wondering how they were able to make such strange sounds.

"Chen Laoshi" meant "Professor Chen," which was how Charlie had been instructed to refer to his new Chinese teacher, a woman in her mid-fifties wearing a matching jacket and skirt, her silver-black hair pulled back in a bun.

"Class," said the teacher, switching to English "we have a new second-year student here with us today. His name is Charlie Creevey and he has joined us from northern California. I'm sure you'll all do your best to welcome him to Puget Academy."

The entire class turned in their desk chairs to look at Charlie. He felt the blood rush into his face and wished that he could melt under his desk and stay hidden in the puddle he formed. Unfortunately, it didn't seem like he would melt any time soon. Instead he said, "Um, hi?" to the staring faces.

"Class, please open your books to page ten. We'll begin where we left off yesterday." Charlie's relief at having everyone's attention turned to their textbooks was short-lived, however, as soon as the students began to speak.

The sounds that began to come out of everyone's mouths were so completely incomprehensible that Charlie found himself panicking. He didn't know if he would be able to learn Chinese. Everyone else seemed so far ahead.

Today was his first day of school. Beverly and Randall had spoken with their friend, Principal Wang, at Puget Academy to see about space for Charlie. It had taken several phone calls to make it all work out. The school had a waiting list, but at the last minute a local family had to move back east because of a job transfer, creating an open slot.

"You're in, kiddo!" Beverly had said to him with a wink. "I didn't even have to use any you-know-what to make it happen."

It was very different from Clarkston High back home. First of all, he had to wear a uniform. Charlie had felt very strange in his white button-down shirt and navy blue slacks, until he saw all the other guys wearing the same thing. The girls wore white shirts and plaid skirts. A few of the students wore navy sweaters. Even though Puget Academy wasn't religiously affiliated, the uniforms reminded him of the Catholic school back home.

"You'll want one of those sweaters soon. It's gonna start getting cold and damp here around mid-September," Randall had told him.

Another thing that was different about Puget Academy was its size. There were only four hundred students, approximately one hundred per grade. Clarkston High had had well over fifteen hundred.

And another thing: everyone seemed so nice. It wasn't like all the kids back home were mean. But many of the older kids pushed the younger ones around. People scurried around with their heads down, hoping to avoid altercations. Yelling and fighting were common in the hallways.

At Puget Academy there was a strict no-tolerance policy. Principal Wang himself had explained it to Charlie in a very grave voice.

"The minute we tolerate even minor altercations, Charlie, it's a slippery slope to chaos, violence, and bullying. That's why we enforce it so strictly."

Apparently he hadn't been kidding. As Charlie walked down A wing, the main section of the school where the administration offices and most of the lockers could be found, he noticed that the students who walked down the halls were mostly smiling, carrying their books and talking to each other in small groups. No pushing, no shoving. Just alert, focused, happy students.

Also, there were lots more Asian kids than at Clarkston. Part of this was because the Academy promoted three years of Chinese language class, which was more than almost any other high school in greater Seattle. Many of the Chinese families in the area wanted their kids to learn the language in school.

Charlie had been strongly encouraged to take Mandarin.

"China isn't just part of our future, Charlie. It's part of our current geo-political environment," said Principal Wang. He explained that he had grown up in a household where his parents spoke Chinese, but the kids only spoke English.

"We wanted to be like everyone else. Unfortunately, I didn't start learning the language of my own culture until I was an adult. At Puget Academy we want to offer students the chance to get an early start."

"Mingtian," said Chen Laoshi to the students.

"Mingtian," they repeated.

"Ming ten," Charlie whispered, trying out the words for the first time.

"Jintian," said Chen Laoshi.

"Jintian," the class repeated.

"Jin ten," Charlie tried to say. He had no idea what he was saying, but Chen Laoshi was pointing in the air about a foot in front of her, then back to where she sat.

"Zuotian," she said, pointing behind her.

What the heck was she saying?

"Zwo ten," he tried. None of what he said sounded right. He was glad that his voice was getting lost in the sounds of the whole class but was scared that he was going to be singled out.

Charlie took notes as best he could, worried that he would never be able to catch up with the other students. It wasn't until the very end of class, as he was putting his things into his backpack, that he realized what Chen Laoshi had been saying.

"Mingtian jian. See you tomorrow," she called as the students began to file out into the hallway. She had been saying, "tomorrow," "today," and "yesterday." He wasn't exactly sure which one was which, but felt relieved that he had understood something. As he picked up his notebook, he wished his buddy Mike were here with him right now. Mike would think learning Chinese was so cool.

"Charlie," said Chen Laoshi as he headed out of the classroom.

He walked over to her desk. "Oh. Um, hi. Er, *ni hao*," he said, hoping he had pronounced "hello" correctly.

She smiled. "Very good, Charlie, very good. Although, because I'm your teacher, you should say, '*nin hao.*' It's how kids in China would say it to their elders, to show respect."

Her correction was firm, but gentle. Charlie felt relieved.

"You've barely missed a week of class, Charlie. I know you'll be able to catch up quite soon. But don't dally. The first semester takes a good two weeks to get fully underway. There are lots of early semester activities going on for the rest of the week. But then the workload starts picking up pretty quickly. It's best to keep your head above water."

"Yes, Ma'am. Er, thanks. *Shay-shay,*" he tried.

"It's '*xiexie.*' *Buxie.*"

"Oh. *Buxie.*"

She smiled. "No, Charlie, I was correcting your pronunciation. 'Thank you' in Mandarin is pronounced *xiexie*, not *shay-shay*. And the correct response would be '*buxie*,' which means, "you are welcome." Try it again."

He thought about what she had said. *"Xiexie?"*

"Almost. Remember you have to learn the sound of each word, and the tone too. '*Xiexie*' is the fourth tone. You used the second tone, which in English sounds like you are asking a question. Say it emphatically. Almost like you are angry."

Charlie's head was starting to feel light. Some of the other students, he noticed, were standing by the doorway watching him. *"Xiexie."* He tried again.

"That's correct. Good job. And my response is, '*Buxie.*' You are welcome. If you have any questions whatsoever, please ask. I want to make sure you keep up here at Puget Academy."

He slipped his backpack over his shoulder and headed out the door, wondering what Chen Laoshi meant by keeping up. Outside in the hallway a few of the students introduced themselves.

A blonde girl with braces named Loreen laughed and said, "Dude! Don't worry about it. You should have heard all of us last week. We were way worse than you. The only one who could get it right was James, but his parents are Chinese, which is totally not fair. Where's your next class?"

She and two other kids looked at the printout of Charlie's schedule and walked him to B wing, on the second floor, which was where his biology class was. He thanked them, then took his schedule over to the teacher, Mr. Setera, and explained that he was a new student.

The rest of the day was easier. Most of the classes seemed a little further along than he had been back in California, but none of them were as impossible as Chinese. All of the teachers welcomed him, which was nice, though it was more than a little troubling when they kept encouraging him to ask for help so that he could keep up.

He was just glad that he had survived his first day.

CHAPTER 17

How Was Your Day?

THAT NIGHT HIS AUNT AND UNCLE moved around the kitchen together, preparing dinner and bumping in to each other. They laughed as they did it, even though they pretended to fight.

"Randall, will you please move? You're standing right in front of the cutting boards."

"Well, I have to wait my turn. Someone is hogging the grater, and …"

"Hogging it? There are two more under the cupboard by the sink and you know it, Mr. Trying-to-Get-Out-of-Work."

"Me? Trying to get out of work?" he turned to Charlie. "Would you tell her that this is my dinner we're making tonight, with ingredients I bought at the store? I don't think it was your aunt who marinated the flank steak. And let's see, I don't think she chopped the veggies for the salad, made the shortcake for dessert, sliced up the …"

Beverly bumped him in the side with her hip. "Don't listen to the man, Charlie. He just talks a lot."

They were loud, these two. At home, meal preparation was mostly a silent affair. Usually it was his mother who was in charge, while he helped out here and there in between his homework. Sometimes his mother turned on the evening talk radio; other times, only the sound of her knife chops or the squawk of the hinges on the old oven door could be heard in the kitchen. They were used to working together in quiet unison.

He was surprised to find himself enjoying the noise Randall and Beverly were making. He wondered why his mother never had anyone over to make dinner with her. None of her friends, and certainly never a date. He didn't know why. He wondered if she ever felt lonely, as he watched these two move about their beautiful kitchen, teasing each other.

He also felt embarrassed about his house back in Clarkston. He had known that the place wasn't anything that would show up in magazines, but he had been proud of it. A rambling old Victorian with a sagging front porch and high ceilings, it was a place of nooks and crannies, old plumbing and plenty of storage in the basement for gardening supplies and his mother's bolts of fabric.

But when he compared it to Beverly and Randall's house, it just seemed shabby.

He hated to admit it, but he felt the same way at school. He had overheard so many people talking about their summer vacations to exotic places or the cool jobs their parents had. A few kids had asked him about California.

"Ooh, are you from L.A.? I love L.A. My parents went to college there."

"Are you from the Bay Area? I think San Francisco is so pretty."

He had shaken his head and tried to tell them that he was from a small town not far from the California–Nevada border. He was pretty sure it wasn't anything like L.A. or San Francisco, though he had never been to either city (he didn't admit that part). In the 1800s it had been a miner's camp. Now it was basically a hick town. He knew he wouldn't tell anyone that his school had a 4-H club or that he had won second place when he was ten years old at the county fair. They had raised goats that year, and he had brought a young billy in to claim the prize.

"Charlie," said Randall, interrupting his thoughts, "we're having wine with dinner. Would you like something? Nonalcoholic, of course. I could make you a cool mocktail with pomegranate juice in it."

"Oh, no, no really, water's fine."

"Charlie, let him. Your uncle thinks he's a master mixer. He won't let up until you try one of his 'mocktails,'" she said, making air quotes with her fingers.

"Ignore the woman, Charlie. Just because she and her 'community,'" Randall teased back with his air quotes, "are a bunch of foodies, you'd think no one outside of their fancy little club knew anything about cuisine."

"Well, your uncle does know how to cook. Thank God for that. It's the only reason I keep him," she said, then yelped and hopped out of the way as Randall pretended to snap her with a dishtowel.

They used so many words. He almost imagined that their lips were set to double time and that his mother had long ago changed her setting two or three notches down. Maybe when you lived this far north you had to talk faster. He wasn't sure.

The mocktail was really good. There was fresh ginger and lime in the drink, mixed with soda water and pomegranate juice, which he had never had before. It was sweet and tart, and spicy from the ginger.

"It'll put hair on your chest," Randall said, winking at him.

"We'd love to hear about your maiden voyage at Puget Academy, if you'd like to talk about it," Beverly said as she walked past her husband and took a lemon from the bowl sitting near the stove, the casual tone in her voice not matching the eager light shining in her eyes. He could tell they were both excited to hear about his day but were trying not to overwhelm him with questions. Maybe his mother had told them that he was as shy as she was, or maybe they just knew to take it easy. Regardless, he appreciated that they didn't throw as many words at him as they did with each other.

His uncle had grilled the beef on the barbecue out on the deck, which was where they sat down for dinner. The sun wouldn't set for a few more hours, and the water of the Sound was slate blue.

The beef was rare, tender, and incredibly delicious. He ate three helpings, along with salad and vegetables.

In between bites, he began to answer questions about his first day at school. They were intrigued by Chinese.

"It sounds so hard," Beverly said.

He was surprised to find himself saying more than just simple yeses and noes. "It's weird. You not only have to learn how to say a word, but you also have to know what tone it is. Like the word for 'thank you.' If you say the sound *'xiexie,'* but you make your voice go up, like asking a question," which he demonstrated, "you're saying one thing. I can't remember what. But if you make it go down, like you're angry," and he demonstrated again, "it means, 'thank you.'" He found himself warming up to the topic of Chinese. Maybe it would become one of his favorite classes.

"Is that why when I hear Chinese, it sounds like people are singing?"

He shrugged. "I guess so. It took me a while to figure out that the teacher was trying to teach us how to say 'yesterday,' 'today,' and 'tomorrow.' By the time I finally understood, class was over."

They chatted about the rest of his day and about Randall's upcoming travel schedule. Randall was a pilot for Alaska Airlines, which was based out of Seattle. He would be flying to L.A., then Mexico the next day, and flying home late Saturday night. Charlie was finding it quite easy to talk to these people.

"Charlie, did you have all the school supplies you needed today?" asked his aunt.

He nodded.

"Good. Please speak up if there's anything else you need. Okay?" She stood up from the table and walked to the deck door. Before opening it, she turned back to him and said, "I bought you some things today that I thought would be useful. I figured you could use them for school, and it'll make it easier for us to communicate with each other. Be right back."

She stepped inside the house. He looked over at Randall, who just winked at him and tried to hide his smile behind a mouthful of shortcake.

"Aren't these late-summer strawberries good?" he asked.

At that moment his aunt walked back out onto the deck carrying a large white plastic bag over to the table. She set it on the ground next to him, then sat back down in her chair. She too seemed to be trying to hide her smile. She was better at it than her husband.

He leaned over on the edge of his chair and looked in the bag. Inside were two white boxes, one quite large, the other the size of his old thesaurus.

"Oh my god!" he said. "Oh my god!"

"It was easy. There's a store nearby, so …"

"Oh my god! Are you serious? Seriously serious?"

He jumped up out of his chair and pulled the boxes out of the bag. Beverly had bought him a laptop and a cell phone.

He had wanted his own laptop, but they hadn't been able to afford one. He and his mom shared an old desktop at home, "which is more than plenty for our needs," she would always say. "And why everyone thinks they need high-speed Internet these days …"

She had never let him have a cell phone, even though all his friends did. "It's just a waste of money," was another favorite of hers.

"Do you like it? Is it okay?"

"It's awesome! It's so great. Thank you so much."

Then he paused, feeling the same worry that he did before when he didn't have any money for school clothes. Worry, and shame.

"I, uh … Can I pay you back? After I get a job and stuff?"

This time it was his aunt's turn to stifle a laugh. Randall shushed her and spoke up.

"Listen, Charlie, about all that. Let's clear the table and then go inside for a talk. Just so that you know where things stand. Okay?"

Charlie brought the bag with the unopened laptop and cell phone into the dining room and set it on the floor, worrying about what they were going to say to him.

CHAPTER 18

The Money Talk

THE THREE OF THEM SAT in the living room together. Charlie looked over at the fireplace, wondering if his aunt was going to do any more fire tricks tonight. He doubted it. Beverly and Randall sat side by side, occasionally opening then closing their mouths like carp in a fish pond, trying to find the right words for whatever it was they wanted to say. It didn't seem like the right kind of moment for displays of witchcraft.

He was nervous. He could feel shame creeping into his face; shame that he was poor, shame that he came from a hick town, and even in the hick town, he and his mother lived on the outskirts. They were even more country than most of the other people of Clarkston. And his mother was so strict with money all of the time. He was afraid he was going to get into trouble or at least get a stern talking-to from Beverly and Randall. He knew that didn't make sense, since they had just given him two very expensive gifts. But he wasn't used to any of this and didn't know how to behave. He wanted to walk upstairs, go in his room, and close the door behind him. It was very hard to sit still and look them in the face.

Finally, Randall broke the silence. "Charlie, do you know that I'm Jewish?"

He stared at his uncle. He certainly hadn't expected him to say that.

"Rand, really. What does that have to do with anything?" asked Beverly.

"Just let me, okay? I think it might help start off this conversation."

His aunt started to say something, then shook her head and waited for her husband to continue.

"Do you, Charlie? Do you know that about me?"

"Um, no."

"Okay, I am."

Charlie had never met a Jewish person before. But he didn't want to admit it out loud. It would make him sound like a Clarkston hick if he did.

"The reason I brought it up," he said, glancing at his wife before turning back to him, "is because some people hold stereotypes about Jews as being cheap or overly focused on making money. This is ironic to me because those same people fail to step back and look at the real reason for this, at years of oppression, at …"

"Rand, while this is true, I'm not sure why this little lesson is appropriate right now," said Beverly, making a "get on with it" gesture with her hands.

"Right. Okay. Sorry. Anyway, at times throughout history, Jews, as well as many other kinds of minority groups, have found themselves looked down upon, or outcast, by the societies where they lived. This meant that they never knew if, or when, they might have to flee their homes in the middle of the night to avoid being killed by angry townspeople.

"If you're constantly worried that you might have to escape in the night, you'd probably try to save money, keeping it hidden in little bags or the lining of your clothes. You know, saving for a rainy day.

"Or you might buy and save gold. Gold is interesting, because it tends to hold its value better than local currencies. I mean, wow, look at all the governments over the years that have fallen. And when they fall, sometimes, whammo, all that cash you had saved up is worth nothing."

"Rand," Beverly groaned, elbowing her husband in the side.

"Okay. Jeez. I'm getting there!

"Anyway," he continued, raising his eyebrows and tilting his head toward his wife with a "Can you believe her?" look on his face, making Charlie laugh in spite of the fact that his head was swimming and he didn't know why Randall was saying all of this.

"Witches are a little like this too. You've probably heard fairy tales of townspeople with torches descending on some little cottage in the woods at night to drive out, or even kill, the old woman who lived there. Just because a cow was born with two heads. Or because someone's baby died, a baby that she had treated for whooping cough.

"Over the centuries, many witches haven't been safe living in towns, surrounded by regular people. We talked about this the other night. Fear can run deep among witches, fear that the townspeople might turn on them at any moment."

Beverly didn't look impatient anymore. She simply stared at her husband as he spoke, the vertical line between her eyes deepening.

"One of the implications of all this is that many witches live like vagabonds. They never settle down, they keep to themselves, always on the go, never forming lasting friendships."

Beverly interrupted. "Many of us feel like we have to be on the run all the time. Even now, when it's so much easier to live what would seem like a normal life on the outside, it's just sort of witch culture to move from place to place, with either a small family or just by yourself, keeping your head down and trying not to draw attention to yourself."

"But you don't do that," Charlie said, wondering what all this had to do with him and money.

"No, you're right. Our ancestors built quite a community here in Seattle. And there are certainly many other places like this all over the world. But it's still common for witches to be loners."

She paused, looked at her husband, then back at him. "Kind of like your mother," she said gently.

"Oh," said Charlie. He had been so wrapped up in Jews and witches, laptops and money, that he hadn't made the connection.

"The reason why I brought up the Jewish thing, Charlie," Randall continued, "is that many witches also do their best to be frugal, to save money, to keep savings on hand in case of emergency. Even if they're like your aunt here, who has an established life and is a vital member of her neighborhood, they still might save a lot more than non-witch types.

"Does all of this make sense so far?" he asked.

Charlie nodded, though he wasn't sure it did.

"Okay. So if you take a people who for generations have saved money in order to have extra cash on hand for emergencies, as well as to pass down to their children and their children's children, well, witch families might end up saving a lot of money. You can imagine it, right?"

He nodded again.

"If you combine that with the fact that witches for the most part tend to be careful, they don't make willy-nilly decisions about investing, but focus on long-term growth over short-term ROI …"

"Charlie," Beverly cut in while she patted her husband's knee, "what your uncle is taking forever to say is that we have money. A lot. More than we could ever need. My ancestors saved it and made it grow, and each time they passed it down from one generation to the next, it grew more. So that by the time it came to my generation, as I said, there was, is, a lot."

Randall looked at her, then back at his nephew. "What that also means is that half of that money is your mother's. She hasn't claimed it, but that doesn't mean it isn't hers. And what that also means, basically, is that since we have no kids, you're the only one of the next generation. So all of that money is yours too."

Charlie felt his jaw drop open. He knew his aunt and uncle had been trying to tell him not to worry about money, that they had enough. It was kind of obvious when you looked at their nice house and the neighborhood they lived in. But the part about his mother, and about him …

"What? No, no, it's yours. I didn't, uh, I didn't have anything to do with it. I never even saved any of it. I … what?"

"Take it easy, buddy. We're not trying to scare you. I know everything is brand new and strange. We didn't want to just drop all of this on you at once. But you've talked about money and getting a job a couple of times, as well as paying us back. We just want you to know that there is plenty for all of us, for your aunt and me, for your mother if she would like it, for you too. For your schooling, for a computer, for your food and clothes, for a car when you're ready to drive.

"It's not like we're going to give it all to you and tell you to go crazy, Charlie." Randall laughed. "That wouldn't be very responsible of us. It sounds like your mother has done a wonderful job instilling in you the value of saving money. That's great.

"We just want you to know that for right now, you can relax a little. You're taken care of. We can only imagine how much is on your mind. A new place to live, a new school, all the things we talked about the other day with your mother and your aunt. All that witch stuff. We want you to have one less thing to worry about."

Charlie looked back and forth from his uncle to his aunt, then down at his hands. The three helpings of beef and the extra dessert sat like a lump in his stomach. Even though he liked how they seemed to respect him enough to talk to him like a person instead of a little kid, he didn't know how he felt about what they said. It just seemed too weird. His mother had a lot of money? And he did too? How could that be true?

"Did we tell you too much, Charlie?" asked his aunt.

"Um, I guess not. Well, you said it was my money too. But not really, right? I mean, not to sound disrespectful, but," he said, then paused. What was he trying to say?

That he didn't believe them? No, that wasn't it. As strange as all this sounded, it was more believable than some of the other weird stuff he had had to swallow in the past few days. That they were going to give him a crazy allowance or something? No, it was just that …

"But that money really isn't mine until you two, and my mom … until I'm the only one still alive, right?"

"You mean as an inheritance?" asked Randall. "Technically, yes. Or at least not until you're eighteen years old. But we don't think about it that way. That pool of money is for all four of us. Right now. And someday it'll just be for you, when we're gone."

CHAPTER 19

Carson Park

CHARLIE WALKED DOWN WASHINGTON STREET on his way to his second day of school. It was a bright sunny morning, though he could feel a cooler layer of air beneath the warmth of the day. His uncle had told him they never knew how long summer would last in Seattle. Sometimes it could go until late September, and other times it ended right about now, not even mid-month and the weather would turn cold, gray, and rainy.

"And then that's what we're stuck with for about eight to ten months," he had said with an odd mixture of annoyance and affection in his voice, as if Seattle weather were a fussy yet lovable infant.

A fresh-faced woman in a light blue T-shirt and shorts who appeared to be in her early twenties was jogging toward him, the white cord of her earbuds shining in the sun. Her dark blonde hair was pulled back into a ponytail, and she smiled at him as she passed by. He turned around, not sure if he was supposed to know who she was. She winked at him, then kept moving.

He wondered if he found her attractive. She was obviously older than him, but not by too much. She seemed to have a great body and a really pretty face.

"Yeah, I think I could find her attractive," he said. This made him feel happy. And a little hopeful too.

People were outside watering their lawns and hanging flowerpots. He still wasn't used to a neighborhood like this, with houses so close together, with sidewalks and people who greeted him as he walked by. His home back in California sat alone at the end of a lane. The nearest house was about two miles away. He loved to walk around on their acreage or cross the state highway nearby and go up into the hills. It was seldom that he ever saw anyone else near the house unless it was in a car driving by.

Here, every moment seemed to bring with it so much new information. Last night he had learned that his aunt and uncle, his mother and he, were rich. Or had a lot of money. He didn't even know how to think about it other than that it was weird. He should feel relieved, right? I mean, isn't that what everybody wanted? More money? He didn't know what to do with the news except add it to the growing pile of things that were now supposed to be true about him: having a family in Seattle and a mother who was a witch who had hidden him from bad people by lying about her background; going to a prep school and learning Chinese; having lots of money.

His head spun with it all. He wanted some things to be normal. Or regular. Or even better. If everything could slow down a little bit, he would feel like he could catch his breath. He found himself wondering what his mother was doing right now. The raspberries along the south side of the house still needed to be picked. Maybe she was making jam with them. Or maybe ... but the now familiar mixture of pain and confusion pounded into his heart when he tried to picture what she was doing, making it difficult to think; he pushed the thoughts out of his mind and instead looked at his surroundings.

To his right he saw the Olympic Mountains, far beyond Puget Sound, snow still capping their peaks this late in the season. Did his aunt and uncle like to hike? Maybe they could all go camping up there one day and look around.

One thing that hadn't changed was his desire to explore his surroundings. Whenever he had finished his chores back in Clarkston, he would spent as much time as he could wandering the rolling hills near his house. He liked to be alone in nature. This was only his second time walking the eight or so blocks to school and back. Maybe he would take off after class today and go around the neighborhood.

Beverly had said there was a nature preserve down the street from them.

Then a thought brought him up short:

Is it safe to be by myself in nature? Is it safe to be by myself anywhere? Will something try to get me?

An image of a four-legged creature, teeth sharp, maw wide, smelling of wood and fur, flashed through his mind.

He shuddered as panic arose, marring his previously calm contemplative walk to school. Then he remembered Beverly, looking out the window in her bathrobe, saying, "I use my muscles. They are very strong."

And just like that, the panic subsided a little.

Maybe there was nothing to worry about?

He shook his head to clear his thoughts, then glanced at his watch and saw that he only had fifteen minutes before the first bell rang. He hurried his steps and crossed Admiral Way ("At the crosswalk, please," his aunt had said. "It's a busy street."), then switched over to Forty-Sixth Avenue. Soon he saw cars pulling up to the curb, dropping kids off in front of Puget Academy. Yesterday he overheard a boy in one of his classes say that he lived on a nearby island and had to take the ferryboat every day to cross over Puget Sound to get to P.A. Charlie couldn't imagine taking a boat to school.

"Well, you couldn't imagine being a rich witch living in Seattle either, and here you are doing it," he muttered to himself.

"Charlie!" he heard someone yell his name. He glanced up and saw Loreen, the girl from his Chinese class, waving at him. He took a deep breath, put on a smile, and headed into his second day of school.

* * *

As he walked home later that day, he found himself yawning and debated whether or not he should go for a hike. His homework load had grown in two days, and he finally understood why all the teachers had talked to him about keeping his head above water. If things kept going the way they were, he would soon be drowning in homework.

Even though he still had trouble finding each of his classes and he couldn't remember all of his teachers' names, everything had been more familiar today than yesterday. That was a relief.

As he approached Beverly and Randall's place, he looked up at the house. He couldn't believe how big and beautiful it was. Two full stories, a sweeping deck at the back with a full view of Puget Sound and the Olympic Mountains beyond, a large flower garden on the north side of the house and an even bigger one, filled with herbs and late summer vegetables, in the back. Most of the houses in the street were big, but Beverly and Randall's house seemed to be almost twice the size of its neighbors. True, no one had four acres out here like they had had in Clarkston, but the lots seemed pretty spacious for a city.

He walked up to the front porch and unlocked the door with his own key.

"Hi, Charlie," his aunt called from somewhere in the house. "Hey, look, I'm glad you're home. I was just about to write you a note. I have to go to a meeting. Help yourself to snacks in the fridge, okay?" She rounded the doorway from the kitchen, slipping her purse over her shoulder. She was dressed in cream-colored pants and matching jacket.

"I'm running a little late. You okay to be here by yourself?"

"Oh sure. Yeah."

"Great. I thought I'd take you out to dinner tonight if you'd like. There's a new Japanese restaurant in the Junction that I've wanted to try. How would that be?" she said as she grabbed her keys from the small table in the foyer.

"Fine. Yeah." He had never had Japanese food before nor did he know what the Junction was. "Um, I thought I'd go explore that nature preserve you told me about and maybe take Amos with me. Is that cool?"

"What? Oh sure. He would love it. His leash is in the coat closet. Just walk to Admiral, take a right and follow it down about four or five blocks. It's called Carson Park, and it's on the left-hand side of the road."

She opened the front door, and then looked over her shoulder. "I should be back around six thirty or seven, okay? Eat anything you want, but don't spoil your appetite for dinner tonight, all right? See you!" And with that, she smiled and closed the door.

He stood in the foyer, listening as the engine of her Volvo started up. He heard her back down the driveway.

And then there was silence. It was the first time he had been in the house alone. He was surprised how quiet it was. And how relieved he felt. As much as he liked his aunt and uncle, he wasn't used to talking to people so much. The quiet felt thick, like sunlight, like sinking into bed after a full day of picking fruit in the orchards. He set his backpack down on the floor and stood there, letting the light from the window above the door warm the top of his head.

Thinking about picking fruit made him think about his mother. Thinking about his mother reminded him that he had a new cell phone. He pulled it out of his backpack and looked at it.

Maybe I should call her. See how she's doing. See if she's okay.

Was she safe back home by herself? If she had let her witchcraft weaken over the years, how could she protect herself if something happened?

The more he thought about it, the less scared and the more frustrated he grew.

"She left me," he said out loud. "She should call to see how I am!"

He put his phone back in his backpack, trying to convince himself that he was doing the right thing.

Fifteen minutes later, after dropping his stuff off in his room and changing out of his school uniform, Charlie ate some chicken and an apple, then grabbed his house keys. He opened the coat closet and removed Amos's leash. Before he could call out, he heard the click-click-click of the dog's nails as he ran along the wooden floor from the dining room to the front door. Charlie smiled. It looked like he wasn't the only one who wanted to get out and explore today.

* * *

Carson Park was less of a big square lawn, like the one in the center of Clarkston, and more a series of small hiking trails that ran from the entrance at Admiral Way into a very dense canopy of trees. Charlie saw that there were a few cars parked along the street near the main gate as he and Amos walked in, but there weren't many people actually hiking today.

Maybe Fridays are quieter around here, he wondered.

The landscape was completely different from anything he was used to in California. In Clarkston at this time of year, everything was brown and dried. There were large oak trees, fields of grass baked hard from the relentless summer sun, and the dusty smells of sage and pine.

Here, everything was green. Even this late in summer. There were huge leafy ferns bordering the sides of the road. He couldn't identify most of the trees. Many of them were covered in moss.

At times Amos pulled on the end of his leash, rushing ahead and whining as if he wanted to race up and down the trails. At other times the big dog would stop short to smell bushes and ferns along the side of the dirt trail. Charlie realized that if he didn't keep them moving at a steady pace, they would never get anywhere.

Lost in the green wonder of it all, with no real thought in his head, Charlie was surprised as the narrow path, lined with thick berry bushes and fuzzy ground cover, curved to the right and opened up into a wide paved road. The air cooled noticeably, and he could smell salt water nearby.

Suddenly, the hairs on the back of his neck stood up. He stopped. Amos ceased yanking on his leash and sat still near Charlie's feet, a low rumble coming from his belly.

Up ahead, a bend in the road ran off to the left. A large dog came into view from around the bend. Its teeth were bared. It was growling.

Charlie stopped breathing. Fear chilled him as it flew like an ice storm up his legs and into his chest.

The dog's fur was pale, almost white, and it looked out of place as it walked straight at them, head down, tail held high.

Amos's growl grew louder. He rose up from his sitting position and stood on all fours, then stepped in front of Charlie.

Charlie didn't know what to do. The dog looked like it might attack them. He tried to remember what you were supposed to do in the event of an animal attack, but his mind was blank.

A rustling sound in the bushes to his left caught his attention.

Out of nowhere, an elderly woman, dressed in shorts and a polar fleece vest and carrying a large walking stick, stepped out onto the path just in front of Charlie and Amos.

"Hello there, young man," she said to him, before turning to face the dog.

"No! Be careful. There's ..." Charlie tried to warn her.

But the woman paid him no heed. Instead she took a few steps forward and banged the butt of her walking stick on the paved road three times.

"Shoo! Go on! We don't want your kind here."

The approaching dog stopped about twenty feet from them. It continued growling but moved no closer.

The woman took several more steps forward. She was now less than ten feet from the dog.

"Go on! Leave! Now!" She raised the stick above her head.

The dog made a short yelping noise, turned on its heels and ran, tail tucked between its legs, until it disappeared around the bend in the road. Charlie caught the faint whiff of something wet and woodsy, as if it had been raining in the forest.

The woman turned back to him.

"Th-th-thank you," Charlie stuttered.

"My pleasure, young man. My pleasure," she said as she walked back toward him, her voice warm and calm, as if she had just shooed a deer from her strawberry patch. "We should all be able to roam freely in these woods without that riffraff trying to ruin a perfectly good day."

She was much older than Charlie had thought. Wrinkles covered her entire brown face, pulling at her mouth and gathering near the corners of her eyes, where she was smiling.

"Okay, time to be off. Enjoy yourself in these woods today. You'll have no more trouble," she said, then pushed past him and walked back through the thick foliage. He watched until he could see her no more. It was as if the berry bushes on either side of the path swallowed her up.

* * *

That night in bed, his stomach full of interesting and weird food with names like *uni* and *nori* and *tsunomono*, Charlie thought about the dog in the woods. It had seemed very angry, like it was going to attack. He thought again about the German shepherd in his kitchen, with the same mean muzzle. Was that dog in the woods today one of the bad guys?

He felt stupid calling the dog a "bad guy," but he didn't have any other words for it. He had tried to ask Beverly and Randall more about who these "bad guys" were, but his aunt had told him that more would be explained later. He had wanted to insist, to glean as much information as he could, but her tone of voice told him that he would get no more from her on the subject.

If it had been one of those bad guys, then why had it come after him?

Who was that old woman who had come out of nowhere and scared the dog away? Was she a witch?

Why hadn't he told Beverly about the dog? Probably because he figured she wouldn't tell him anything about it anyway. Was that the only reason? He wasn't sure.

He fell asleep and didn't stir until the sun shining in his face woke him up the next morning.

Since it was a Saturday and he didn't have to go to school, his Aunt Beverly took him shopping downtown for more clothes. He found himself less and less shy around her. She had a relaxed attitude about most things, and unlike his mother or any other grown-up he had ever known, talked to him like he was a person who had opinions about things. Like he was an adult.

She asked him what kind of clothes he liked. He wasn't really sure. She took him to several different stores, giving him her opinion now and then and also asking the salespeople what they thought.

"You know, you're very handsome, Charlie," his aunt said to him once as he walked out of one of the many dressing rooms of the day, this time with a new dress shirt on. "That shirt shows off your hazel eyes nicely. And I think the salesgirl would agree with me," she added, nodding out to the floor where the girl had gone to see if they had pants in Charlie's size.

It was the last thing he had expected her to say. He felt his cheeks burning and tried to stammer out an answer. "Oh, um, I don't really, uh, think that …"

"Oh, Charlie, I'm sorry. I didn't mean to embarrass you. Look at me, just blabbing my big mouth off."

"Oh, it's okay, really." He tried to smile at her, but only succeeded in ducking his head to his chest, then walking back into the dressing room.

After that, they didn't talk much. Charlie was pretty sure his aunt had said that to try to boost his confidence. It seemed like everyone was always trying to boost his confidence. He didn't like it. It felt like too much pressure, like he was supposed to act a certain way, different from how he was.

And the comment about the salesgirl made him nervous. Did she really think he was cute? Should he have done something about it? Nothing like that had ever happened to him before. Did you just go up and give someone your phone number? Now that he had his own phone, maybe he should. Or could. Or would?

"Hi, here's my phone number. What's yours?" he tried to imagine himself saying. But he couldn't. It just seemed too embarrassing.

CHAPTER 20

The Lunchbox

"CHARLIE," BEVERLY SAID AFTER THEY had finished carrying the last of the shopping bags into the dining room area and setting them down. Armed with a pair of scissors each, they had set themselves the task of cutting off tags and removing stickers from all of his new clothes. Charlie tried not to look at the prices. He could just imagine his mother saying, "You spent how much on a winter coat? That'll barely last you the season. And then what are you going to wear next year?"

Charlie had been excited about all of the new clothes they had bought. But thinking of his mother's reactions to the purchases dampened his enthusiasm. Maybe they had spent too much money. Maybe he should have insisted that two pairs of pants were enough, not the six pairs that Beverly ended up buying him.

Maybe I should call her, he found himself wondering again.

But I don't really want to.

Lost in his own thoughts, he was surprised to hear what his aunt said next. Had she been listening to his thoughts? Could witches do that?

"Your mother left something else for you. It's a small lunchbox that she used to carry around with her everywhere, even after she left middle school. We all thought she had outgrown the thing and should let it retire, but she wouldn't part with it. She told me that she brought it with her to California." His aunt stood up and walked out of the dining room. He could hear her footsteps echo down the small hallway past the kitchen. A door opened, most likely to one of the closets off the kitchen pantry.

Why would his mother want to give him a lunchbox? Was there something witch-related in it?

Beverly walked back into the dining room and sat down next to him. She placed the lunchbox on the table. "She asked me to give this to you after you settled in. I have no idea what's inside. She said it might help you understand her a little bit more."

He looked at the lunchbox. It was, or at least had been, pink. The paint had faded and chipped in places, revealing the metal-plated finish beneath. The word "Celeste" was stenciled at the top in deluxe cursive font. Beneath the letters stood a bright-cheeked doll in a frilly dress.

It reminded him of the lunchboxes kids used to carry to school when he was little, covered with pictures of superheroes, football players, angels. Inside would be thermoses of juice, egg salad or bologna sandwiches wrapped in plastic pouches, store-bought granola bars or chocolate kisses. He had always wanted one, but his mom made him carry everything in the canvas backpack she had made for him. "It's much sturdier than one of those cheap boxes, Charlie. You'd just break one of them, and then we'd have to buy another one."

Yeah, well look how long yours lasted, he thought to himself.

"Your mother was nuts about that doll Celeste when she was a little girl. She had the doll itself, plus her clothes, two dollhouses, the works," Beverly said, shaking her head. "Somewhere along the way she stopped playing with all that stuff, but for some reason she never let the lunchbox go."

Charlie nodded. He reached down and pressed the metal button near the worn plastic handle. The lid popped up an inch or two, releasing the smell of stale grape candy and pencil shavings.

Where had his mother kept this lunchbox? He knew every inch of their house in Clarkston, every nook and cranny. Or thought he did. But then he reminded himself how much she had kept hidden from him.

Whatever, he said in his mind, trying on an attitude of nonchalance. It didn't seem to fit him as well as the shirts and pants and the jackets and the shoes that he had tried on earlier that day.

Beverly leaned over the box with Charlie. "Oh my god, I forgot about all that stuff!" she exclaimed.

Inside were pastel-colored gel pens, bright fruit-shaped erasers, a few pencil stubs, and a tattered notebook. There were two photographs. One of them was obviously a school photo of his mother, maybe from high school. The second, curled from age, showed two young girls standing on a rocky beach, blue water shining in the background. They stood arm in arm, smiling at the camera, though the sunshine in their eyes forced them to squint. Both of them were wearing bathing suits.

"Who's that?" Charlie asked.

Beverly picked up the photo and laughed. "Look at them! Oh, they're so little. That's your mother, Charlie, on the right. She's probably about eight years old there. With her best friend Jeanine. Jeanine Petrovich. That must have been on one of the camping trips Jeanine's kooky mom Sue took the girls on. Sue was a single mom and used to have gatherings at her house where she tried to get her friends to buy vitamins, or candles and whatnot. My parents didn't like her. They tried to keep Lizzy from spending too much time there."

Beverly sighed, then shook her head. "You know, I think Lizzy liked going over to Jeanine's house because she felt normal there. Not just because Sue and Jeanine weren't witches. As much as my parents used to badmouth Sue, I'm sure she was very welcoming to Lizzy. To all her daughter's friends. Our house ... well, it was a cold place. My mother was a nice woman, but things could get pretty tense, as your mom and I told you the other day. Dad, when he wasn't busy running meetings and stirring up trouble, was a stern father. He drove us pretty hard. I think Lizzy probably felt loved at the Petrovich's in a way she never could at home."

Sadness spread over Beverly's face replacing the delight that had been there moments before upon discovering the contents of the lunchbox.

Charlie looked down at the two girls in the photograph. He tried to find his mother in the image of the young girl, but couldn't. She was skinny and had shoulder-length red hair, but that was where the similarities stopped. There was a squirrelly joy exuding from the girl, a goofy confidence in the way she stood. It was hard to imagine that his mother was ever this age, let alone someone who stood on a beach with her hip jutting out, arm around the waist of her best friend, who had dark brown hair, was soft where his mother was bony, with a round belly protruding above her bathing suit bottom. It was hard to imagine his mother having a best friend.

A bright color from inside the box caught Charlie's attention. There was a yellow sticky note on top of the notebook. It must have been hidden by the photographs.

Charlie, the note began. He felt his stomach flip. Not another note from his mother. He dreaded what else she might have to say.

Charlie, read this notebook. I've marked which pages. It might help explain some things better. Love, Mom.

He looked up and saw Beverly watching him. For a moment, neither of them spoke. Even though he knew he would read the notebook and would talk about it with Beverly and Randall, for a moment he thought about closing the lunchbox and handing it over to his aunt, saying, "No thanks. No more curve balls. Mom's done enough already. I don't want any more of this."

"Well," Beverly said, her smile reminding him of his dentist's smile, the one she gave him before injecting him with novocaine. "Looks like you have some reading to do."

CHAPTER 21

Dear Diary

Nov. 1, 1995: Well, they're here again. Dad's got 'em all downstairs. Still not sure what they're doing, but I gotta find out.

Nov. 3, 1995: Mom's so lame. Left her grimoire out again. Maybe she's doing it on purpose, knowing that her sneaky daughter will look at it. Probably feels bad I'm not getting the "education" Bev got. But I bet there's something in there that will help.

Nov. 3 (later): It worked! It said I had to use a seriema feather. Who ever heard of that? So I just used one I found down on Alki

Alki? Charlie wondered. It was strange to read the word, knowing that it was a real place, just a few minutes' drive from Beverly and Randall's place. A place that his mother had been to before.

He looked out the window of his bedroom for a moment, wondering if his mother used to sit here, on this window seat, watching her neighbors come and go. Maybe she even wrote in her diary on this seat.

He had looked at several of the pages in the notebook before the spot that his mother had marked with the sticky note that read "Begin here." It was mainly just a bunch of stuff about school, about hanging out with Jeanine Petrovich, or about how Beverly was bossy, her mother was stupid, and her dad was mean.

Charlie took a deep breath and continued reading.

So I just used one I found down on Alki Beach. It's not from a seagull, though I have no idea what it is. It's white. That must have counted for something. Anyways, I couldn't figure out half the spell, but I just kept saying it until the Words came out, and used the feather over the water in the scrying bowl. I wasn't sure if it worked until I walked downstairs and not even Maggie could tell I was there.

God, this is a long entry! Anyways …

"It should be 'anyway,' not 'anyways.'" Wasn't she always correcting him when he said it wrong?'

I went downstairs, where Dad was talking with Mr. Corcoran, Ms. Kahn, and Sir John (I HATE that guy!). I didn't go in Dad's office, but I could hear them inside. He usually closes the door, but this time, I was lucky.

They were all, Demetrius, how do you know it'll work and how can you trust her? And you know Dad. He was all Of course it'll work, don't worry about it. Such the salesman.

He kept saying Matt buddy (and I couldn't believe Mr. Corcoran was in on it), it'll be fine, have I ever steered you wrong? And Mr. Corcoran wouldn't answer. Sir Creepy John with that nasty pervert voice kept laughing and saying they were all going to get screwed.

You know how Ms. Kahn gets. Demetrius, what are the hard facts? Where's the data? And Dad kept on going Phoebe, Phoebe, what facts? What hard data? She's a pioneer. She's out there doing what no one else has had the guts to do. The data will come later when people like you watch it and can run studies.

This was his mother talking? It didn't sound like her. The person who wrote in this notebook sounded like a snotty teenager who … but wait. That's right. She is a teenager. Or, was a teenager, when she wrote this stuff. Charlie was finding it difficult to reconcile the words in the diary with the stern, quiet person he knew his mother to be.

What had made her change? And just what, exactly, had been going on down in the basement?

So they keep on going, blah blah blah. I don't know what they're talking about, but I know who. It's Grace. They're all so spellbound by her. Well, not literally. But everyone thinks she's so great. I don't like her. There's something wrong with her. Bev said I was just jealous because she's so pretty. I told her to eff off (though I didn't just say "eff" ha ha ha) but maybe Bev is right. Or a little. You should see Grace. It's ridiculous. Like something right out of Vogue. And she's so nice to everybody and stuff. But I don't buy it.

Nov. 5, 1995: I snuck downstairs again. They're going up to Edmonds, to Grace's place, for some sort of meeting, or to see whatever it is Dad thinks is such a good idea. He left the address just sitting there. I hope he doesn't know I snuck in and got it later.

I checked out the bus schedule. It'll take me like forever to get there, but I can't take Mom's car or she'll know I'm up to something. Same goes for a broom. Mom can always tell if one's been used. But I'm going. I gotta figure out what this is all about.

Nov. 7, 1995: Oh my god, oh my god, OH MY GOD!!! I don't know what to ... You can't even believe it. I gotta get out of here. It's all so terr—

The entry ended there. Charlie turned the page, only to find it blank. He skimmed through the rest of the diary, but it was blank too. Nothing.

Did his mom make it up to Grace's place? If so, what happened? Did she figure it out? Did Demetrius catch her?

He tried to remember what the adults had said about Grace. All they had really mentioned was that she was bad and that other people worked for her. Or something like that.

Charlie sat back on the window seat and sighed. He didn't know why his mom had given him this stupid lunchbox. The diary didn't tell him anything. Well, that's not true. It had some clues in it, he supposed. But nothing was clear. It was even murkier now than ever.

So his mom spied on her dad and his friends. So what? So she snuck up to Grace's. What did any of this have to do with him?

He felt so angry at his mom. Why did she have all these secrets? About who she was? Who he was? About what happened before? Why did she have to be so tight-lipped about everything?

Charlie slammed the diary shut and put it back in the lunchbox. He flipped the metal catch near the handle. It made a satisfying snap sound.

"Who was Maggie?" Charlie asked Beverly later, after she read the notebook and they were sitting at the kitchen counter having tea. "And what's a 'grimorey?'"

"Maggie was our cat," she said without looking at him. She was staring out the window, though Charlie didn't think that she was actually seeing anything.

"It's not 'grimorey.' It's 'grimoire.' A French word. It's just a fancy name for a witch's spellbook."

Charlie could hear the ticking of the large grandfather clock in the entryway. He sat still, afraid to ask more, but for once in his life was more uncomfortable with the silence between him and another person than he was with breaking it.

"Beverly?"

"Yes?" she said, now looking at him, her eyes clouded in thought.

"What do you think happened? Why did she stop writing?"

"I don't know, honey. Your mother left the lunchbox with me the night before she left. She said it would help you understand things and asked me not to go through it before you did. I thought there would be more information, but …"

"Do you think she made it up to Grace's? She, uh, she said that she was going to sneak up to Grace's to try to figure out some stuff. Some stuff that involved her dad. Uh, your dad too."

Beverly looked at him for several moments before she spoke. "If I had to guess, I would say she did. She must have discovered something, something so terrible that it made her run away from home."

Charlie had thought the same thing. His aunt's answer only confirmed it.

"The last entry in it was November 7 …"

"November 7, 1995."

He nodded.

"That was the night she ran away. I'm sorry, Charlie. Your mom has chosen once again to keep us in the dark. I've tried to call her a few times, even though she asked me not to. She hasn't picked up or returned any of my calls. Now with this," she said, pointing to his mother's notebook lying on the counter, "I want to try her again, but I have a feeling she'll keep ignoring us. Don't worry. I know she's safe. If something happened to her, I'd know. It's a witchy sister thing," she finished, then smiled to reassure him.

Beverly shook her head as if to clear it of bad thoughts, then shrugged. "Looks like we'll just have to be patient, huh?"

CHAPTER 22

The Market

THE SUNDAY FARMERS MARKET filled the space of two large parking lots. There were booths with white awnings displaying art, fresh pork and lamb, fruits and vegetables, a couple of cheese stands, and several little kiosks selling things like soap and shampoo.

The market bustled with people. Charlie was surprised. The weekly markets in Clarkston covered more surface area, and even had livestock for sale, but were nowhere near this packed.

"God, this place is nuts," Randall said as he waited for an elderly man to finish loading his car with purchases and vacate his parking spot.

"Well, it'll be one of the last weekends of great weather before it starts raining. Everyone wants to enjoy it while they can," his aunt replied as her husband backed into the space. The three of them stepped out of the Volvo and headed over to the market.

They began to peruse each booth, his aunt and uncle planning the evening's meal while choosing produce. They were having some friends over for dinner that night and wanted to make something special.

"Remember how I said that Beverly's community is made up of food snobs?" Randall had said while they were still back at home gathering their canvas shopping bags for the trip to the market. "Well, you just wait until tonight. They'll be in fine form."

"And what, may I ask, is wrong with that?" Beverly asked, making sure that Amos had enough water in his drinking bowl before they left. "We're foodies, that's all."

Randall rolled his eyes at Charlie.

"I saw that!"

"You can't get away with anything, living with a witch. I call it the Darren Stevens syndrome."

"I heard that!"

All three of them had laughed, even though Charlie didn't know who Darren Stevens was.

Beverly and Randall ran into some friends near a booth selling fresh flowers. After introductions were made, the adults kept talking about the weather, the produce, and local politics.

"We'll be here forever talking about boring stuff, Charlie," Randall said to him. "Why don't you go have a look around? Take one of these bags with you in case you want to buy something."

"We can meet back up in thirty minutes over by that fountain." Beverly pointed to a low cement structure wedged between a bank and a pharmacy.

Charlie nodded, looked around, then headed in the direction of the produce stands.

People. So many people. Pushing and shoving to taste samples of late summer fruit, to fill their bags with purchases.

"I'll weigh those cucumbers for you!"

"Really? Just add a few cups of the cider right into the bowl? Or do I have to heat it first?"

"Excuse me, excuse me, I just want to try some of that."

He let himself be jostled about, surprised to find that he was enjoying the crowd rather than being afraid of it. He liked the feeling of being among so many people without anyone looking at him or asking him questions. And with so many noises, so many good smells, he was able to take his mind off of his mother's journal and her frustrating mysteries.

He walked over to a small booth that sold local salmon, both fresh and smoked.

"Like a sample?" asked a tall man with a trim red beard standing behind the table.

"Uh, sure."

The man spread something white over a round cracker, then placed a bit of fish on top.

"This is our smoked chinook, the last of the season, with a little chive cheese."

Charlie bit into the cracker, which was hearty and thick. The cheese filled his mouth with a tangy richness. But what surprised him was the rich, oily taste of the salmon: slightly salty, but almost like it had been barbecued. He thought it might be the best thing he had ever eaten.

"Pretty good, huh?"

He smiled and nodded.

"A four-ounce package, that's the small one, is thirteen fifty."

That's expensive, he thought, on the verge of opening his mouth and saying so. His mother would never pay for anything that cost this much. Maybe she would insist on catching the fish and smoking it herself, just to prove how ridiculous vendors could be with their fancy products and outrageous markups. Maybe she would even make a few choice comments about the kind of people who bought extravagant unnecessary things like this.

But a flash of anger filled him; not indignation at the fish seller and his prices, but at her. She was the one who had up and left him in the middle of the night without even saying goodbye. She had kept an entire world of secrets from him, knowledge of her own background and therefore his own too. And somehow her little lunchbox was supposed to answer all of his questions?

He had spent years listening to her prattle on about careless spending, about incapable people and their lazy habits. He had swallowed all of it whole, had sucked up her do-it-yourself arrogance without ever questioning the source.

And yet who was standing here in front of him offering him something good to eat? His mother? No, she had lied to him, lied to him about basically everything in life and had been too chicken to admit to it, had instead dumped him off with random strangers and driven away, had acted worse than all the "stupid people" she had ever complained about combined, had …

"How much is the bigger one?" Charlie heard himself ask, the words rushing out of his mouth before he could stop himself. He didn't even hear the man's reply of, "Twenty-three dollars."

He felt a thrill rush through him, welling up, felt himself turning giddy. His mother wasn't here and, for all he knew, might not be coming back anytime soon. (Or ever? The thought tried to shove its way past his growing excitement, but he pushed it away.) She wasn't here to police him even if she wanted to. Maybe that's what it means when your mother leaves you with strangers: that you can do what you want and stop worrying about her reaction.

The salmon vendor took Charlie's silence for reticence.

"I know it's kind of pricey. Tell you what," he said, opening his hands palms up, eyes crinkling at the corners as he smiled, "for twenty-four dollars, I'll give you the larger smoked Chinook, a tub of the chive cheese, which is normally four fifty, and throw in a box of crackers too."

Charlie smiled and quickly nodded. He didn't know if he was getting a good deal or not, but he didn't care. He took out his wallet and handed over the two twenties that Randall had given him that morning.

"This is the first thing that I bought in Seattle. Smoked salmon!" he imagined himself saying to the salmon vendor. Like shy people the world over, Charlie held many conversations inside his head, all of which turned out better than reality. No one ever embarrassed him during these fantasy chats. They only included him in their collective fold. He imagined himself saying it, imagined the red-bearded vendor clapping him on the back and congratulating him on his choice.

Of course, he said none of this. Instead he placed his purchases inside his canvas bag, thanked the vendor, and turned away.

But he could still taste the rich flavor of the salmon. He smiled. It tasted like freedom.

*   *   *

Charlie wandered over to where a small crowd had gathered near the produce stalls.

"... must be from last year's supply," he heard a woman say.

"No, ma'am. These are early Braeburns, I assure you. Try one and tell me if it isn't the freshest apple you've ever tasted," another voice said. It was male, and younger than the woman's. Charlie couldn't tell where it came from, but an unexpected thought ran through his head: *I like that voice.*

As he stood there, he saw a sign that read "Ramirez Yakima Produce" above a stand selling several different kinds of apples. People were trying small slices. He could see the back of the black-haired person passing out the samples, only a few feet away from him.

That person turned and caught Charlie's eye.

He looked to be about Charlie's age, or maybe slightly older. He was taller than Charlie's five feet nine inches, probably over six feet. His skin was cinnamon-colored, and he had wide eyes, nearly as wide as Beverly's, but much darker. His teeth were bright white as he smiled at him.

Charlie's mind felt empty in that moment, all thoughts draining away. People were pushing against him to try the apple samples, but he just stood there, looking back at the boy. For some reason he held his breath.

"Hi, I'm Diego," he said to Charlie. "Wanna try a sample?"

CHAPTER 23

Rubbing It In

CHARLIE WALKED OVER TO WHERE the boy stood and took a small slice from the plastic container he held.

"They're really good this year. It was a hot summer over in Yakima. My uncle couldn't believe they were coming in this early, or this sweet," he said.

Charlie looked up at Diego's face, focusing on his lips. They were thick, and they moved quickly as he spoke, blocking, then exposing, the boy's white teeth.

Like the sun behind curtains, he thought.

What are you doing, staring at him like that? he berated himself, horrified. He put the fruit sample in his mouth.

Sweetness flooded over his tongue, causing Charlie to momentarily forget his embarrassment. The flavor of the apple was softer, had less sharpness, than the Granny Smiths he was used to eating. And instead of clashing with the taste of the salmon, it blended with it, causing his mouth to water.

"Pretty good, huh?" said the boy, then turned to offer samples to other passersby. Charlie was struck by two feelings at the same time: relief at being spared further embarrassment and dread that the boy would never speak to him again.

Both feelings disappeared when, moments later, Diego turned back to face him and asked, "What's your name?"

"Oh. Charlie. Charlie Creevey," he said. A small fleck of apple flew out of his mouth when he pronounced the "ch" sound of his name. Heat flared in his cheeks. He was sure he had turned as red as the tomatoes two stands over. It was all he could do not to run out of the farmers market as fast as his legs would carry him. Diego either didn't see the piece of apple or chose not to mention it.

"You live around here?"

"Uh, yeah. Yeah, over on Washington." Charlie said, relieved to hear that he sounded normal. "I, uh, I go to Puget Academy."

"What?" The boy stopped. He walked over and handed the sample container to an older man with a thick mustache, then came back to Charlie.

"No you don't," the boy said, laughing. "I go to P.A. I've never seen you before."

Charlie blushed. "Oh. Um, I just moved here. From California. I live with my aunt and uncle."

"Wow, that's great!" Diego said. "Welcome to Seattle. How do you like it so far?"

Diego was the first person not to mention anything about Los Angeles or San Francisco when Charlie said he was from California. He answered the boy's questions easily, though he couldn't remember exactly what he had said.

They fell in to talking about school, about the late summer weather, about what Charlie thought of living in West Seattle, and he noticed that there was something very easygoing about Diego, about the way he convinced people to try the apple samples, about the questions he asked Charlie, about the things he said.

Most people overcompensated for Charlie's shyness by either becoming overly cheerful and chatty or quiet themselves. He hated it and wished he could just be normal so people didn't feel that they had to change around him, but so far he hadn't been able to overcome being so bashful. When he tried to be more talkative, it only made things worse.

Diego didn't seem to notice, or at least it didn't bother him. Charlie found himself relaxing, even as the shoppers crowded around them. Even though the boy had been a total stranger up until a few minutes ago, he found himself wanting to tell him things, about his mother, about his fears and concerns, about …

"*Ven aqui, mi'jo,*" shouted the man with the mustache. "*Necesito ayuda.*"

"*Vengo, vengo,*" Diego turned his head and yelled back at the man. "*Momentito.*"

"Hey look," Diego said to Charlie. "I gotta get back and help my uncle. We'll be closing up shop here in a little bit. But my friends are having a P.A. party Tuesday night. Wanna come? They do it every year as a bit of a kickoff for the new school year or as a funeral for the end of summer. It's all legit, the parents will be there and everything. It'd be turbo-bitchin' if you came."

Charlie laughed, having never heard "turbo-bitchin'" before.

"Oh, um, yeah. Yeah, sure," Charlie heard himself saying, shrugging his shoulders, as if he always got invitations to parties, as if confident people like Diego asked him to do things all the time.

"Cool!" Diego said, and for some reason, Charlie believed that he meant it.

"Gimme your cell number," the boy said. Charlie's mind went blank.

"I, uh, I forgot it," he blushed. "The number. Not the phone. I forgot the number. It's stupid," he said, pulling the phone out from his pocket. "I, uh, I just got it and …"

Diego laughed and took the phone from his hand. He touched the screen a few times and typed in a number. Then he began typing. "D-I-E-G-O R-A-M-I-R-E-Z," he said, spelling his name out loud. "Now I'm in your contacts. Call me later today and I'll give you the 411," he said.

"*¡Diego! ¡Ahorrita!*" the uncle yelled.

"Gotta go. Really great meeting you!" And with that, the boy pushed through the crowd and started taking cash from the shoppers impatient to finish with their apple purchases and be on their way.

Charlie put the phone back in his jeans pocket and walked away, his mind once again empty of thoughts. His face felt funny, like it was bigger than the rest of his head, like it was ballooning outwards, full of so much air, that at any minute it would detach itself from the rest of him and float up toward the blue sky.

He wandered from stand to stand, not seeing much but hoping it looked like he was shopping.

"This stuff is really good for your skin," said a voice nearby.

He looked down and saw that he was standing in front of a small table displaying organic sunscreen. A heavyset, middle-aged woman with bleached-blonde hair and a pink plastic visor was sitting on a folding chair and pointing to the different bottles and tubes on the table. She was talking to him.

"All of them are SPF 50, some scented, some unscented. Which kind would you like?" she asked him. Her eyelids were covered with thick green eyeshadow, and she wore a pink T-shirt with a faded decal of a stuffed teddy bear and the words, "I love you BEARY much," on the front.

"What? Oh no, I don't need any ..."

Before he could say anything more, the woman squeezed a dollop of white lotion from a tube in her hand onto Charlie's arm and started to rub it all over his skin.

"This has a nice pine scent. Guys love it," she said, continuing to rub.

Charlie wasn't sure what to do. He wished the woman would stop, but he didn't want to appear rude by just yanking his arm back and walking away.

"There, isn't that nice? Can't you just feel all of that ...?" she stopped, mid-sentence.

Her eyes left Charlie's arm and slowly scanned up his chest, to his chin, then his eyes, like she was looking for something.

"Hey! You're a ..." she said. She stopped her rubbing motion and increased the grip on his arm.

Charlie felt the same prickling sensation on the back of his neck that he had at Carson Park a few days ago.

He tried to pull his arm away, but he found that he couldn't move.

The woman's lips started to mumble something, saying words that were too quiet to make out. His field of vision narrowed to a dime-sized circle of light surrounded by complete darkness. Tiny sparks began to dance across the blackness. He felt sick to his stomach. He wondered if he was going to pass out.

"What's going on?" Charlie heard someone saying next to him. A woman's voice. It was sharp, and familiar, but he couldn't remember whose it was.

The sunscreen vendor let go of Charlie's hand and sat back in her chair. Instantly his head cleared. The tiny lights disappeared as the day's sunshine glared in his eyes again.

"Beverly!" the woman said, sounding surprised. "Nothing! Nothing's going on. Everything's fine, honey." She looked very frightened, though she tried to hide it with a smile.

Charlie watched as his aunt leaned down over the table until her face was only a few inches from the woman's, pointing an outstretched finger at her pink T-shirt.

"Don't you 'honey' me, Mavis. This boy is mine, all right? Mine! You wouldn't want to touch something that is mine, would you?" Her words sharp like steel.

He watched as the woman's lips quivered, causing her double chins to jiggle. Her eyes flickered between his aunt's face and her extended finger.

"No, no, really, Beverly, really, I wasn't doing anything. Anything. Please, you gotta believe me, I …"

"This is the only warning you get, Mavis. You and all your bosom buddies. Understand? You screw around with me and mine, I'll screw around with you and yours. Bad. Got me?"

The woman started to whimper, and tears sprang to her eyes. "Yeah, yeah, I g-g-got you, I won't, uh, we won't, we wouldn't … wouldn't do …"

"Good. I don't want to see you back at this market. Not in this neighborhood either. Take your crap and get out of here."

"All right. All right, Beverly. You got it." The woman's hands shook as she started to gather her wares together. Nearby shoppers had begun to look over at the booth with curiosity.

Beverly turned to face Charlie. Her eyes, which he had come to know as kind, held him fast with their violent brown glare. For a split second he thought she was going to strike him.

"We're done here," she said, her voice snake-soft and scary. She led him away from the table.

* * *

"I got the last item on our … what's going on?" Randall asked as he stepped up to them, several filled canvas bags swinging from each arm.

"We're going," said Beverly, already walking toward the street.

"But we haven't …"

"We're going. Now!" she said over her shoulder. Her hand searched around in her purse until she found her car keys.

Randall looked at him for an explanation, but Charlie couldn't find any words. He was still shaken by the dizzy nauseous feeling. And by the way his aunt had completely terrified the vendor.

"What happened back there?" Randall asked again as his wife pulled the car away from the curb.

"Later. We'll talk about this later," was all she would say as she turned left, then right, and drove the car north toward home.

CHAPTER 24

An Echo

ONCE THE SHOCK OF THE WHOLE experience wore off, Charlie began to wonder if he had done something wrong. His aunt was very angry, and he was worried that it was at him. He was also afraid of her. While he had been wary of her when his mother had introduced Beverly as his aunt and while he had been in awe of how she had bewitched the candle, he hadn't been afraid of her. But Charlie had just seen flint in her eyes, and he was pretty sure that it wouldn't take but a small spark to set her ablaze. He would bet that the sunscreen vendor had been thinking the same thing.

Charlie lay on his bed, pondering what had happened between his aunt and Mavis. The two women had known each other. But they were clearly not friends. Maybe Mavis was a bad guy too. They seemed to be popping up everywhere.

He knew he should be doing his homework, but he couldn't stop thinking about the events at the farmers market. He wanted answers, and he figured he knew where to get them, even if the source of the information wanted to tear his head off.

Gathering his courage, he walked down the carpeted staircase. As he approached the kitchen, he could hear his aunt and uncle talking in low voices. They stopped as he walked through the doorway.

"Hey, buddy," his uncle said.

"Um, can I help with anything? Making dinner or whatever?"

"Oh no, Charlie, thanks. We've got it under control," said Beverly.

He took a deep breath and opened his mouth.

"Can I, uh, ask you something?"

They both nodded.

"Um, are you like, well, mad at me or something? Because I was talking to that sunscreen lady?" He felt stupid asking the question. Whenever adults were mad at you they told you so. No use stirring the hornets' nest if he could avoid it. And yet, things were too confusing. He thought he might go crazy if he didn't get more information.

"What? Oh, Charlie, no. No! I'm sorry you thought that. No, you were fine, perfectly fine. She, she just ..."

"Is she one of those bad guys you and Mom were talking about the other night?"

"No. Not at all. Mavis is, well, Mavis is a bit of a head case. A minor hassle really."

He waited, not really knowing what that meant.

"She's nothing to worry about, Charlie. She has some talent in her blood, but it's not much. We call it an 'echo' when someone hasn't been popped before but still has traces of the ..."

"Beverly," Randall scolded, "knock off the mumbo-jumbo crap. Charlie doesn't know what 'popped' means. Sooner or later you're going to have to explain it all to him. The more you wait, the more confusing it'll be for him to ..."

She cut him off. "I know. I know. Don't you think I don't know it, Rand? Give me a little credit, for God's sake."

Charlie watched as Randall held up his hands in a conciliatory gesture. "Okay, okay. All I'm saying is ..."

She turned to Charlie, and the late afternoon sun turned strands of her dark hair a deep red. Her menacing look from the farmers market was gone now, replaced with something softer, though he wasn't sure what. Reluctance? Apology? Acceptance of what Randall had said?

"Charlie, there's so much to talk about," she continued. "I don't even know where to start. I don't know how much I should or shouldn't say. All the kids in our community have grown up with this stuff, so when they learn something they already have a foundation to build on. For you, it's all so new. I'm afraid I'll tell you too much and frighten you."

"And I'm afraid she won't tell you anything, leaving you in the dark," added Randall.

Charlie wasn't sure how much Beverly should say either. A part of him wanted to know everything, including who the bad guys were and how to make candles float. He was tired of being told that there was too much to know. There was a whole new world for him to discover, and waiting for it was so difficult it nearly made his bones ache.

But another part of him was scared. Everything still felt like it was moving at light speed. If he could just slow things down a little and catch up with all the changes happening, he might feel like he was standing on solid ground. He worried that the more Beverly told him, the shakier and crazier things would feel, like after reading his mom's notebook. Everything led to more questions, not less. He wanted it all to stop. If she told him more, it would speed things up.

"Well, um, tell me what you want to tell me. Since I don't know anything, it'll be better than being totally clueless."

Beverly finally smiled, and he was reminded of how good she had been, how good both of them had been to him, letting him stay at their house, buying him clothes and a cell phone, a laptop …

"Look, why don't I tell you a little about Mavis, so you can understand what that was all about? The friends who are coming over tonight will want to know what happened at the farmers market, so there'll be more to the story then, okay? I'll be as brief as I can, but just interrupt me if you have any questions or don't understand something."

"And I'll just chop some vegetables for dinner and look pretty," said Randall, blinking his eyelashes and grinning broadly.

Beverly frowned.

"Oops. Sorry. Bev, I know it's hard for you to figure out what to say and not say. I'll get dinner going, but you know I'll add in stuff too. I can't keep my mouth closed."

"It's why I love you so much, honey." Beverly said in a completely unconvincing voice. But she leaned over the counter and kissed him anyway.

Charlie was surprised to find that he wasn't embarrassed by their kissing. Maybe with all the other weird things going on in his life, this didn't even merit his face turning red. He considered this to be a vast improvement.

Beverly poured three glasses of water, handing one to Charlie and one to her husband.

"Have a seat, kiddo," she said, indicating one of the bar stools. He sat down, eager to hear whatever it was that she had to say.

"Okay, here's something you should know," she began, after taking a long sip out of her own glass. "Witchcraft runs in people's blood. It's passed from family member to family member. This means that not just anyone can be a witch. Randall couldn't if he tried."

"And believe you me, I've tried," he said, slicing into a red pepper. Charlie watched as white seeds fell away from the bright flesh.

"But just because someone has the blood in them," Beverly continued, "doesn't mean that they can do anything with their abilities. They have to go through a process that we call being 'popped.' Another witch basically helps their craft come to the surface. It's kind of complicated, and not important right now, but suffice it to say that there are people out there in the world who are 'unpopped,' meaning they have the blood, or the legacy, in them but maybe don't know it, or can't access it, or don't want to.

"Now, some of these people have what we call an 'echo.' It means that in spite of not being popped, some of their abilities leak out. It's why some people claim to be psychic. Others seem to experience better luck than most. And others might be extremely talented in the work that they do, maybe as surgeons, or as firefighters, even professional athletes. They just seem better than the rest. This could be because of the echo in them."

Beverly paused a moment, then continued. "Mavis is an echo. She is sleazy, always running scams here and there. She didn't even know about being an echo until she was an adult. By that time, it's usually too late to be popped. People are just too set in their ways to be able to have their full abilities come to the surface. It's like they calcify, and nothing can break through to bring their witchcraft out.

"But I'm pretty sure her whole life she's been able to do minor things, like make really great skin concoctions, maybe even get lucky now and then at pull tabs or the smaller state lotteries."

Charlie had no idea what pull tabs were, but he didn't want to interrupt his aunt's momentum. His own excitement was growing as he listened to all that she was saying.

"Sometimes people like her are called 'kitchen witches,' which isn't a nice thing to say to someone."

Charlie heard the term and suddenly remembered the dog in the kitchen, taunting his mother. It had said, "Or what? You'll bake something? You'll come at me with a rolling pin? Please, Elizabeth, we both know that you are nothing more than a kitchen witch these days."

His lips begin to tremble, and shivers ran up and down his arms.

"Charlie, what is it?" he heard his aunt saying. "You're turning pale."

Her voice brought him back from the kitchen down in Clarkston to this bigger, more modern one. He saw his aunt and uncle staring at him, the knife in Randall's hand paused above the cutting board.

He shook his head to clear away the images in his mind.

"That dog, you know? The one that came into our house and …?"

"Yes?"

"He called my mom that. A kitchen witch. Before she made him, uh, made him turn into a man. He said it to her."

"What?" Beverly snapped, coming around from the corner of the counter as if she were about to confront the man himself. "Idiot! He had no right to say anything like that to her!"

"Hon, calm down, okay?" said Randall. "Just take a breather."

She paused, then looked at her husband. Charlie watched as she inhaled. "Okay, sorry. Charlie, your mother is not a kitchen witch. She was fully popped and had been developing her abilities for a few years before she ... before she left Seattle. She stopped, so she isn't very strong. But she has access to her full legacy. That dog didn't know what the hell it was talking about.

"Anyway, there are people like Mavis all over Seattle, all over the world, really, who have some latent talent and use it to trick folks. They run seedy psychic shops, become fake fortune tellers. They do other scams too. We keep an eye on them. For the most part they don't have enough ability to cause any real damage. Just more of a nuisance, really.

"Today I just let Mavis know that I was on to her and gave her a very strong warning to stay away from you. She knows I can come after her and make her life miserable, should I want to. She wouldn't want me or our community watchdogs to track her. I'm confident that she'll back off and not cause any more problems."

"Why did she do that to me then?"

"Do what, honey?" she asked, knitting her eyebrows together.

"Put her hand on my arm like that?"

"Oh, she could probably tell that you had some unpopped abilities and wanted to find out more about you."

"But she made me feel really dizzy and kind of sick to my stomach, like I was gonna puke or pass out or something."

"What? That's impossible! She doesn't have that kind of ability. How could she ...? Charlie, are you sure that's what she was doing?" Beverly asked.

"She grabbed my arm and started rubbing sunscreen on it. I didn't know what to do, so I just stood there. She was talking to me, then she looked at me funny and said, 'Hey, you're a ...' and she stopped rubbing my arm. She held on to it though and started saying these words, words I couldn't really hear. I felt all dizzy, and like all the lights started to go out."

"Damn it!" Beverly slapped her closed right fist into her left palm. "That changes things."

"What is it, Bev? Isn't she just an echo?" asked Randall.

"Yes," she said, but her voice trailed off as she looked out the window over Puget Sound.

"Beverly, don't go quiet on us now. What is it?" Charlie's uncle pressed.

"It's just that," she said, her voice muted, her face still turned away, "it's just that she shouldn't be able to do what she did. Something is up. Something is definitely up." Charlie watched as her face hardened like it had at the market. His skin broke out in gooseflesh as he too looked out the window, half expecting to see Mavis standing outside on the deck, staring in at them.

His aunt turned from the window and faced them both.

"That's enough for now," she said, and the tone of her voice made it clear that there was no room for discussion. "We'll continue this when the others get here."

Charlie didn't think that it was enough. He wanted to know what was "definitely up," wanted to know what she was thinking, wanted to know what Mavis had been doing and what it all meant.

But Beverly had already turned to stare out the window again. When he opened his mouth to say something, Randall cut a glance at him and shook his head, mouthing the word "no."

Charlie sighed, accepting the fact that the conversation, at least for now, was over.

He tried to imagine what getting popped was like. Images flooded his mind: a cork being removed from a champagne bottle; his friend Mike teaching him how to make popping noises by flicking his finger out of his mouth with his cheeks puffed out; watching Polaroid pictures develop in front of his eyes from his mother's old camera; a human face breaking through the surface of still water.

Was it like any of those things? Did it hurt? Would he be able to get popped?

He walked out of the kitchen while his mind raced with thoughts of echoes and popped witches, of people sneaking around behind Beverly's back, of the dizzy way he felt when Mavis grabbed hold of him and wouldn't let go.

CHAPTER 25

Invitation

CHARLIE WENT BACK UPSTAIRS to change his clothes for dinner. He saw his cell phone sitting on the bed and suddenly remembered meeting Diego. He had forgotten about him after what happened with Mavis.

He frowned as he sat down on the bed and picked up the phone. He was still shaken from what Beverly had been saying downstairs. He probably shouldn't call the boy now, even though Diego had told Charlie to get hold of him about the party.

The more he thought about it, the more he was sure that Diego had just been playing the nice guy. He probably felt sorry for Charlie, being the new kid and all, and wanted to help him out, like a charity case or something. Why else would he have entered his number into Charlie's phone?

He was about to give up on the whole idea when an image of the boy's face appeared in his mind: the bright eyes, the warm brown color of his skin, the smile that seemed to be an invitation to kindness and adventure. He tried to erase the picture from his head, but it wouldn't disappear.

He thought about the easy way Diego had chatted to him and how Charlie didn't have to explain himself when they had talked.

Maybe we really could be friends, he thought. And before he could talk himself out of it, he found Diego's name in his contacts and called him.

"Hello?" said the voice on the other end of the line, in a cheerful, slightly breathless way.

"Uh, Diego? Is this Diego?"

"Yeah ..."

"Oh, um, yeah. Hi. This is Charlie. The uh, the guy from the ..."

"Charlie! Charlie Creevey! Oh good, you called back. I didn't think you were going to."

"Why not?" Charlie forgot that he had told Diego his last name. Sometimes kids teased him about it. He had heard "Creepy Creevey" his whole life. But Diego didn't tease him. Charlie liked how it sounded when the boy said it, as if he had filed it away in his memory as something important.

"Oh, I'm weird that way, that's all. Hey, do you still wanna go to that party Tuesday night? Did you ask your aunt and uncle?"

"Uh, no."

"No, you don't want to go, or ...?" he asked, his last word rising up into a question.

"No, no. I mean, no, I didn't ask them yet. But I'd like to, uh, yeah, I'd like to go, if, you know, if that's okay and all."

"Totally okay, you goofball," the boy said and laughed.

Charlie smiled. He had never been called a goofball in a nice way before.

He lay back on the bed and looked out the window. A gust of wind swayed the birch trees in the front yard, making their leaves flash from green to silver to green again.

While the boys began to chat, the whole experience of Mavis, of witches being popped, of people with echoes, faded into the background. They talked about school, about their teachers, about Seattle. Diego was a junior and had taken Chinese for two years.

"Ni juede xuexi Zhongwen nanbunan?" Diego said, sounding completely different, like maybe he was Chinese or something.

"Um, I have no idea what you just said," Charlie replied.

Diego laughed. It was a gentle laugh, not cruel, just a sound that seemed to mean he was enjoying himself. It was a sound Charlie liked.

"I asked you if you thought studying Chinese was difficult."

"Yeah, definitely. I mean, sometimes I don't even know what Chen Laoshi is saying until class is over, and then it's too late."

"Don't worry. You'll get used to it."

They talked some more until Charlie heard the doorbell ring downstairs and remembered that he hadn't changed his clothes yet.

"Uh, Diego, look, I think I should go. Some people are coming over for dinner."

"Hope they taste good," he said. "Ha ha ha."

"Okay, now who's the goofball?" Charlie replied. He wasn't used to teasing people, and the words felt as foreign in his mouth as Chinese did.

But Diego laughed again, harder this time.

"Okay, man, take care. Hey look, the party starts at seven. I can come by and pick you up at six forty-five. Why don't you have your aunt and uncle call me? They can talk to my mom to make sure it's all cool. Adults like that kind of thing."

"Sure, sure they do," Charlie said, just like a kid who was used to asking his mom if he could go to parties.

Charlie pressed "end" on his phone, then got up and walked over to the window. The wind had died down, and the street in front of the house was quiet. People must be settling in for their Sunday evenings together, he thought. Just before he turned around, he spied a small cat sitting on the curb on the opposite side of the street in front of a thick expanse of green trimmed lawn. The cat seemed to be staring right at him, and its tail stretched out from the side of its sleek body. As he watched, another cat approached and sat down next to the first. Both animals seemed to be looking directly up at the window where he stood.

"That's weird," Charlie said out loud. He left the window and went over to his closet to find something to wear for dinner.

CHAPTER 26

The Accidental Spy

THE SUN SAT POISED ABOVE the Olympic Mountains. The colors of the pre-sunset sky mingled with oranges and purples, pinks and maroons. They would look cheap painted as makeup on a woman's face, Mavis thought, but even she had to admit that it just made the sky look prettier.

There wasn't much that she found pretty these days. Everything looked washed out and gray, even without the constant drizzle that would certainly be settling in any day now. Mavis sighed, shifting her weight on the park bench, which was growing steadily colder.

She had wanted all of this, hadn't she? She had wanted to be more, had told herself for years that if she could, life would be better. It would be easier. More colorful even. She wouldn't be so broke all of the time.

Well, that hadn't happened yet. Who cared if she could actually do more now? She used to be able to live in relative obscurity, deciding how her days went, even deciding who she got to pal around with. She and her friends would mostly complain about everything, always wanting things to be different. But at least they got to complain when they wanted to.

But now, no. Now her time was dictated by others. She felt like an indentured servant, with the terms of her unwritten contract changing all the time, getting worse.

And the money never came. That was the biggest rub. You had to have a good plan in order to liberate people of their hard-earned cash, and in order to have a good plan, you had to have time. She was a fool. She had only thought about being able to do more, to have more, to finally upgrade herself to be more like a real ...

"Hello, Mavis," said a soft voice in her right ear. She jumped, her hands clutching at her ample bosom.

"Jesus!" she wheezed. Unable to catch her breath, she started coughing.

The young woman sitting on the park bench next to her laughed, clear notes ringing true in the cooling twilight.

"It's just me, honey. Relax."

Mavis remembered Beverly saying, "Don't you 'honey' me." She almost opened her mouth and repeated the line, but she cherished her existence too much to start the conversation like that.

"Do you always *(cough)* have to *(cough)* sneak up on me like that?" Cough, cough.

Another laugh. "I thought you'd quit smoking."

Mavis sucked at the air, trying to stay calm. She had once thought she could hold her own with these people. Now she did her best just to remain unscathed.

"I did. Damage's been done, though," she said, pointing to her lungs.

Mavis turned her head to look at the woman. Claudia was young, black, with tight curly hair springing from her head in coils that reached just below her earlobes. Her eyes were the color of jade and would have been beautiful on a normal human being. On Claudia they were exquisite. Painfully so. As was everything about her, from her high cheekbones, to her mahogany-colored skin, to her lithe figure. She had a warm, sugary scent about her. She looked like she belonged in a multivitamin commercial or an ad for a Caribbean cruise.

Looking at her was a mistake. Mavis held her hand over her mouth to feign another cough. Instead she mumbled a few Words and relaxed slightly as she felt a thin veneer surface between them. It helped Mavis to find her balance again. Claudia could suck her in and enchant her in a heartbeat if she wanted to.

"Mavis, dear, why the distance? You know you're safe here with me."

"Ha! That's a laugh. Like the sheep is safe with the wolf?"

"Like the sheep is safe with the shepherd, dear one. You know that."

Several retorts sprang into her head, but she kept her mouth closed. She was learning. She had spent her entire life saying whatever she wanted, whenever she wanted. The luxury of all of that easy tongue-wagging was nearly gone. Bank account drained, so to speak. The price of getting what she always thought she had wanted was watching her freedom and time drift away from her, slipping right through her fingers. And it was too late to do anything about it.

"What can I do for you, Claudia?"

The young woman sighed, and her sugary smell filled Mavis's nostrils. It made her want to cry, to let her head drop down onto Claudia's firm breasts and be held while she wept and told her everything.

But Mavis knew that she had to keep whatever autonomy she still had these days.

Claudia patted Mavis on her hand. The woman's skin was warm. What it must be like to let those fingers run along your skin, to let her palm press down into …

"What do you want?" she asked, wishing this were already over, wishing that she were home alone, in her robe and slippers, watching *American Idol*, a hot mug of tea and a plate of cookies her only companions.

"Just a report, sweet 'ums. That's all. What's new in the neighborhood?"

Mavis still wasn't sure why they needed people like her to report in on goings-on. Claudia and the others dripped with so much power that it was like sitting next to a nuclear reactor. Couldn't they just divine what they needed and leave her alone?

But clearly she was missing something. There was some need they had that she and the others provided. The other halfies, as she liked to think about them. What a joke, though. More like a half of a half of nothing.

She told Claudia about the different networks operating around the city, about how they had infiltrated the courtrooms downtown, about the new school board superintendent that they had put in place, about the kids over on Beacon Hill. To be honest, it wasn't much. But she had to stretch it out to make sure that Claudia knew she was doing her job.

Mavis had considered not mentioning the unpopped boy at the farmers market. She really didn't want to be on Beverly's bad side any more than she already was. But if she didn't, and her little omission were discovered, she would be on Claudia's bad side too. And when you were on Claudia's bad side, it was only a matter of time before you were on her bad side, and when that happened …

Jesus, she thought to herself for the hundredth time that day. *Can't I just get out of this? Can't I just go back to being a hag with no real abilities to speak of? I just want to be home, I just want to be …*

She stopped. Whining to herself would only have her lose focus. Not a good thing to do when sitting on a park bench, now in the dark, with someone like Claudia. Besides, she needed to make sure that Claudia and the others knew she could still provide value. She told the woman about her encounter at the farmers market.

Claudia listened quietly. Even though Mavis looked straight ahead out over the dark waves of the Sound, she could feel the twin emeralds of Claudia's eyes pressing against the side of her face, pulling at her.

When she finished talking, Claudia said, "So. Mama bear felt threatened today, did she? Interesting." Her last word seemed to linger. Mavis could almost see it as a smoke ring, thick and solid, floating up in the night air.

"Thank you, Mavis. You've been a very helpful kitten today." Claudia stood up from the park bench.

"Don't mention it," Mavis replied, hoping she sounded nonchalant.

"Keep up the good work, okay?" The beautiful young witch cooed at her as she turned her back on the park bench and walked across the cement path, leaving a faint waft of wet wood lingering in the air.

Mavis couldn't resist glancing over her shoulder. Weak yellow light from the lamppost a few feet away showed Claudia reaching into her pants pocket and pulling out something the approximate size of a single chopstick. She threw it to the ground, and Mavis heard a cracking sound, then watched as the chopstick shot out into a full broomstick, its bristles extending outward in a soft whoosh.

The witch picked up the broom from the ground, placed it between her legs, then waggled her fingers in Mavis's direction.

"Toodle-oo," she said. Her face was covered in shadow, but Mavis knew she was smiling. She pushed with her feet and sailed off into the night.

CHAPTER 27

Dinner Party

GLASSES CLINKED, CANDLE FLAMES flickered, Amos sighed on the floor near the table. They sat in the dining room, all six of them. The sun had nearly set, and Randall dimmed the lights until they shone with a soft glow.

At first Charlie thought that he shouldn't be wearing jeans and a sweatshirt. The silverware sparkled on the table, and to him the dining room looked like the kind of restaurant he had seen on TV, the kind he had never been to before. But the others were also casually dressed and seemed very relaxed with each other.

His aunt and uncle sat on either side of him. Across from him and to the left sat Daniel Burman, a thickly built quiet man with hair cut close to his scalp. He worked as a detective in the Seattle Police Department. His eyes were pale gray and seemed to bore into whatever caught their attention, including, at times, Charlie. The man appeared to be in his late forties or early fifties.

Next to Daniel sat Rita and Jeremy Lostich, a married couple in their late twenties or early thirties who owned several coffee shops around town. "Local and fair trade, of course," said Rita, winking at him and laughing. He didn't know what that meant but found himself smiling back at her. She had curly dark blond hair that fell halfway down her back. She smelled of spice and wore a loose sleeveless shirt. A small ring pierced her nose. She had a generous laugh.

Her husband Jeremy had a beard and shoulder-length dark hair, which he wore parted down the middle so that it hung down and over each side of his forehead like opened curtains. He had kind eyes and an easy smile. Charlie thought he could play the role of Jesus in an Easter movie.

"The Lostiches are my favorite hippy-chic couple," Randall had told Charlie as he had made introductions.

Where the Lostiches were quick-witted and giggly, Daniel Burman remained solemn, almost brooding. Neither, however, appeared bothered by the other. Only Charlie seemed surprised by the contrast.

The guests oohed and aahed over his aunt and uncle's cooking. The meal was halibut, steamed in a banana leaf, with rice, soy sauce, green onions, ginger, chilies, and sesame oil. They had roasted summer squash, and there were fresh greens with berry something-or-other that was tart and refreshing. ("It's just a fancy name for a sauce, Charlie. Remember, these witches are insufferable!" Randall had teased.)

Charlie was pretty sure his aunt had informed the guests ahead of time that he was shy, because they didn't pry him with questions. Rita told him that she had lived for several years in the Lake Tahoe area and knew the foothills quite well.

"I used to hang out in Nevada City as a teenager."

"Yeah, N.C. is pretty cool."

"Did you ever go to Fairplay?"

"Yeah, it's about forty-five minutes away from Clarkston. Closer to Forkville," Charlie said. Then he remembered the newscast he had seen with his mother and the photo of Ted Jones, the Forkville high school senior beaten and left by the roadside. He had forgotten all about him in the tumult that had preceded coming to Seattle.

Daniel was staring at him from across the table, as if waiting for him to say something. The candlelight made his gray eyes look silver. Instead of saying more, Charlie looked down at his plate and stabbed the last bite of fish with his fork.

"Well," said Rita. "I heard a rumor there was dessert?"

Randall and Beverly served homemade green tea sorbet with ginger cookies, accompanied by late-summer peaches from the farmers market, which brought more expressions of delight from the guests.

"So what happened earlier today, Ms. Geehan?" Jeremy asked after licking a drop of sorbet from his spoon. "You were so cryptic on the phone."

Charlie looked up at his aunt. Geehan? That was her last name? It dawned on him that he hadn't known his aunt and uncle's last name even though he had been living with them for over a week already. Maybe he had heard it during the mad dash to get him registered at Puget Academy. He couldn't remember. There was still so much he didn't know.

Beverly began. "Randall, Charlie, and I went to the West Seattle Farmers Market this morning. I was pricing some orchids. When I looked up I saw Mavis O'Malley, of all people, sitting behind a booth, holding onto Charlie's arm."

All three dinner guests reacted.

"What?" said Daniel.

"No way!" said Rita.

"You gotta be friggin' kidding me," said Jeremy, his rough response tarnishing his Jesus-like image.

"It's true. Charlie," now Beverly turned to him, "it would be easier if you told this part of the story. Do you mind?"

He had hoped that he wouldn't have to talk much in front of these new adults, let alone recount the events at the farmers market. But everyone was looking at him. He opened his mouth to say something, but his throat was bone dry.

He took a long sip of water from his drinking glass, then felt his face redden as his mouth made a loud sucking noise.

"It's okay, buddy," said Randall, ignoring the sound. "Just tell them what you told us."

"Yeah, well, um, I just wandered by her booth, not really paying attention to anything, you know?" He left out the part about meeting Diego.

Everyone nodded, so he continued, explaining how Mavis had grabbed his arm, what she had said to him, how he had felt dizzy and couldn't see very well.

"That goddamn hag!" Rita exclaimed, slamming her hand down on the table, causing the dishes and silverware to rattle. "What was she thinking, doing a drain like that?" Charlie wondered if maybe the Lostichs weren't as "peace and love" as Randall had led him to believe.

"More importantly, how did Mavis O'Malley learn to do a drain anyway?" asked Daniel.

"My thoughts exactly," said Beverly.

"What happened after that?" asked Jeremy.

Beverly took over the recounting of the incident. "I walked right over to her and told her that if she messed with me and mine, I'd mess with her."

"You didn't!" said Jeremy, impressed.

"You bet I did. I told her to leave the farmers market and not come back. I know it scared her."

The adults all looked at each other, then at Charlie.

It was taciturn distant Daniel Burman who spoke next. "I'll get my inside team to investigate. Something is afoot among the echoes here in Seattle. I don't like it."

CHAPTER 28

How Do I?

BEVERLY LED CHARLIE THROUGH a trail at Carson Park, Amos pulling hard at the leash in her hand. It was Monday, after school. "We'll get there, buddy, we'll get there," she said to the dog.

When Charlie had walked into the house earlier that afternoon, his aunt had approached him from the kitchen.

"Would you be up for a walk with Amos and me today? There's something I'd like to show you, and I thought it would be fun to have a little outing at the same time."

The weather was cooler today. Charlie had watched a cold full moon rise in the near-black sky the night before from his bedroom window soon after he had explained what Mavis had done to him and the table-side discussion had wound down.

He felt a chilly touch of autumn in the air as they walked along. The afternoon light glowed and the undergrowth shone bright green against the dun walking trail, as if everything were preparing for the full color display of the upcoming season.

"… and the reason I decided to keep my last name was because it was part of who I was, part of my community," Beverly was saying.

Charlie hadn't been paying attention, caught up as he was in the lushness of the woods.

"Wait, so your last name is 'Geehan' but Randall's is 'Ruben'?"

"That's right. 'Geehan' is my family name. It's your Mom's too. Or it was before she changed it to 'Creevey' to hide her identity. Amos! Get away from there!" Beverly yelled, then laughed as she yanked on the leash trying to keep the dog from sniffing at a small pile of animal scat on the trailside.

Charlie wasn't really sure why she was telling him this, but he found himself enjoying the conversation nonetheless. More than once in the last week he had observed Beverly talking to him like he was someone with thoughts and opinions about things. He had never really regarded himself that way, but maybe he was that kind of person. Or maybe he could become one.

"So that's why you both decided to keep your own last names?" he said as they stepped over a sodden log laying in the middle of the path. Amos took the opportunity to lift his leg on a bunch of devil's club, a stalky spiked plant that Beverly had pointed out earlier.

"That's right. Randall has extended family all over the U.S. and Europe. He isn't religious, but his Jewish roots are very important to him. He likes being part of that group of people, or 'tribe' as he calls it, even if he doesn't know most of them. It gives him a sense of place in the world. A sense of belonging.

"It's the same thing with me. The legacy of my family is such a strong part of who I am. It ties me to my community. Not just the Irish part, but the witch part too. I thought about changing my name to 'Ruben' when I got married, but it felt like I would be losing who I was."

Charlie wondered if that meant he was Irish too. Like everything else, his mother had never told him about his ancestry.

They took a right turn and ducked under several cedar branches, which hung over the path like mossy green flags.

"Can I, um, ask you some more questions?" Charlie asked once they had begun to follow a wider trail.

"Shoot."

"Well, really … I have a bunch."

"Go ahead."

He paused, then took a deep breath.

"I'm a witch, right?"

"Yes. Or, more technically, you have the legacy in you. Your mother carried it very strongly, so you do too."

"What about my dad? Was he a witch?"

Beverly didn't say anything for quite some time. He wondered if he had said something wrong. The trail climbed up for about a hundred yards, so when they reached the top they were both out of breath.

"Whew!" she said, hands on her thighs, inhaling and exhaling deeply. After a moment, she continued.

"I don't know. I didn't even know you existed until last week. I thought your mother would be more forthcoming, but ..." she trailed off.

Then she surprised him with what she said next.

"Your birthday's in August. August 18." It was a statement, not a question.

"Yeah," he replied, wondering what that had to do with anything.

"Well, if you do the math, November is nine months before August. And November is when Lizzy left Seattle. That means that somewhere around the time your mother left and when she got to California, she ..." Beverly paused.

"Oh. She met my father?" He finished. It hadn't occurred to him to count the months backwards from his birthday after he had read his mother's notebook.

"That's what I figure. But that doesn't really tell us anything about him, does it? Lizzy wasn't dating anyone at the time she left town, at least not that I knew of. I had hoped there would be more clues in her diary. But your mother can be very, shall we say, secretive?" Charlie heard the frustration in her voice. "You'll have to ask her about it, since it's her story to tell."

Then she smiled at him.

"But I do know that you have the legacy in you. Even if your father wasn't a witch. The blood in our family is strong," she said proudly, then continued along the path.

Charlie wished he could find out more about his father but knew that Beverly was as much in the dark as he was. So he switched topics.

"Well, how do I become a witch then?"

"I thought you'd never ask," his aunt said as they walked farther into the woods.

CHAPTER 29

The Leap

CHARLIE FELT THE AIR GROW COOLER around them, and the trail that they had been following, narrowed by brambles and the tree limbs crowding in on either side, expanded into a wide cement lane. He could hear the sound of a stream somewhere to his right as well as cars passing nearby.

It was the same spot as last week where he had encountered the dog and the elderly witch who'd shooed it away.

He tensed, expecting at any moment to see the same dog rounding the corner up ahead.

Beverly pointed up toward the break in the trees. "See that?"

At first, Charlie only saw the leafy branches of the trees and the late afternoon sunlight filling the open spaces, turning everything green-gold. Then a massive concrete base, covered in graffiti, rose into view leading up to the criss-cross of girders and eventually a wide rust-colored bridge spanning the airway at the point where the lane veered left and out of sight.

He was surprised to realize that he hadn't even noticed the bridge last week because he had been distracted by the dog's presence. After the woman had told Charlie that everything was safe again, he had turned around and led Amos back home, having lost his stomach for more exploration.

Walking closer, Charlie saw that the base marked the far left edge of the lane while its twin sat a good fifty yards across from it.

In between the two bases, a small stream gurgled along, two steep banks flanking it on either side, and a wide stretch of dirt led from the stream bed to the opposite bridge base.

It created a strange feeling. Most of these woods were cramped with trees, small paths running here and there. Other than at the wider entrance at the mouth of the park, you had to walk single file on all of the trails. But here everything spread out. The bridge seemed to pull at the treetops, stretching them higher into the air, creating an expansive unexpected canopy.

"I always liked it here, this surprise," Beverly said. "You're just walking along with all this foliage blocking everything and then, suddenly, a bridge!"

She explained that it was part of Admiral Way, that he had driven over it with them when heading down from their house to Alki Beach. He remembered seeing it, with a sidewalk on either side for pedestrians. That would explain the car sounds he could hear. It was strange to be underneath it now.

Beverly walked over to a wooden bench that sat on the bank overlooking the stream. She tied Amos's leash to one of the bench legs, then sat down and motioned for Charlie to join her.

The dry bank of the stream at their feet sloped sharply down about five feet, where it touched the pebbles of the stream bed. Another bank rose up on the opposite side before leveling off into the expanse of dirt ending at the farthest bridge base. Charlie could see empty beer bottles scattered near the base as well as small piles of fast food wrappers.

"You know, I'd chastise the kids who come here and litter like that," she said to him, "except that it would be the pot calling the kettle black. I used to do the same thing when I was young," a slight smile playing on her face. "But don't tell anyone I told you so. Deal?"

"Deal," he smiled, enjoying sharing this secret with her.

"Charlie, when I was your age, I had already known about the legacy for a long time. I didn't need to have it explained to me in such a rushed way, like we're doing with you.

"Even so, we kids would compare stories. Some of what we told each other was true, and some of it we made up, either to act like know-it-alls or just to scare each other. I did a fair amount of that story swapping right over there, under the bridge."

"Like what?"

"Oh, my friend Janey told me once that her mother always knew when she was going to do something bad, so for years I believed the woman had eyes in the back of her head. Or Mark Ferguson got us all to believe that his dad had single-handedly stopped a band of thieves from stealing diamonds out of a downtown vault."

She laughed and shook her head, the afternoon light shining on her dark hair.

"It wasn't until I grew up that I learned those stories had just been, well, stories. Made-up myths. I'm telling you this so you'll know that I won't make things up when you have questions, okay? I'll do my best to be as accurate as possible.

"But," Beverly said, then stopped. Charlie watched as her brow furrowed and her eyes seemed to grow slightly darker. "There are certain things I can't tell you. Sometimes it's because I don't know the answers. As you'll soon discover, there are many things out there that we don't understand. Mysteries. Other times it'll be because I won't tell you. Certain things you are just going to have to learn for yourself."

She looked up at the bridge and paused, as if she were counting the cars passing by overhead. Then she turned her head and continued.

"But feel free to ask anything that you'd like. If I can't or won't answer, I'll try to tell you why not. How does that sound?"

"Good. Yeah, pretty good," he answered. He already knew that she grew uncomfortable when the topic of his mother came up, about why she had run away and what had happened before he was born. So he decided to move on to something else.

"So, um, does that mean you will or you won't tell me about becoming a witch?"

She laughed.

"Nope, I can tell you about that. Or at least enough to satisfy you, I think. We talked yesterday about popping, and echoes, and the craft being in someone's blood. Well, the craft is definitely in your blood, Charlie. You'll be popped when you're ready."

"When will I be ready?"

"When you reach a certain age. It's different for everybody, but mostly it coincides with puberty."

"But aren't I, I mean, right now …?" He stopped, blushing, caught between his desire to become a witch and the horror that his aunt might decide to talk about the birds and the bees with him.

"Probably. There's a man named Malcolm who knows about all of that and does the popping. I can't do it, nor can any of the other witches in our community. We don't have that ability."

"Will he be …?"

"I sent him a message about you. He should be back in town in a week or so."

"Does it hurt?"

"What Malcolm does?" She smiled, then shook her head. "No, it doesn't hurt. But it's a bit strange. What happens is, well, it's sort of like …"

She looked off into the distance, trying to find the words.

"Imagine that all your life you could only see out of one eye. The other one was completely blind. So you couldn't see everything fully, and you developed habits to compensate. Popping is like finally getting that bad eye fixed. Sure, it's great, because you get full vision, but it's also disorienting. You aren't used to it at first. And all those ways of compensating are habits that don't die off instantly.

"Or imagine being deaf all your life, and then suddenly you can hear. It's hard to get used to all that noise, and you don't know how to block it out right away. It takes time to adjust. Not forever, but a while. Does that make sense?"

Charlie nodded, but only because she expected him too. He couldn't imagine what it would be like.

"Once Malcolm pops you, there will be lots of us to guide you, to help you adjust. But that's really only the first step. Just because you get popped doesn't mean you can do everything right away.

"Let's go back to the one-eye example. Think of it like learning to paint. Getting popped is like getting your full vision back, but it doesn't mean you know how to draw shapes or how to mix colors. Or even how to hold a paintbrush. It just means you have the aptitude for it. You'll still have to learn a lot."

She stopped talking. Charlie could hear her words echoed softly back from the far bank of the stream.

"Sometimes, someone's ability can leak a little during stressful situations. That's probably what happened to you with that stone pendant down in California. When that man attacked your mother, a part of your ability leaked out.

"Or take Mavis. Most likely something traumatic happened to her when she was young, causing a part of her ability to surface. Or whatever blocked her eroded away a little over time as she grew older. That can happen too.

"At least that's what I thought until you told me what she did to you yesterday. Remember when Rita called it a drain? It's when you siphon off someone's potency for a little while. Kind of like draining their blood. The one doing the draining gets a jolt of power, while the one being drained feels weak for a while. Mavis is just a minor scam artist with very little real talent. She shouldn't have been able to do what she did."

"Then how did she?" Charlie asked, leaning forward so that his elbows rested on his knees. He felt a chill run up his spine and shuddered, remembering how Mavis had gripped his arm, how nauseous and dizzy he had felt. He ran his hand along his forearm right at the place where her fingers had dug into his skin.

"That's what we don't know. We keep an eye on echoes like her so that they can't cause any trouble. If something changed in her, we should have known about it."

"What kind of trouble?"

"Oh, petty stuff, the kind I told you about yesterday in the kitchen. Winning minor state lotteries, horse-racing scams, those kinds of things. Daniel's going to look into it. Besides his regular detective work, he keeps track of what's going on in the witching world. He's good at what he does. If anyone can find out more about her, he can.

"Anyway, you don't need to worry about this right now. You have your schoolwork cut out for you, and when Malcolm gets back, you'll have your craft to learn about. It takes a lot of practice, believe me.

"In the meantime, will you wear this?" Beverly reached into her shirt pocket and pulled out a thin silver bracelet. "It's the main reason I brought you here today."

"What is it?"

"This will hide your potential from other witches so that they can't guess about you the way Mavis did. It would also alert me if you were in any kind of trouble."

"How does it work?"

She winked at him. "It's a secret. Wait until you're popped and then we can revisit the question, okay?"

Charlie nodded, then slipped the bracelet onto his wrist. He thought he would feel something, maybe a slight buzzing or a tiny vibration to indicate that it was actually working. But it just felt like cool metal on his skin.

"It doesn't seem like it's doing anything."

Beverly laughed. "Don't worry. It is."

He liked the way the thin band looked on his wrist, the tiny blond hairs of his arms contrasting with the silver color.

"Well, um, thanks," he said.

"You got it, Bucko."

"Why did you have to bring me here to give it me?"

"I didn't. I just thought a walk sounded nice, and I wanted to show you where I used to hang out."

He smiled at her. They sat together for a while, enjoying the stream in front of them and the occasional birdsong in the trees overhead.

Then he remembered something and started jiggling his feet in anticipation.

"Oh, could I, well, do you think that I could ..." he started, feeling his shyness descend like a heavy blanket. His foot accidentally kicked Amos, who was lying in the dirt in front of them. The dog yelped and stood up.

"Oh, Amos. I'm sorry, boy" he said as the dog dropped his head beneath Charlie's hands. He rubbed the dog's neck, enjoying how his dark fur looked purple in the late afternoon light.

"Don't worry. Amos is a big dog and is used to getting bumped. Aren't you, buddy? Aren't you?" she said, joining Charlie in giving the dog a good back rub. The dog moaned in pleasure.

"What were you going to ask?" said his aunt after a moment.

"Oh. Do you think I could go to a party tomorrow night?" There, he had said it before he could chicken out.

"A party? Well, sure. Is it at someone's house?"

"Yeah, it's some kids at Puget Academy. I got invited by someone, by this guy, Diego, from school. I don't know the people having the party. But their parents will be there. Diego gave me his number. He said you could call him and his mom to ask about the details."

"Well, how thoughtful. Sure, why don't we call when we get back? What a nice thing for you to do, Charlie. You'll get to know more kids at school," she said, giving him a smile of encouragement.

Charlie nodded but didn't look at his aunt. A part of him wanted to tell her about the brown-skinned boy and how they talked to each other, but he didn't know what to say, especially since he didn't know what he thought about it all.

"Before we go back, Charlie, I wanted to show you something else. Something witchy."

Excitement rose from his belly to his cheeks. Would it be like the candle trick?

"It's very important that others, people who aren't witches, don't find out about this. It would scare them too much. And it's important for us to protect our identity. But I can tell if we're alone and the coast is clear."

She stopped and tilted her head, as if listening to something in the distance. Then, after a few moments, "We're good."

His aunt stood up and faced him.

"You know how I said we kids used to swap stories over there, under that bridge?" she said, pointing to the expanse of dirt across the stream from where they sat.

"Yeah?"

"How do you think we got over there without getting wet?"

He shrugged. He hadn't thought about it.

"Like this," she said. Turning away from him, she bent her knees and jumped into the air. Instead of coming down in the middle of the shallow stream, her jump extended into a long arc that carried her clear over the stream bed and another good twenty feet beyond it. Her feet touched down next to the huge base of the bridge, landing her in a crouched position. She looked over her shoulder and smiled at him, then stood up and turned around.

"Whoa! Whoooa!" Charlie yelled, jumping up and down like a little kid on Christmas morning.

"Don't tell your uncle I did that, okay? I wouldn't hear the end of it," she yelled back at him.

"Whoa! Okay, I won't. But ... whoa!"

Amos barked at Beverly, his leash forcing him to run back and forth in small circles.

"Come on, come on, boy. You know you want to swim a bit. Come on," she called to him. "Charlie, undo his leash, will you?"

Charlie unclipped the lead from Amos's collar while the dog shivered in anticipation. Once set free, he leaped over the side of the embankment and threw himself into the stream, splashing and frothing the water for the short trip across before lumbering up the far bank and racing across the dirt to where Beverly stood.

"Good boy!" she exclaimed, then shielded herself with her hands in a very un-witchlike gesture as Amos shook water from his fur. "Ugh! I should have known better. He always does that!" She laughed.

After a moment, she looked over at Charlie. "Wanna try it?" she yelled. "The coast is still clear."

"What, you mean like Amos?"

"No, silly, like me."

"But I can't ..."

"I know. But I can. All you have to do is jump and leave the rest to me."

"Oh my god," he whispered. He stepped to the edge of the bank. Suddenly it seemed much higher, and Beverly appeared very far away.

"Come on, it's fun!" she shouted.

Fear took root in Charlie's chest and branched out like a tree. Or maybe it was excitement. He remembered his seventh grade science teacher, Mr. McPheeters, telling them that people's bodies respond to fear and excitement in much the same way: you start breathing faster, your hands get sweaty, your heart pumps harder ...

"Wanna?"

"Um, okay. Okay!" he yelled back. "What do I do again?"

"Just jump. I've got you."

"When?"

"Any time you're ready."

"Just jump?"

"Yeah. Just jump."

Charlie squatted down like his aunt had done. He paused, and in that moment everything grew brighter. A cluster of ferns off to the right of the stream bed glowed green. A single strand of spider web stretching from a fallen tree to a blackberry bush reflected light like a glass rod. Even the air seemed to change, growing thinner and cleaner.

He took a deep breath.

"Oh my god, oh my god, oh my god," he said, blowing the words through his clenched teeth.

And then he jumped as high as he could.

Instead of feeling the pull of gravity that would have cut his leap short, he felt something akin to invisible hands or a firm burst of wind pushing on his hips, his shoulders, the backs of his legs. He thought he might lose his balance and fall into the stream, but instead he soared right over the water. The pushing sensation continued as air blew against his face, just like it did when he rode his bike on a windy day.

His legs, slow to the fact that he was being swept along in a witch's embrace, pumped hard in midair as if to help.

"Unnnhhh!" he grunted, his voice straining to express the shock, the delight, the sheer miracle of such a launch.

And then, before he knew it, he landed with a soft thump as if he had just jumped from a low ledge. He wobbled for a moment before catching his balance.

Beverly was looking at him from where she stood four feet away, her eyes wide, a huge smile on her face.

"Whoa. That was like, totally, whoa!" He yelled, unable to find other words to capture the thrill. Before he could stop himself, he threw his arms around his aunt, and together they jumped up and down, laughing and yelling, "Whoa!" not caring in that moment if anyone could hear them, while Amos encircled them in leaps and wiggles, barking and wagging his wet tail, their collective noise rising all the way up to the September sky, like an exaltation, like a prayer.

CHAPTER 30

A Storm Is Coming

THAT EVENING, CHARLIE AND RANDALL drove to Costco to buy Charlie a printer for school. The windshield wipers kept up a steady rhythm against the drizzle as they drove down the long stretch of Admiral Way that would lead to the West Seattle Bridge.

"Your aunt told me that you two talked a lot about the legacy," Randall said, before looking out Charlie's passenger-side window at a woman in an SUV trying to merge into their lane. "Come on, princess, come on. Take your own sweet time. There you go." He winked at Charlie. "Sorry. Beverly says I have a bad habit of talking to drivers who can't hear me. She always reminds me that I'm the pilot, not the air traffic controller. Really, I'm just trying to help people.

"Anyway, do you have any questions for your old uncle here? About all of this stuff? I'm certainly not one of them, but I do have an outsider's perspective, which might help."

Charlie looked out the window as they drove over the bridge. It was hard to believe that it had only been a week since he and his mother had driven over this same bridge in the opposite direction as they arrived in West Seattle for the first time. It seemed like months.

"Well," Charlie dove in, his curiosity winning out over his shyness, "what about getting popped? Do you know about that?"

"A little, yes. I've never seen it happen. They don't exactly sell tickets to their events. But I've heard people say things about it. What do you want to know?"

"Beverly said it doesn't hurt, but that it's weird, like getting to see for the first time, or hearing things after you've been deaf."

"Yeah, that sounds about right. To me it seems like a combination of losing your virginity and having a bar mitzvah all at the same time. The adult community is proud of you, but you're pretty shocked and surprised by it all.

"Maybe," he added, flipping on the turn indicator and taking the Fourth Avenue exit, "it's like all of that and a really weird drug trip too. Uh, I shouldn't be talking to you about sex and drugs. Maybe I'm supposed to. Don't do drugs, okay? And as for sex … I'm not ready to talk to you about that." He smiled.

Charlie's ears and the back of his neck grew hot. He wanted to learn whatever he could from his non-witch uncle but knew that if the man talked any more about sex, he might just open up the passenger side door and jump out.

"Awkward silence," Randall said, and they both laughed.

"Anyway," he went on, "I've seen kids after they've been popped. They're very spacey, like you are after you've had surgery and are still goofy from the anesthesia. Have you ever had surgery?"

Charlie shook his head.

"They're silly for a while and can't quite figure regular things out. So they're watched, and eventually everything goes back to normal. Well, not exactly normal. They're popped and can learn to do some really amazing stuff. But their minds go back to being mostly like they were before."

"How long does that part take?"

"The spaced out feeling and coming back to normal? Seems to be anywhere from a few days to a week."

"No, I mean the popping part. How long does that take?"

"Well," he said, pondering the question. "Here's what's strange, Charlie. The witches aren't very big on ceremony. You know all those stories about the hocus-pocus and the big cauldrons? All that witch crap from the movies? It's hogwash. They just seem to sit down and mumble their words, which you can never hear anyway, and then they're done. Wham, bam, thank you, ma'am. You should see some of the ceremonies at a Jewish temple. They can go on forever. But not our witch friends. They're an efficient people."

Randall turned into the massive Costco parking lot. "It's always a hassle to find parking here. Let's see. Okay, Mr. Volkswagen, you coming or going? Okay, you're staying put, aren't you there, little buddy, okay, hmm ... ah, there's a spot, yep, let's just ... hey! Looks like Missy Ford Focus just stole from us. Ah ..." he said and then found a place to park between two large trucks. He turned off the car and faced Charlie.

"Beverly thinks I come here only for the hot dogs. I tell her she doesn't know what she's talking about. But she might be right. Don't you think the drive and the hassle of parking are worth it? Tell me you've had a Costco hot dog before."

Charlie shook his head.

"You're kidding me! Boy, you are in for a treat. But I warn you, those witchy foodie people will give you grief if you try to extol the virtues of the Costco dog. Confess to them at your own peril."

Randall grew serious. "Remember the other night, when I got mad at your mom and your aunt? And I mentioned how hard it was for me to accept Beverly's true identity?"

Charlie nodded.

"I thought that maybe if I told you the whole story, it might help you some."

"Yeah, sure," Charlie said, excited to learn more.

Randall looked out the window at the shoppers running into the store to avoid the rain.

"I met your aunt when I was just starting out as a pilot. My shift was over, so I flew as a passenger from Seattle to San Diego, where I was living at the time. She told me later that she was headed down for some sort of witch conference. As it happened, I was lucky enough to sit next to her.

"Holy schmokies, I fell head over heels the first five minutes we started talking. We didn't shut up the whole flight. When we landed and she got ready to leave, I asked for her phone number. I called her that night and we had our first official date."

He smiled as he stared ahead out the windshield as if seeing that first plane ride, not the gentle rain, the mass of cars parked in the lot, or the people wheeling large flatbed carts loaded with bulk toilet paper and guacamole.

"We dated long distance for a while, and then when things got more serious, I moved to Seattle. Her family and friends didn't like me very much. I thought it was because I was a new pilot and didn't have much money. Little did I know the real reason, that the community frowns on witches and non-witches being together. Of course, she didn't tell me any of that at the time. But she kept insisting that she wanted to be with me, so I just said, 'F-.' Oops. I said, 'Screw you all. We'll date if we want to.'

"We decided to get married. I didn't know how much pressure she was under to let go of the relationship. But eventually she persuaded her community to let her marry me. I found out much later that she had to go through a formal process where she promised that the safety and security of the witches would always trump anything else. That if our marriage ever threatened the secrecy of her community, she would choose them over us."

"How could your marriage threaten them?" Charlie asked.

"If I found out who Beverly was and divulged the secret to non-witches, they could all be exposed. So Beverly had to agree that if her non-witch husband ever spilled the beans, they'd make sure I never talked again." Randall's forced laugh bounced off the car's interior.

"Oh," Charlie said, the realization sending a small shiver down his back. He couldn't imagine the Lostiches silencing someone. Maybe Daniel Burman, but not Jeremy and Rita. Was it like the stories he had heard of Mafia killings? Or was it some spell the witches would cast to keep his uncle from talking?

"Yeah, right. Creepy. But like I said, I didn't know any of that at the time, and you know what they say—ignorance is bliss. So, we got married and lived for a while in a house over in Madison Park, like we told you the other night. Technically it's not that far away, but it can feel pretty removed from West Seattle. She was going back and forth a lot, and I was working long shifts and irregular hours as a pilot, because I didn't have seniority at the time, so I had to take any flight I could get."

He paused, running a hand over his mustache as if to flatten it, as if all this storytelling caused the hairs to stand on end. He turned his head and looked out the window at the truck next to them. Then he faced Charlie.

"I'm not proud to tell you this, but I began to get suspicious. Beverly kept strange hours. Stranger than mine. I knew there was something going on that she wasn't telling me. And look at her. She's a beautiful, talented, brilliant woman. Rich too. Deep down, I guess I couldn't believe that someone like her really wanted to be with an average Joe like me.

"So, I did the typical guy thing and began to worry that she was having an affair. I didn't confront her at first. But the longer we lived together, and the more she kept her weird hours and her secrets, the more I was sure that's what it was.

"'You're kidding, right? You can't be serious,' she kept saying when I told her what I suspected.

"But I didn't buy it. I begged her to tell me his name, where he lived, how many times a week they got together, if she had known him before she met me.

"She kept telling me that I was crazy, that there was no one else. She said she loved me and only me.

"But I kept at her. I'd say, 'Then what the hell is going on? What am I supposed to think? All these "family meetings" you go to'" Randall said, making air quotes with his fingers. "'Why don't you ever bring me? Why do you keep so many secrets from me?'

"She finally confessed that there were things she hadn't told me, but they didn't have anything to do with having an affair. Furthermore, she said they didn't threaten our relationship and hoped that I'd just forget about it. But I wouldn't let it go.

"'What is it?' I kept asking. 'Are you in trouble? Are people after you? Do you need money to pay them off? You could take our savings if you need it.'

"As you can see, I was just shooting in the dark.

"After days of this, she finally said, 'No, it's nothing like that, Rand. Believe me. Look, give me a few days, okay? Then I'll fill you in a bit. I just need some time to figure things out first.'

"Later that week she took me down to one of our favorite spots, just a little picnic table on the beach where no one else ever came. We bought fish and chips at a local shop like we had a million times before. It was raining much harder than it is right now, but like usual we had our trusty rain gear on.

"I was nervous. All I could imagine was that she was some sort of drug smuggler, or was plotting to take over the government or something. Or maybe she was a jewel thief," Randall said, shaking his head. "I know it sounds ridiculous. But I had no clue what she was going to disclose. Witchcraft isn't exactly the first thing that comes to mind.

"Anyway, after we'd eaten for a while in silence, she finally spoke.

"'Rand, do you love me?' she asked me, looking right at me with those big beautiful eyes of hers.

"I told her that I did.

"'Do you trust me?'

"I told her that I trusted her.

"She then proceeded to tell me right then and there about her family, about the legacy, about who she was and what she could do. I don't remember most of what she said though a few things do stand out: broomsticks, not bad people, but good, good people, spells and incantations, for the benefit of humanity and whatnot."

He paused, looking out the window again. The sudden silence seemed strange to Charlie. There had been so many words for the past twenty minutes, and now nothing. He caught himself holding his breath. He had to know what Randall had said in response. It seemed important, not just for his aunt and uncle, but for himself and his own future.

Finally, when he could handle the tension no longer, Charlie spoke. "What did you say? What did you say when she told you all that stuff?"

Even in the semidarkness of the car, Charlie could see the lines on his uncle's forehead deepen, could see the crow's-feet at the corners of his eyes grow longer.

"Well, it wasn't my best moment. Not by a long shot. At first I laughed. Then I told her she was crazy, not only for saying what she was saying, but for expecting me to believe it. I asked her if she needed professional help. I talked about medication.

"She told me later that as she sat there, listening to me accusing her of being a nutcase, she got angrier and angrier. I guess it had been a relief to let the cat out of the bag. She thought she could just tell me and everything would be right as rain. I was the first non-witch she'd ever talked to about all of it. It hadn't occurred to her that I'd laugh at her. That I wouldn't believe her.

"I know now how much I hurt her. Can you imagine? Finally telling the person you love most in the world who you really are only to have him behave like a complete jackass?

"Like I said, I know all of this now. But let's just say at the time I wasn't looking at the situation through her eyes. I was busy wondering how I could convince her to see a psychiatrist.

"Anyway, you've seen her get angry, Charlie. You know what she's like," Randall said, crossing his arms and looking at his nephew.

Charlie nodded, swallowing.

"You know how she goes very still, like the quiet before a storm?"

He nodded again, riveted to every word Randall was saying.

"After a long silence, she stood up from the picnic table. She put her hands on her hips, and even though she was wearing a raincoat, she looked scary. Intense. In that focused way she can get.

"She said, 'You want me to show you, Rand? You want me to show you I'm not the crackpot you think I am?'

"'Yeah, Beverly, go on. Show me some of this hoo-ha you're trying to convince me is real,'" said Randall, his voice mocking.

"You said that?" asked Charlie in disbelief.

"You bet I did. What would you have done? Your wife, whom you thought was having an affair, but now you think is nuts, wants to show you that she isn't?"

"Yeah, okay. Good point."

"She looks up for a minute, like she's listening for something, then makes this big sweeping movement with her hand," Randall said, demonstrating for Charlie, "and I swear to God, all the food on the table, all the little bits of fish and chips, the coleslaw, even the gobs of ketchup and tartar sauce, they shoot up into the sky like pebbles, and they just hover there, above her head, while she has this wild look in her eyes, staring at me. Before I can even register what's going on, a huge flock of seagulls swarms above us and eats it all up."

"Whoa! What did you do?" Charlie asked excitedly.

"At first I just sat there, blinking my eyes, with all that seagull squawking going on above us. I couldn't make sense of what I saw. I tried to convince myself that it hadn't happened. Maybe I'd missed something, maybe her arm actually hit the food, you know, and swept it up in the air. Maybe it hadn't really floated. Or a huge gust of wind did it. It's amazing what you tell yourself when you don't believe what's right in front of your nose.

"'You still don't believe me, is that it? You still think I'm crazy?' She started yelling at me, her hood back, her hair getting soaked. I gotta tell you, I did get a little afraid then. Or at least really really confused. Like maybe I didn't know which end was up anymore.

"Before I knew it, Beverly's hands came smashing down on the picnic table. The entire thing cracked down the middle lengthwise and collapsed in on itself. I fell back off the bench, but my feet got tangled up in the base of the table and I couldn't get away.

"'Do you think I'm crazy now?' she yelled at me. 'How 'bout now? How 'bout now?'

"She started doing things, Charlie. Her body changed shape, or color, I can't remember. Things flew at me. A small section of beach near us turned liquid, like a tar pit. I heard voices, I saw images of people I knew, floating in the tide pools nearby."

"What did you do? Were you still stuck under the table?"

"No, I managed to untangle myself and sort of crab-walk away from her, but she kept coming after me, yelling, asking if I still thought she was crazy.

"I'm not proud of what I did next, Charlie. All I can say is that I completely and utterly lost my shit. I just lost it."

Charlie waited, eagerly watching his uncle's face staring out the window, his brow furrowed, his large hands formed into fists and tapping on the steering wheel, his mouth opening then closing slightly as if he couldn't decide whether or not to bite into something. Minutes passed. So many, in fact, that he wasn't sure Randall was going to finish his story.

Finally he looked at his nephew.

"I left. I got up, ran across the street, got in my car, and drove away as fast as I could. And I didn't come back for a year."

"You what? You left her?" asked Charlie, incredulous. "You left Aunt Beverly? For a whole year?"

Having been left as a boy by his own father, Charlie had developed rules and laws about what you did and didn't do with your family. First and foremost was that you never left them. To do so was one of the most reprehensible things a person could do.

"I did. I never contacted Beverly. I never asked about her. I never …"

"But why? Why did you leave? Why didn't you come back?" Charlie interrupted. He knew the answer, knew that his uncle had been terrified. But he was angry at Randall for abandoning Beverly, angry for thinking that the best thing to do was to pack up and leave. Even more so, he was furious at his own mother for having done the same thing, for slipping away without telling him why. How could she?

But he didn't know how to express any of this, so for now all he could do was to ask the obvious.

Randall stared at the boy then turned his head away, as if he couldn't bear to look in Charlie's eyes.

"I'm not saying that what I did was a good thing. But you of all people should understand. I literally could not believe what Beverly had done. I felt like I was going crazy, like everything I knew about the world, about reality, about how things worked, was slipping away from me. It felt like I couldn't hold on to anything real, like I was losing my mind.

"I didn't think, 'Randall, you should get up and drive away and abandon your wife for a year.' I wasn't thinking at all. I was scared out of my gourd. All I wanted to do was to get far away from her, from what she had done, from what she was …"

The sharp burst of a car horn somewhere off to the right caused both of them to jump.

"I'll see you back at home!" they heard a young woman shout from the parking lot. "Don't forget to buy the folding chairs!"

Randall continued. "I drove for about two and a half hours that day, until I couldn't go any farther. I pulled into a motel outside Portland and holed up for a few days. I didn't sleep much. I kept seeing all those crazy things in my mind, and I was afraid she was going to come and get me."

"What do you mean? That Beverly would hurt you or something?"

"I know it sounds crazy now. But I couldn't connect what I had seen with the wonderful woman I'd married. Maybe she was someone different. Or maybe she'd changed somehow, and that the good normal Beverly wasn't around anymore. All I knew was that I was afraid and I wanted to be away from her.

"Initially I assumed it would be for a couple of days, or maybe a week. I always thought that I'd just pick up the phone from the motel and call her—this was before email and cell phones, remember—but I kept putting it off.

"The airlines put me on probation because I called in sick too many times, but eventually they took me back. I got an apartment in Portland, then signed up for as many flights as possible, working like a madman. Maybe it wasn't the best way to deal with it, but the work helped me to forget what I'd seen. And somehow I thought Portland was far enough away for Beverly not to find me. Ha! She told me later that she used a spell to make sure I was okay and then just waited for me. It was really hard on her. But she was afraid that if she showed up in Portland, she'd only drive me further away. She knew she had to wait, to let me find my way back to her. And she also knew that I might not come back.

"Charlie, you gotta understand. This was pure survival on my part. I'm not saying what I did was good, except that I think it kept me sane. Remember when you first saw the talking dog? How it just didn't make sense?"

He nodded, still able to recall the sensation that the ground underneath him had flipped upside down, that his mind was going to split in two, that the reality he knew was running away from him like a herd of frightened gazelles dashing off into the thick protection of the jungle.

"On the one hand, I think what I did was a mistake. It was really hard on Beverly, and on our marriage. Also on me. But what Beverly did was a mistake too. She'd be the first to admit it. She lost her cool and showed me too much. So on the other hand, what I did might not have been a mistake. My brain cracked open, and it took me some time to put it back together again. It's not like there was an advice column I could write to for help. 'Dear Abby, my wife's a witch. What should I do?'" His laugh sounded hollow.

"I think if I had stayed and tried to understand it all right away, I might not have been able to handle it and would have eventually left. I don't know.

"Believe me, Charlie, she and I have been over and over this. We've apologized more times to each other than I care to count. We've wondered if things didn't work out the way they should have. It's easy to be a Monday-morning quarterback now, but at the time, neither of us knew what to do.

"I've read a lot since then about how our brains work. When something so unbelievable happens, our mind just can't accept it, so it tells us to do what it needs to survive: 'Run! Get away! Or at least make up some logical explanation for what you're seeing!' Because if it can't, or if you can't get away, then you really can go crazy.

"That the law of gravity exists, that if you put something on a table, it'll stay there unless someone else removes it, that bones and body tissue keep their shape unless there's a tear or a break ... having to accept witchcraft meant having to let my mind be blown, and that, my friend, is one of the hardest things to go through in this life.

"It's why the witches try to educate their kids when they're young, before they've formed strong views of the world. It's why they let echoes just be echoes instead of trying to pop them as adults. Adult brains become rigid, hard-set in their belief systems. Cracking them open can have serious mental, and even physical, results.

"So your mind has been blown, Charlie. True, you're much younger than I was when it happened, and you're a lot smarter than me. But still, your mind has been blown wide open. You gotta go easy on yourself, kid. This is not just a simple thing to accept, like scientists discovering a new island in the Pacific Ocean. This is having to swallow a whole new way of seeing how the world really works. And no matter how understanding Beverly and the other witches try to be, they'll never get what it's like for us outsiders to accept it all.

"Now, Beverly would kill me if she knew how much I was talking and lecturing at you. She would say I should stop and ask you if you have any questions. So, do you have any questions?" Randall asked, a shy, but friendly smile on his face.

Charlie looked out the window, feeling calmer now than when he had first learned about his uncle leaving Beverly. Even if he didn't like the fact that Randall hadn't contacted Beverly during all that time, he could understand, all too well, what it felt like to go crazy.

"Um, how did you two get back together?"

"I called her one day, out of the blue. I didn't have a plan. I just missed her too much. She answered the phone, and hearing her voice was incredible. It was her, the Beverly that I knew, not the scary one from the beach. She started crying, I started crying, and the rest, as they say, is history."

"Was it easy to come back home and understand it all?"

"No. It wasn't. We had to make a deal with each other. She wouldn't show me anything or tell me anything unless I asked, and I wouldn't flee in the middle of the night without at least telling her that I wanted to. It was hard for the both of us in the beginning, but we figured it was what we needed to make things work out.

"We took it very slowly. Over time, we became a couple again. Stronger than we had been before. When her mother died, we moved into the family home in West Seattle. I even became friends with some of the other witches. But I didn't ask many questions. And believe me, the witches weren't that fond of showing me things. It worked out for the better.

"Look, Charlie, I think we've had enough talking for tonight. Or at least I think I've talked at you enough. Let me text Beverly to tell her that we got to chatting, and then let's go inside before Costco closes."

He fished in his jeans pocket for his phone. "Got gabby, will be later than expected," he said as he typed, then hit send. "There! Now let's go get us some hot dogs!"

The two of them stretched their legs in the parking lot. Randall looked up at the darkening sky.

"All that warm dry weather we've been having? It looks like it could be on its way out any day now. This," he spread his arms and looked up at the sky, "means that the season of wet will soon be upon us. And," he said, looking out at the dark gray clouds piled low on the horizon, one on top of the other, "my guess is that a storm is coming."

CHAPTER 31

The President

THE BELL RANG AND THE STUDENTS began putting away their books and papers.

"*Hao le,*" Chen Laoshi said. "*Mingtian de gongke jiushi di ershi dao di ershiwuye, dongbudong?*"

"*Dong,*" said the students. Charlie knew enough Chinese now to understand that the homework was to do pages twenty through twenty-five.

As he walked out into the hallway he was surprised to see Diego standing to the side of the door with a big smile on his face.

"Hey," Charlie said, embarrassed.

"I'm your stalker for the day!" Diego said, looking down at him and laughing. "The office told me you had Chinese this morning."

"Oh." Charlie didn't know what else to say. Diego seemed so big and bright standing there with students walking around him, some of them greeting him.

Diego's smile faded. "You busy with something? Or just creeped out that I found you?"

"No, no," Charlie said, trying to find words. He was happy to see Diego. But nervous too. Why was he nervous? It didn't make any sense. "I still feel like everything's so new, is all," he said, fingers playing with the bracelet that Beverly had given him.

"That's a cool bracelet! Where'd you get it?"

"My aunt gave it to me."

"I want one. Can she get me one too?" he asked, encircling his hand around Charlie's wrist and pulling it closer to inspect the silver band.

Diego's skin felt warm. Warm and safe. Charlie shivered, then pulled his hand away.

"She, uh, she said she picked it up somewhere, kind of, um, far away. Maybe on a trip in Europe?" he said feeling stupid, sure that Diego could see through his lie.

Diego looked like he was about to say something about the bracelet, then shrugged and smiled.

"What's your next class?"

"Biology."

They started walking down the hallway.

"I have a meeting with the school advisor for the GSA in ten minutes, so I have time to walk you to class. Do you know what the GSA is?" Diego asked, his voice rising slightly in pitch.

"Oh yeah, sure," he said, having no idea what it was.

"Well, I'm the president of it. Two years running."

"Oh wow, that's great," he said, hoping Diego wouldn't ask him a question about it and reveal his ignorance.

As they walked, several students and a few of the teachers said hi to Diego. Clearly he was popular. So why did he want to have anything to do with Charlie?

"We still on for the party tonight?"

"Yeah, yeah. Thanks for letting my aunt call you."

"Sure. What are you going to wear tonight?" asked Diego.

Charlie felt himself shrink. None of his friends back home ever asked him what he was going to wear when they went to do something. He hadn't thought about it. Should he have? He felt so utterly stupid about everything. He didn't know what the GSA was, no one said hi to him, and he didn't even know what to wear to a party. And this popular guy was walking him to biology class.

"I hadn't thought about it," he said, shrugging his shoulders and trying to make his voice sound nonchalant.

Diego looked over at him, then stopped walking.

"Look, Charlie, if you don't want to go, that's okay."

"No, no, it's not that. It's just …"

"What? Is something going on?"

Charlie looked down the hall at all the students in their uniforms, laughing, walking in groups, heading to class. Everyone seemed to know where to go. And what was expected of them. Charlie thought about what Randall had said in the car last night. "It felt like I couldn't hold on to anything real, like I was losing my mind." He doubted any of these kids had had talks the night before about witchcraft with their uncles while sitting in the parking lot at Costco. Or about having to accept things that seemed straight out of a fairy tale.

"Diego, it's all just so new, you know? Being here, trying to, to fit in …"

"Hey, I didn't mean to embarrass you about what you were going to wear. I mean, it's no big deal, it's just a stupid party," he said, waving his hands in front of him as if to push something aside.

Charlie looked down at the floor. It wasn't about the clothes, or any of that really. But it was kind of Diego to try to reassure him. Once again, he felt the desire to tell this boy everything that had been happening to him. He knew he couldn't, knew he wouldn't, but that didn't mean he didn't want to.

"It's okay," said Charlie. He smiled. "I do want to go to the party. It'll be cool to meet some new people. And," he said, surprising himself, "hanging out with you."

Diego's brown face grew darker as he blushed. "Really? Dude, that's awesome," he said, his smile growing so bright that Charlie wanted to shield his eyes.

"I'm sure it's not easy being new and all. But stick with me. I'll show you the ropes around here and introduce you to some cool people."

They walked the rest of the way in silence, if heading down hallways between classes with lockers slamming, kids laughing, and teachers talking with each other could be considered silent. It was uncomfortable because Charlie didn't know what to say and it felt like something had been decided between them, even if he didn't know what it was. But it wasn't awful. He was used to awkwardness between him and the rest of the world. Besides, it felt surprisingly good to tell Diego that he wanted to spend time with him. And even better that the boy seemed to appreciate it.

*   *   *

As embarrassed as he felt asking Beverly to help him choose clothes for the party, the idea of showing up looking like an idiot seemed even worse.

Beverly looked surprised when Charlie walked into the kitchen and said, "Um, this is kind of stupid but, could you maybe help me pick out something to wear tonight?"

"For the party?" Her voice was loud and excited. But she took a breath, and he could tell she did her best to tone it down. "Sure. Yeah. I'll be up in just a minute, okay? I'm sure we can find something from what we bought the other day."

Charlie could tell as she turned her back on him and pretended to look at the pile of mail on the kitchen counter that she was trying to hide her smile.

He walked upstairs feeling a little stupid, but also happy. He really liked his aunt and uncle and knew they were doing their best to make sure he felt welcome in their home.

Together he and his aunt pulled out some pants, a few shirts, and a sweater that they both liked.

"I don't know if I'm supposed to wear jeans, or nice pants, or what. Everybody at school just wears a uniform."

"This is what I do when I'm not sure. I try to figure out what kind of party it is, and then just dress a little nicer than what I think I'd be expected to wear. Not a lot, just a little. The way I look at it, I'd rather be a bit more overdressed than underdressed."

"But don't you just, I don't know, do something when you want to find out? Like something, uh ..."

"Witchy?" she asked, then laughed. "Charlie, if you think witchcraft helps people avoid embarrassing situations, you're wrong. Even witches make social blunders.

"But I'm pretty sure that if you wear that shirt with these pants, and a sweater in case it gets cold, you should be fine. Or just bring along that leather jacket we bought. You'd look nice without standing out too much."

"Really?" he asked, relieved. "I feel like I stand out all the time. It would be nice to ..."

"I think you'll blend in just fine."

* * *

After taking a shower, Charlie changed into his clothes and checked himself out in the full-length mirror. He decided he looked all right, or at least what he was wearing looked all right. His hair seemed to stick out everywhere. He wondered if he could learn a spell to get rid of his stupid curls. He sat down on the edge of his bed. The clock on the nightstand read ten after seven. Diego was over twenty minutes late. Maybe he had decided not to come? *That would be a relief*, he thought. But if so, then why did he feel more than a little disappointed?

He walked over to the window and looked out past the front yard to the street beyond it. He had been checking the last several nights to see if those two cats were still around, looking up at him in that weird cat way. But there was no sign of them.

It seemed like it was getting darker earlier and earlier, even in just the short amount of time that he had been in Seattle. Autumn seemed to come faster here than it did back home.

You are home, a voice said inside his head. The voice sounded remarkably like his own.

He heard the sound of a car and watched as a shiny silver BMW pulled up in front of the house. Diego got out and looked at the front door. Charlie stepped away from the window so he wouldn't be caught waiting for the boy to show up even though that's exactly what he had been doing.

The doorbell rang and he heard Randall greet Diego.

Charlie took a deep breath, then opened his bedroom door and walked downstairs.

* * *

"Sorry I'm late. I begged my mom to let me take her car tonight instead of my beater Honda. At first she wouldn't let me, but finally agreed on one condition—that I only drive five miles an hour," Diego laughed as his hands slid over the steering wheel. "Your aunt and uncle seem really cool. Way more laid back than my mom. I mean, she's good to me and all, but she can get a little uptight."

"Yeah, they're nice," Charlie said, looking out the window as they drove down block after block of residential streets.

"What a cool house you live in! Ours, it's more modern. My mom's kinda into the chrome-and-glass look, you know?"

"Uh-huh." Charlie nodded, having no idea what chrome-and-glass houses looked like. He tried to picture it but could only imagine something like a big Christmas tree ornament.

"Really cool leather jacket," Diego said, reaching over and touching the sleeve. "Where'd you get it?"

Charlie told him a little bit about the shopping trip with his aunt.

"Why did you move to Seattle?" he asked. "I keep meaning to ask you."

Charlie told him the story that he and Randall and Beverly had worked out together. "The school district where we live isn't that great, and my mom wants me to get a good education. My aunt and uncle knew about Puget Academy, so they said I could come live with them. We decided kind of last minute."

"Right on," said Diego, nodding. He seemed to believe the story.

"I'd better start looking for parking. They live on this block, but it looks like a lot of cars are here already."

Charlie tried to swallow, but his throat was too dry. He didn't know so many people would be coming to the party. What if he said something stupid and looked like a fool in front of his new friend? What if everybody made him talk about California? What if they made him the center of attention all night, and he couldn't get away?

He began to feel nauseous. Maybe they could just keep driving. Maybe he should ask Diego to take him back to Washington Street.

"Well, we're here," Diego said as he pulled on the parking brake and got out of the car.

The house was made of dark brown brick with a sloped roof and a large grass lawn in front. The houses in this neighborhood didn't seem as nice as where he lived on Washington, but it was still nicer than what he was used to in California.

"Mr. and Mrs. Tanner are the hosts tonight. Do you know Kayla and Brandon Tanner at school? He's a sophomore and his sister is a senior. They've been doing this since Kayla was a freshman at P.A.," Diego said, acting like a tour guide as they walked up the cement walkway to the front door. Charlie could hear music coming from inside.

"I think the parents get more excited about this party than anyone else does," whispered Diego on the doorstep as he rang the doorbell.

"Diego Ramirez, welcome, welcome," said a barrel-chested man in a button-down shirt with sweat stains on the front. He had a pin on the front of his shirt that read "Proud P.A. Papa. "You just keep getting taller and taller, don't you? Come in, come in. Who's your friend?"

"Hi, Mr. Tanner. I'd like to you to meet Charlie Creevey. He's a new sophomore, a transfer from California."

"Charlie! Ted Tanner. Come in, welcome, welcome," Mr. Tanner shouted. He wondered if the man was hard of hearing. He took Charlie's hand in his own and gave it a bone-cracking squeeze. Charlie smiled back at the man, whose face was red. "California! Well, well!"

The boys stepped into the house. The air was much stuffier than outside. Kids their age were walking up and down the stairs or crowding around a table filled with food.

"I've just been dancing in the living room. Pardon my mess," Mr. Tanner said, referring to his shirt. "Gingy, Diego Ramirez is here with a new student!"

A woman with frizzy blonde hair came out of the kitchen wiping her hands on a towel as she walked toward them.

"Look at you, Diego. I swear you take handsome pills every morning." She put her arms around him. He hugged her back, laughing as he did.

She looked at Charlie, and her smile remained, but her face looked surprised. "I don't think I know you," she said. "I'm Ginger Tanner."

"Hi, Mrs. Tanner," Charlie said, relieved when she shook his hand instead of hugging him. "I, uh, I'm a new student, just started last week. My aunt and uncle live here in West Seattle and I'm living with them for the school year."

"How nice, how nice. Let me take your coats." She walked them toward the entry closet. "We usually hold this party the first week of school, but Ted had some thing in Spokane, so we couldn't do it until now. Glad we didn't miss you," she said to Charlie.

Coats were hung, more introductions were made, and the boys were ushered over to the food table. They began filling their plates, while P.A. friends of Diego's came over to greet him and to meet Charlie.

Charlie felt himself relaxing. The noise and activities reminded him of the fall festival back at school in California where kids ran amok in the decorated school auditorium and parents staffed booths and craft tables. The Tanners' party was on a much smaller scale but was crowded enough that Charlie could watch the activities without being the center of attention.

"I'd like you to meet somebody," Diego said as he carried his plate over to a room off the kitchen. There were three kids on folding chairs, talking to each other. Diego headed for a small love seat right near them.

One of the kids, a girl with long blonde hair and a pretty smile, looked up and saw Diego.

"Honey!" she shouted, and stood up, nearly knocking his plate of food from his hands.

"Mwa! Mwa!" they said, kissing each other on the cheek.

Charlie was surprised. Diego hadn't said anything about having a girlfriend.

"And you," said the girl, setting down her glass of soda and walking over to him, "must be Charlie. I've already heard so much about you!"

Diego smiled broadly, and the girl laughed.

"Charlie, I'd like you to meet Tawny Rose. Tawny, this is Charlie Creevey."

"Nice to meet you," Charlie said, taking her hand.

The three of them sat down together. The other two kids left, and soon Diego and Tawny were talking about everybody at school. Every so often they would turn to Charlie to say things like, "Wait until you meet her," and "We have to tell you what happened in chemistry last week."

Charlie dug into the nachos, the potato salad, and pieces of summer fruit on his plate. He found it pleasant to be sitting next to the two friends, hearing them talk but not being required to join in. He enjoyed watching some of the other kids come and go from the den where they sat. At one point Mrs. Tanner came in carrying a very large pitcher filled with a cloudy liquid.

"Coconut juice, anyone? It's apparently all the rage. Charlie, do they drink it in California?"

"Um, I dunno," he said, hoping she wouldn't single him out with any more questions. He relaxed as she floated out of the room, shouting, "Coconut juice, anyone?"

"The Tanners," said Tawny quietly, "do this party every year. And every year Kayla begs them not to. Charlie, if you haven't met her yet, she's easy to spot. She's the girl with the permanent scowl on her face. Everyone else, including Brandon, has fun. I think she's just embarrassed because she wants her parents to be more hands-off."

A few really tall, older-looking boys walked into the room and called Diego's name. He looked up, started laughing, and ran over to where they stood. Right away they started doing a complex series of handshakes, part mutual and part competitive.

"So," Tawny turned toward him, "like I said, Diego has told me a lot about you. How are you adjusting to P.A. so far?"

"It's pretty good." Charlie wondered if she were scrutinizing him. She wouldn't be jealous of her boyfriend spending time with him, would she?

"I don't know if I've ever met your aunt and uncle before," she said, biting into a potato chip.

"Oh, um, they don't have any kids, so they haven't really hung out at P.A. before.

Silence followed. Charlie realized he should probably ask her a question. It seemed like the polite thing to do.

"Where do you live?" he said, hoping the question wasn't too stupid and boring.

"Not far from here. Head south on California, and I'm near the dead end."

"Cool. How long have you and Diego been going out?" he asked, the question sliding from his mouth before he had the chance to wonder if it was rude or not.

CHAPTER 32

Alliances

TAWNY, WHO HAD BEEN TAKING a sip of her soda, coughed and spat some of the liquid onto his arm and her plate of food. She coughed several more times, trying to catch her breath.

"Sorry! Sorry!" she croaked, patting at his arm with her napkin. It struck him as funny too, and they both giggled while they tried to mop up the mess.

When Tawny finally recovered enough to talk, she looked directly into his eyes.

"Oh, um, Charlie? We're not going out. We're friends. We are definitely not going out."

She seemed to be emphasizing her words, looking at him intently. He knew he was missing something, but he wasn't sure what it was.

Diego came over and sat down next to them. "Those guys are nuts!" he said, laughing and shaking his head. He obviously hadn't seen Tawny choke on her drink.

They fell back into conversation again, talking about more teachers, classes, and school stories that Charlie didn't know anything about. Tawny didn't mention Charlie's dating question, but he found her sneaking glances at him every so often, her eyes guarded.

"I think I'll head downstairs to watch the foosball tournament," she said. "You guys wanna come?"

"Charlie?" asked Diego.

"Sure."

As they headed downstairs, they could hear kids laughing and shouting. "You cheated! You can't move the ball like that!"

The basement was a large carpeted room with board games, a large foosball table, a pool table, and a big-screen TV showing a kung fu movie. Kids were spread out all over the place, talking in groups or playing games.

"Will you guys shut up?" a girl yelled over her shoulder to the gaggle of students shouting at the foosball game in action. "We're trying to watch a movie."

When the game ended in a loud cheer, Diego asked Charlie if he wanted to be a team. They moved to one side of the table while the winners of the last game got ready on the other.

The ball dropped and Charlie, who had been playing foosball nearly his entire life at the community center in Clarkston with his buddy Mike, blocked a shot from the forward and then spun the handle of his defense line. The ball flew into the goal before anyone could block it.

"Dude! You scored! Goal!" Diego shouted, imitating a Spanish-speaking soccer announcer.

The ball was dropped in again. Charlie took a second shot and scored.

"No fair!" shouted one of the kids on the other team. "You gotta give us a chance."

Soon Diego and Charlie won the game and took on a series of players.

At one point, Tawny stepped in to play with Charlie. She was just as good as Diego, and they maintained their winning streak.

"What's this I hear about champions at my foosball table?" bellowed a voice coming down the stairs about fifteen minutes later.

Mr. Tanner and a much younger facsimile of himself stepped up to where Diego and Charlie stood.

"Let's take 'em, Dad" said Brandon. And with that, a wild game of foosball erupted, father and son on one side of the table, Charlie and Diego on the other. The other kids in the basement gathered around. Charlie remained calm, enjoying the fact that he could keep his focus on the game and not on who was watching him. Maybe parties could actually be fun, he thought to himself as he blocked a shot on the goal.

In the end, the Tanners emerged the victors.

"But we've never had someone give us such a run for our money," Mr. Tanner said, patting them both on the back.

Kids started to head upstairs as Mrs. Tanner announced that it was nearly ten thirty and time to wind things up.

"It's a school night, everybody. And besides, we promised your parents we wouldn't keep you out too late."

"Thanks for helping to keep my husband's ego in check," Mrs. Tanner said moments later, handing the boys their coats as they stepped out onto the front porch.

Charlie had been sweating downstairs during the foosball match. The cold night air felt good on his face. He turned around and looked back into the house drinking in the warmth, the new friends, the evening. He was surprised to find that he didn't want the party to be over.

"Come on, Charlie. I told your aunt and uncle I'd have you home before eleven," said Diego.

They walked behind several other P.A. students leaving the party. Out in the street, car doors opened and closed as the calls of "goodnight" and "see you tomorrow" echoed up and down the street.

A boy and a girl holding hands near a small red Honda grabbed Charlie by the arm as he walked by their car. He recognized them from Chinese class.

"Dude, you rock at foosball! Nobody ever goes head-to-head like that against Team Tanner. Wait until we tell Chen Laoshi tomorrow," the girl said, smiling at Charlie. "I'm Hannah."

"Hen hao, hen hao," said the boy.

"Xiexie nimen," Charlie replied, unable to hold back his smile.

He walked over to Mrs. Ramirez's BMW, where Diego was talking to Tawny. They looked up at him. Diego was frowning.

"Night, boys," Tawny said as she walked to her car. "Really nice finally meeting you, Mr. Creevey."

"You too. Uh, see you at school," he replied, wondering what they had been talking about.

Charlie climbed in and sat on the soft leather seat. Diego followed, but didn't start the car.

"Uh ... did you have fun tonight?" he asked, his voice quiet. This wasn't the vivacious cheerful boy who had just played foosball with him.

"Yeah, yeah, it was cool. Mr. and Mrs. Tanner are kind of crazy. But nice too. Oh, and I really like Tawny," he added, worried that Diego would think he didn't get along with her.

"Good, good," said the boy. He was looking out the windshield like he was counting the cars.

"Um, is everything okay?" Charlie asked.

"Yeah, yeah. No, it's fine. I just ... Charlie, can I ask you something?"

"Sure."

"Today, when I told you I was president of the GSA, you said you knew what that was, right?"

Charlie felt his stomach tighten. All thoughts of the party vanished. Diego had caught him in a lie and now was probably going to chide him for pretending to know something that he didn't.

"I'm, uh, sorry," he said quickly. "I don't know why I did that. I was just trying to sound cool, I guess."

"Oh. Okay ..." Diego sighed. He looked down at his hands, then ran his fingers along the base of the steering wheel.

Charlie heard another car engine start up, saw its headlights turn on, then watched as it pulled away from the curb, drove to the next block, and turned left. The street was quiet now. White clouds raced across the cold night sky.

For some reason, he was holding his breath. He looked up at Diego, who turned his head and looked back at him.

"Charlie, the GSA is the Gay–Straight Alliance that we have at school. It's, uh, set up so queer kids and straight kids can talk together. Can be friends, instead of bullying each other."

"Oh," said Charlie. He was glad Diego was involved with something like that. Bullying could be a big problem. "That's cool," he added.

"Charlie, you don't get it, do you? I'm gay, Charlie. And I thought … well, I thought you knew."

CHAPTER 33

Just Friends

THE BOYS SAT IN THE CAR without saying anything while the cold began to seep in through the doors. Charlie felt his mind go blank. He could hear someone calling to a dog somewhere off in the distance. Then a low deep rumble from the direction of the water, which Randall had told him was the horn from one of the ferryboats traversing Puget Sound.

Charlie's small voice broke the silence. "I, uh, I didn't know that." He thought about getting out of the car and walking home. It wasn't that far. He figured he would walk in the opposite direction from where they had come and find it eventually. Didn't his cell phone have GPS?

"Yeah, I can tell that now. I feel kinda stupid. I thought that since you knew about the GSA thing, you knew about me too."

He ran his fingers through his hair, so dark now that it blended in with the interior of the car, making it look like the top of his head was part of the shadows. Only his forehead and teeth were visible.

"Are you okay with that? With me, I mean? Jesus, I thought I was through with all of this worrying," he added, more to himself than to Charlie.

"What? With you? Being gay? Oh sure, it's, uh, it's f- ... it's fine." God, he was stuttering like people did in bad movies. He saw the image of Ted Jones lying face down on a road somewhere. Soon Ted's face changed to Diego's, with blood running down his cheeks while several large guys stood around him taking turns kicking his side, his legs, his head.

"No, you're not. You aren't. I can tell. Damn it. I don't want it to be awkward, you know? I hate that part. Everyone rushing around telling me how great it is that I'm out and how proud I should be, while all the time I can tell they don't want to talk to me about it.

"It's not like people hate me. Most people. There are some at P.A. who do. But really. My mom talked to so many faculty members, and even Principal Wang, to make sure it would be a safe place. I didn't have such a great experience in middle school, you know? She'd wanted me to go to P.A. anyway but made sure that the school would do a good job of making it okay for me to be there and be out.

"Anyway, like I said, it's not like people walk up to me and call me 'faggot' to my face or anything like they did in eighth grade. But everyone sort of smiles too much. Even Mr. and Mrs. Tanner. They are totally nice and all, but …"

Charlie sat in the passenger seat, tapping his feet on the floor mat. He wasn't sure why Diego was telling him so much. He wasn't really listening to him. *Maybe I could just ask him to take me home. I could tell him I was tired, and could we talk about it later?*

There was a pause in Diego's chatter. "Well, is it true?"

"Is what true?" Charlie asked, realizing that he hadn't heard Diego's question.

"About you? I thought, I thought maybe you were gay too. I'm sorry, I don't mean to be so in-your-face about it, Charlie. If not, that's cool too. I just …"

"No. No, I'm not gay," he said, scooting closer to the car door at his right. *At least I don't think so. How do you know if you are?*

Diego exhaled then sat back against his seat. "Oh, okay. Look, no hard feelings, right? I didn't mean to make you uncomfortable, I just …"

"No, no, it's cool."

"I hate this stuff. It never goes well. It always gets so weird," Diego said and then slammed his fist against the dashboard. The loud thud made Charlie jump.

"Um, could you just take me home? I'm sorry. I'm just tired is all. Could we maybe …"

"Oh sure. Sure."

"… talk about it tomorrow?"

"Yeah, of course," said Diego, starting up the car, not looking at him. None of the normal aliveness was in his voice, and Charlie had something to do with that. It felt awful.

"Really, I mean it, it's just been a long day, and …"

"No prob. No prob. *Meiyou wenti,*" he said, then flashed a wide grin at Charlie, a grin that failed to touch the boy's eyes.

He pulled the car away from the curb and turned into a driveway. He backed the car up, then drove down the street and out of the neighborhood. *"Meiyou wenti."*

When the car pulled in front of the house on Washington Street, Charlie turned to Diego to apologize. He wasn't exactly sure what he was apologizing for, but he knew it was something important.

But Diego spoke first. "Look, can we just drop this? It was totally my fault. My mistake. I kind of blunder into these things. I didn't mean to drop so much heavy stuff on you," he said, and this time his smile filled his whole face. He was talking loudly.

Diego reached across Charlie and opened the passenger-side door. "We're both a little tired. I'll, you know, I'll see you at school tomorrow. In our boring old uniforms, but oh well, same shit on a new day, right?" he said, winking.

The amount of things Charlie wanted to say and do in that moment overwhelmed him. He wanted to pull the door closed, tell Diego to turn up the heat, and just drive around the city for a while.

He wanted to get Tawny in the car with them. Maybe she would sit in the front passenger seat while Diego drove, and Charlie would sit in the back. He would listen to them as they talked about school. He would learn to talk just like they did. They wouldn't expect anything more from him than to just sit there.

He wanted to scream at the boy, "What do you want from me? What does everybody want? Why do people always want stuff?"

He wanted to whisper in the boy's ear that his aunt could jump over a stream bed, could make things float, and that pretty soon he would be able to do these things. He wanted to whisper, "I'll show you when I learn, okay?"

And a deeper part, a part that scared him almost as much as talking dogs, wanted to take the boy's face in his hands, to smell the gel in his hair, the hot breath in his mouth, the way the scent of the soap he used still lingered on his skin. He wanted to run his finger over the freckle on the boy's right temple, the one that looked like a small comma, and press on it. He wanted to open his own mouth and see if there was a way he could taste the words that Diego said, all of them, the vast variety of them, the ease with which he said them.

He wanted to be this boy's friend. And he was pretty sure that that wasn't going to happen now. He felt flashes of fear and sadness. How had he managed to screw everything up so fast?

But he didn't say any of this to Diego. He didn't know how to say it all without more words coming out, words that might be like *Words*, for they could do things, they could set things in motion, they could have a witchcraft of their own. Charlie had never felt more afraid of what might come spilling out of his mouth than in that moment, and so he kept it closed.

He climbed out of the car and stood on the wet grass near the curb.

"Thanks for the ..."

"Sure, Charlie, we'll see you," Diego said, already turning his head away, already making decisions that might not include him anymore.

The red taillights of the BMW looked like a pair of angry disgusted eyes glaring back at him. He made himself stand there and watch until they turned right a block away and disappeared around the corner. Then he fished for the keys in his pocket, unlocked the door, and walked inside the house.

CHAPTER 34

The Witch of the House

THE ONLY SOUNDS TO BE heard in the neighborhood were typical night noises: tree boughs blowing, late-night television playing, the groan of a refrigerator door opening and closing. Somewhere a child's voice, stuffy with sleep, asked for a drink of water.

Two figures stood listening on a rooftop a block away from their target, the house on Washington Street. Once they were sure that their presence was undetected, they nodded to each other and, holding their broomsticks aloft, jumped to the ground below. Quieter than moonbeams on water, they slipped across the street and approached the house, letting their broomsticks shrink to small twigs and placing them in their pockets as they moved.

They stopped inches from the barrier surrounding the front yard and the circumference of the house. This barrier was invisible to the naked eye. It had been set in place by the formidable witch who resided in and watched over the home, and its purpose was to keep people like them from entering the property. It would have worked, except ...

Except that Grace had given them the way in. Years ago, when she had learned all the community's secrets from its careless and lusty leader, she made sure to study the ways it protected itself.

She had passed these ways on to the two figures now looking at the house. If used correctly, they would be able to breach the wall. And get inside.

They said their Words in unison. Their hands made movements in the air. It did not take long.

At first, just a small snap. Then, tiny fissures spread out along the invisible wall, like cracks on a windshield. The barrier didn't collapse. It was too strong to destroy completely. It simply began to weaken.

The strangers said more Words, made more hand gestures, until a perfectly round hole formed, large enough for them to slip inside. Just like Grace had said it would.

The man, Tony, spun in place and wiggled his hips, his own version of a silent celebration. The woman, Claudia, rolled her eyes. He bowed and made a chivalrous gesture. She nodded, then took a short breath, and caused her own form to turn to vapor. The vapor poured through the hole like smoke through an open window, and before two seconds had passed, she was crouched on the ground inside the property. She paused, listening for any signs of disturbance. When satisfied that she was in the clear, she signaled to Tony behind her, whose own form vaporized and poured through the round gap.

Together they remained near the ground, their senses alert to any alarms sounded. Nothing. Not a change. Nothing to indicate that the home's security had been breached. Still, they waited. The witch inside was known to be quite strong.

*   *   *

Charlie was dreaming. In the dream, he was teaching a Chinese class. He sat at his desk looking at his materials, all of which were written in Chinese characters. He couldn't understand anything.

He looked up from his desk to see that every student in class was Chinese. They sat still, waiting for him to say something. He realized with horror that he couldn't speak anything other than English. Sweat filled the worry lines on his forehead.

One of the students sitting in the front row, a nine- or ten-year-old girl in black braids, raised her hand. Charlie nodded to her.

"Teacher, blah blah wingwang wingwang blah blah wingwang Puget Sound chingchong chingchong witchcraft," she said.

The rest of the students nodded and smiled. What she had said made perfect sense to them, yet he could only make out a few words.

Charlie heard a noise at his feet. He looked down, and saw Amos lying on the floor to the right of his desk. The dog trembled from head to foot. He whimpered. He seemed to be suffering.

Charlie felt a tap on his shoulder. He looked up to see the young girl with the braids standing by his side. "I think you're in trouble," she said in plain English. She was missing her two front teeth.

"You mean the dog, right?" he said to her, confused.

"No, Charlie. You. You're in trouble. *Hen weixian,*" she said.

* * *

Claudia and Tony stood over the boy as he slept in his bed. The curtains from the opened window floated in the night breeze. The large dog lay trembling in the corner, unable to get up or make a noise. A few simple Words had subdued it.

The boy had bright yellow curls spread about his pillow. Apples added color to his otherwise pale cheeks. His face was knotted and tight as he slept, as if he were lifting something heavy.

The two strangers stared at the boy. They were pretty sure it was him. They had been given a clear description. That, and the fact that they knew they were in the right house, confirmed that it had to be the boy they were looking for.

* * *

Two cats ran down a succession of alleys in the neighborhood, loping along in their thin-bodied silent-footed way. They were soon joined by another, then another, and even more still. The cluster ran together for several blocks until a few of them split off down side roads.

One of the cats turned down Washington Street. Jumping into the air, she dug her claws into a tall pine tree in the yard of the large white house and clambered halfway up, then raced out onto a thick branch. Just before reaching the end of the branch, the cat leaped from the tree and landed on a window sill. She pawed loudly at the glass until the human female, the one with the long dark hair, parted the curtains and looked out. The human stared at the cat's face for a moment, until her brown eyes grew round. In a flash she was gone from the window, the curtains closing again.

* * *

Claudia took several strips of the gauzy material that Tony held out in his hands and leaned over the sleeping boy, peering at him until she was inches from his face. She knew not to use any Words on him until she could block his mouth. It might not be needed, but she couldn't be too cautious.

Without warning, the door to the bedroom crashed open. The witch of the house rushed at them, her long dark hair streaming behind her as she attacked, Words hissing from her mouth, hands outstretched.

Tony spun to his side and threw a bladed metal disk at the witch. Before it could touch her, it skipped past her head and stuck itself in the wall behind her. Tony dove sideways as a bolt of light shot from the witch's hands and blasted into the carpet where his feet had been.

Without pausing, Claudia threw strips of the gauze at the boy's mouth and each of his hands. The material fastened itself to his skin faster than a striking snake. The boy's eyes flew open. Before he could sit up, Claudia flicked her wrists, forcing the bedclothes to stiffen and trap the boy's legs.

The witch turned her attention from Tony and flew through the air to her nephew's bed. She slammed into Claudia's body and tackled her to the ground, her hands squeezing the air from the woman's throat. As the witch's mouth moved, sparks shot from Claudia's ears and scalp. She writhed and screamed in pain.

Tony's body blurred as he ran to the bed, threw the boy's bound form over his shoulder like a sack of laundry, then jumped toward the open window.

"Beverly," he said, "Stop moving or I toss the boy out, head first."

Beverly released her grip on Claudia and looked at him, pure venom in her large brown eyes.

* * *

Charlie wriggled in the man's arms. The stretchy material trapped his limbs, and even though he kicked hard at the man's back, it had no effect.

"Get off me, bitch," said the woman pinned beneath Beverly. "Get off me before I …"

From his vantage point hanging over the man's shoulder, Charlie watched as Beverly stood up. She was wearing a long white nightgown. The strangers wore black. *The good guys versus the bad guys.* His aunt stood very still, arms at her sides, her eyes locked on the man and Charlie. The woman got up from the floor and walked over to them, rubbing the back of her neck.

"Here's how this is gonna go," said Claudia. "We leave with the boy, and you stay put. If you even begin to move your lips," she said, pulling a long curved dagger from the pocket of her jacket, "then this goes into the boy. Got it? If so, nod your head to Mama Claudia here," she said, pointing to herself.

Beverly nodded.

"That's good, missy, that's purely psychological," said the man, doing a strange pelvic thrust in Beverly's direction. "You are down with it, Mama, aren't you?"

The woman turned to look at the man. "Shut up, Tony. Come on. We're leaving."

With a swirl of white material, the spot where Beverly stood was now empty. She didn't vanish so much as sparked across the room. A bright blue streak of electricity charged toward them.

The woman screamed, then flew up against the ceiling as a strip of gauze sealed itself across her mouth. Blue light shot along the sides of her body, forcing her to drop the dagger.

Beverly's white nightgown blurred again, coming toward the man so fast that Charlie almost didn't see it. The man grunted and bent over, but turned and tried to move toward the window. Charlie felt himself sliding downwards, his own hip bumping against Tony's.

He fell to the floor on his back and watched as the man's body lifted into the air and slammed against the ceiling directly above, alongside the woman. He yelled out, "Holy friggin' witch!" before a strip of gauze stuck itself over his lips and cut off his words.

Beverly rushed over to where Charlie lay and pulled him away from the window toward the bedroom door.

"Are you okay?" she asked. He nodded, unable to speak.

She turned her head and looked over to the corner. "Amos, buddy, I'll be right there, okay? First I have to …"

A shadow passed through the doorway.

"What the hell?" said Randall, eyes trying to focus in the faint light as he stepped into the bedroom. Charlie could see that his face was puffy from sleep. He must have only just heard the commotion in the room.

"Randall, get back!" Beverly stood up and put her body in front of her husband and her nephew. But the shift in her attention seemed to be all that the two intruders needed. They fell toward the floor and landed feet first, right as cats. Without pausing, they ripped the gauze from their mouths.

Beverly reached her hands out in front of her, preparing for another attack.

But the man and the woman moved to the window. The woman slipped through first and jumped out into the empty air. The man looked over his shoulder and, just before stepping up onto the windowsill, said, "You are one kick-ass lady. Holy ninja witch!" He smiled his toothpaste commercial smile, winked at them, and then he too was gone in an instant. The smell of damp freshly cut lumber filled the room.

Charlie watched as his aunt ran to the window and looked out. Eventually she turned around to face them, shaking her head. "They're gone," she said. "I think we're safe for now."

CHAPTER 35

Midnight Meeting

AN HOUR LATER, THE COFFEE machine sputtered in the corner while fruit and bagels were pulled from the refrigerator and passed around. The kitchen was filled with conversation as Charlie's aunt and uncle, along with Rita, Jeremy, and four other adults he didn't know, crowded around the island in the middle of the floor. Earlier, while still upstairs in Charlie's bedroom, Beverly had snipped the gauze from his hands and feet and carefully peeled it away from his mouth.

"Okay, stand still. I need to check to make sure that you're okay and that they didn't leave anything behind that could hurt you."

She placed both of her hands on the side of his head, leaned in close enough to his face that their noses were almost touching, then inserted a finger inside each of his ears. The sensation was disorienting.

"What are you doing?" he asked, taking a step back from her.

"Charlie, I don't have the time nor the energy to explain this. I know it's weird, and I'm sorry. But please just stand still."

Her expression was all business, and her voice was low and dark. He thought about how fast she had attacked the two intruders, how she had made the bolt of light shoot from her hands. His knees weakened. Without a second thought, he stepped forward and closed his eyes.

Her fingers slipped inside his ears again. He kept his feet planted. For a brief moment, a buzzing pressure filled his head and spread

205

down his shoulders. And then it was over.

Inspected to her satisfaction, Beverly apologized and told him he was clean.

"Oh, and Charlie? For the time being, please wear the bracelet when you sleep, okay?" she said, nodding to his nightstand where he had set the bracelet before turning off his light last night. "We can't be too careful."

Now he sat on a stool at the far corner of the counter as the adults moved about the kitchen in various stages of pajamas, sweatshirts, and overcoats. It seemed part emergency meeting, part adult sleepover.

"I don't know how they got in, okay? Jesus, Emory, I checked the wards last night before I went to bed, like I always do."

"Okay, okay," said a short chubby redheaded man, standing with his hands behind his back and looking at Beverly. "I just assumed those things were tamper-proof."

"So did I!" she yelled at him. "Don't you think I assumed the same thing?"

"Hey, come on guys," said Jeremy, hands spread in a calming gesture. "We're all a little upset. No need to take it out on each other."

The front door opened, and Charlie heard footsteps walking down the hallway. His jaw dropped as his Chinese teacher, Chen Laoshi, walked into the kitchen.

"Hi, Julia," said Randall, giving her a hug. "Want something to drink?"

She winked at Charlie and said, *"Tongxue hao."*

Without thinking, he said, *"Chen Laoshi hao."*

She walked over to him and leaned over the counter. "Yes, it's true, I'm a member of the secret club. We're not all white, you know."

"Oh, I wasn't thinking ..."

But she turned away from him and grabbed a banana from the bowl on the island.

"Will somebody please explain to me exactly what is going on?" she demanded, commanding the same respect that she used in her classroom.

* * *

"I grabbed some of the woman's hair while we were fighting on the floor, and I used it to create a binding."

"But how did you do it so fast? That's what I want to know," said Rita, looking at Beverly with awe.

Now they all sat in the living room, spread over the sofas, small couches, and chairs.

"Oh, please. I was pumped up on adrenaline. Anyway, thanks to a story Charlie told me of something that happened in California, I got the idea to use the binding to stick her to the ceiling."

Charlie couldn't believe that he had in some way helped foil the intruders.

"I think it scared the man—apparently his name is Tony—it scared him enough to try to escape with Charlie in that moment, rather than attack. It gave me the chance to rush over and get some of his hair too."

"So, you could call it a 'double bind?'" Randall interjected.

"Ha-ha!" laughed Jeremy, rolling his eyes. "Your forays into witch humor once again underwhelm us!"

"No, the only double bind came when Randall walked in and wanted to know what was going on. He broke my concentration and I couldn't hold the bind anymore. They came off the ceiling and escaped out the window."

"Nice going, badass," said Emory, swatting at Randall's knee.

"Well, I didn't know what was going on. I heard loud noises coming from Charlie's room and went to investigate."

"You were very brave to walk in there, honey," said Beverly, giving him a peck on his cheek.

"But clearly they were afraid to attack anymore, Beverly," said Chen Laoshi. "You must have shown considerable strength and fortitude."

"They don't get to touch my nephew," she responded, eyes narrowing in menace as if the intruders were still standing in front of her.

They talked more about the breach of the ward, which seemed to be some sort of witch security system that was supposed to keep out what didn't belong. Apparently all of the witches used something like it at home for protection. They debated whether they could rely on them anymore.

"Grace must be behind it," said Emory. "She's the only one who knows the spells," he said.

"I'm afraid I have to agree with you, Em," said Beverly. "I didn't know you could find out how someone else's ward worked and breach the thing."

"This means our ability to be secure has just plummeted," said Chen Laoshi in a low voice. The others looked around at each other.

"Think of the implications," she said. "Grace and her kind storm in to our homes in the middle of the night, wreaking havoc among us, learning our secrets," she paused, then looked over at Charlie, "and taking our children."

Several of the adults looked at Charlie too, and for once he didn't turn his head away or blush red like Christmas tree lights. Instead, he returned their gaze, realizing that there were much scarier things on the planet than being looked at by grown-ups. Strangers breaking into your home at night and trying to kidnap you was now at the top of the list.

Finally he directed his attention back to his Chinese teacher. "Chen Laoshi, what does *'hen weixian'* mean?"

"It means 'dangerous,' Charlie. 'Very dangerous.' Why do you ask?"

"Oh, nothing. I just heard someone say it in a dream."

CHAPTER 36

Community in Jeopardy

IT WAS LIKE A GUN had gone off, for all the adults started speaking at once.

"Uh-oh!"

"What dream? When?"

"Who said it?"

"Do you have other dreams in Chinese?"

His reserve didn't last, with all the adults gathering around him and talking at once. Charlie froze, not knowing what to do or say. Randall pushed himself into the middle of them and said, "Hey! Hey! You're overwhelming the kid. Just slow down."

"Butt out, Randall," said one of the women Charlie didn't know. "This isn't any of your business." She was short and plump and had shorn gray hair and wire-rimmed glasses. She looked like the kind of person you saw staffing the information desk at the library.

"Look here, Joan," his uncle said, pointing his finger at the woman and glaring down at her, "this is my house, and it's my nephew, and it's all my business, so if you can't pipe down when I say to, then you can go ... go ... suck a duck!" he finished, eyes wide and nostrils flared.

The woman's mouth flew shut. She glared back at Randall but didn't say anything.

The rest of the group stared at his uncle, and a few even smiled with respect.

A snort and a giggle came from somewhere amongst the group. Charlie looked over and saw Jeremy with a hand pressed to his mouth trying to stifle his laughter.

When he saw Randall staring at him too, he stopped laughing and looked chagrined. "Rand, Rand, I'm sorry. I'm trying not to … it's just … 'suck a duck'?" And he turned and doubled over.

Beverly responded for her husband. "He was trying not to drop the F-bomb in front of our teenager," she said.

But the tension seemed to have lessened.

"How did you all get here, anyway?" asked Randall, looking around. "It's not like Beverly called you all. There hasn't been that much time."

"The cats," said Rita. "The neighborhood network knew something was going on, and it looks like we all got alerted."

"I'll explain later," Beverly said to Charlie, who had looked at her with eyebrows raised. "There are more important things to talk about right now."

"I think we should call for a general meeting," said Emory. "If Julia is right, there could be serious 'wayshun' or whatever she called it."

The others nodded.

"I think we also need to get Malcolm back home, and quick," said Beverly, looking over at Charlie.

"What for?" Joan asked.

"Because. Right now we have anywhere between ten and twelve unpopped kids in our community. They could be leaking just like Charlie is. Sorry, honey. The reason we all got a little excited back there was that it sounded like you had the kind of dream you can have when you're in prime need of popping. Things leak out. Like it did in the kitchen in California. When a lot of leaking like that happens, it's best to be popped. The longer you wait, the harder it might be to do.

"Anyway, these kids are at their prime and yet unprotected. They're probably giving off some sort of signal to Grace and her people. If we pop them …"

"Then we're just asking for trouble," Joan interrupted. "It's like giving kids a loaded gun. They won't know how to use it."

"Joan, you and I have been over this. Thousands of times! They already are loaded guns. With the safety lock on. Who's to say that something can't come along and knock off the safety? We've got to pop these kids and teach them how to defend themselves."

"It's too dangerous rushing into it like this. You know how wild it can be to have a few popped kids all at once. But twelve? Do we have the capacity to handle it?" Joan asked, rubbing her hands together in worry.

"I don't know," said his aunt. "I honestly don't. But Grace is forcing our hand. If we don't act now, the whole community could be in jeopardy."

CHAPTER 37

The Soccer Field

CHARLIE HAD A HARD TIME staying awake in school the next day. Chen Laoshi's class was the easiest, since it was the first period of the day, and also because several students kept patting him on the back and calling him a foosball star.

"*Chen Laoshi, Chen Laoshi,* you should have seen him! *Hen hao, hen hao!*" they said. She simply smiled before turning everyone's attention back to their newest chapter dealing with Chinese measure words. Charlie had wondered if Chen Laoshi would seem different this morning, but she was her usual self, insisting that the students pronounce the strange words and use correct tones.

By the time he went to biology, he was exhausted.

His lab partner, a thin quiet boy named Jarrod, had to nudge him a few times in the side to wake him up.

"Sorry," Charlie whispered to the other boy. "Slept badly last night."

"I hear you, dude, I hear you," Jarrod said, sounding more like a worldly old man than a fifteen-year-old science geek.

Each time the bell rang and he walked from the classroom out into the hallway, he half-hoped and half-worried that he would see Diego waiting for him. But the boy never showed up. Charlie was torn. He felt very awkward about what happened the night before in the car and wasn't looking forward to facing Diego again. But he was afraid that their short friendship had come to an end due to a misunderstanding. The more he thought about it, the more he realized how unhappy he would be if they weren't friends anymore.

Beverly had asked him to text her a few times during the day at school just to make sure he was all right. She said that Chen Laoshi would be watching out for things and that there were a few others at the school who were community members and could keep an eye out for anyone unwelcome entering the school's premises. When he asked her who the others were, she just smiled and said he would learn over time.

"But text me anyway, okay? It'll make your old aunt relax a bit."

He thought about how she had single-handedly taken care of the two intruders the night before. "Old aunt" certainly wasn't the description that came to mind. Tony's "ninja witch" seemed more accurate.

Over the next two days, nothing out of the ordinary happened. Beverly told him that Malcolm was cutting his trip short and would be back soon. She and some of the others had gone from home to home making new wards to protect the members of their community. Other than that, there was nothing else they could do.

"I know they say that the best defense is a good offense," she said over dinner one night, "but we wouldn't even know where to begin to strike."

"Well, from what you all say about her, Grace will probably be giving plenty of opportunities for more points of contact soon," added Randall. They finished the rest of their meal in silence.

On Thursday after school, two days after the Tanners' party and the attempted kidnapping, Charlie heard a familiar voice as he gathered his things from his locker and got ready to walk home.

"Hi, Charlie."

He turned to see Diego standing next to his locker. Fear mixed with excitement, worry blended with anticipation, all of it flashed through his chest before he could even register any of it. But the simple pleasure of seeing the other boy won out, and he felt his mouth curve into a smile.

"Diego. Hi."

"How ya doing?"

"Good, good. Um, hey, it's good to see you," Charlie said. "Really good."

"Yeah? Well, likewise, my friend. Likewise. Look, sorry about the other night. I shouldn't have …"

"You shouldn't have apologized, and you don't need to now," Charlie said.

"No, wait, that's not what I mean. I shouldn't have … um, can we go outside, maybe talk somewhere else?"

"Yeah, yeah, sure."

They left through the main door and down the side walkway, which led to the rear of the school and the large sports field. The girls' soccer team was warming up at the far end.

They sat down on the side of a hill above the field. Charlie could see the Olympic Mountains in the distance. He had begun to look at it every day. Unlike Mt. Rainier, which was often invisible due to cloud cover, the peaks of the Olympics were clear nearly every day. He liked the regularity of the view.

A massive maple tree towered over the street corner. Charlie noticed that several of its leaves had begun to shed their summer green, their edges showing yellow and red. It was hard to imagine fall colors among all the green in the area. He wondered if things would look very different.

"What I wanted to say," Diego continued, "was that I'm sorry for not being around the last few days."

"There's no need to …"

"Just hear me out, okay? I got scared, Charlie. And I felt stupid. I should have told you directly that I was gay. I chickened out and instead said what I did about being president of the GSA. That was pretty bogus of me. Anybody can be president. It doesn't mean you're straight, gay, or whatever. I was kind of speaking in code, because I was worried.

"The fact that you didn't know isn't your fault. I should have been upfront about it."

A crow squawked in the tree above them, and both boys looked up.

"Then I felt really stupid about what happened Tuesday night and too embarrassed to see you after that. But I've talked to Tawny about it these last few days, and she said I should just tell you instead of avoiding you."

"Oh. I'm glad you did, Diego. I felt stupid about the other night too. And then I thought I'd been, you know, a total jerk, and pissed you off or something, and you didn't want to be friends anymore."

Diego laughed. "And here I thought you didn't want to be friends with me."

"I guess we both got kind of worried, huh?"

A soccer ball came flying through the air toward the hill where they sat.

"Block those balls, Melissa!" Diego yelled as he jumped up, grabbed the ball, and threw it back.

"Thanks, *guapo*," said a girl in the goal box.

"She's a senior this year. She'll probably get a scholarship anywhere she wants for soccer," he told Charlie as he sat down again. "She's the best girls' goalie this school has ever seen and has turned everybody at P.A. into fans. The games are packed!"

They didn't say anything for a long time. They watched the girls practice and listened to the coach yelling at them.

Charlie had a feeling Diego was used to talking more than being silent.

"You want to go for a hike sometime?" he asked Diego.

"Yeah. Where?"

"Well, it's not very big, but I've been taking Amos, my aunt and uncle's dog, down to Carson Park."

"Cool. I haven't been there in a long time. Have you been to Lincoln Park yet?"

"No, where's that?"

"It's down by the Fauntleroy ferry dock. Carson Park has more windy trails and stuff. Lincoln Park is much bigger. It runs along the Sound. Anyway, yeah, cool, I'd love to go to Carson Park. When?"

They decided on a hike after school the next day as long as Diego wasn't busy. Apparently his uncle came over from Yakima on a weekly basis, and Diego would help him out at a few of the farmers markets in the area. His uncle hadn't told him yet whether or not he would need the help.

"That reminds me, about Lincoln Park, going on hikes and stuff. There's something else I want to tell you, since I'm just outing myself anyway," said Diego, then smiled and looked shy at the same time. "I'm a witch, Charlie, and I thought you should know."

CHAPTER 38

Bully, Bully, Bully

CHARLIE FELT HIS JAW DROP. How hadn't he known? Why hadn't Beverly told him? Was this one of those surprises he had to figure out on his own at school? It didn't make any sense. Why wouldn't she have told him? Maybe it was the same way nobody had said anything about Chen Laoshi.

Diego laughed hard. "You look shocked, Charlie. Don't be so surprised. It's not like it's a creepy, black-hat-and-broomstick kind of thing. Have you ever heard of Wicca? It's an earth-based religion. I became a witch a few years ago."

Charlie was having trouble keeping up with the conversation. "Is your mom a witch too?" he whispered, looking over his shoulder.

"You don't have to whisper, Charlie. People at school know. We even have Wicca meetings once a month.

"Anyway, no, my mom isn't. She's Catholic. Like everyone else in our family. I was raised that way. But I didn't want to go to Mass anymore. Tawny got into Wicca in middle school just to piss off her parents, and then she really started to enjoy it. She explained it to me one day, and it just made sense. We started doing outdoor rituals, and I really liked it."

"What kind of rituals?" Charlie asked, beginning to wonder if Diego's concept of "witch" was different from his own.

"You know, nature stuff. The four elements, asking the gods for help with stuff like our parents, or school. We also ask for help to be the best people we can be.

"It's not black magic, Charlie, so you don't have to worry about that. There's this law in Wicca called the Threefold Way, or the Law of Three. It says that whatever you put out into the world comes back at you threefold, so if you wish something bad on someone, it comes back to you three times as bad. So we just concentrate on good stuff. Stuff for our friends, our family, the world, you know."

"Am I creeping you out?" he asked.

Charlie looked at his face. He had a square chin with a dimple in the middle of it. The rule at P.A. was that the boys had to shave every day. Diego's beard was thick enough that by the end of the day, his jawline and sideburns, as well as the skin above his upper lip, grew dark. Charlie barely even had peach fuzz and felt like a little boy sitting next to Diego.

After a moment Charlie laughed. "No, no," he said, shaking his head. He was glad he hadn't said anything about Beverly and his mother, or his own legacy. "Um, it sounds pretty cool."

"Yeah, it is. If you want to, you could come to a ritual sometime. But I'm not trying to get you to join, 'k? It's not like a church where we go around trying to recruit members."

Three upperclassmen were walking up the sidewalk back toward school.

"Hey, Ramirez. ¿Quién está contigo? ¿Tu novio? ¿Tu pareja?" one of the boys yelled.

"Just ignore them, okay, Charlie?" Diego whispered, looking angry and turning his face away from the boys.

"What did he say?"

"Just forget it. He's being stupid is all."

"¡Qué maricones! Bésa le, Diego. ¡Dale un besito!" The three boys started walking toward them.

A sharp whistle cracked through the air. Charlie looked down the hill and saw the soccer coach walking up toward them, whistle in her mouth, a stern look on her face.

"Diego, everything all right? Is Julio giving you trouble?"

The upperclassmen stared at Diego and Charlie. One of them smiled.

"Naw, we're not bothering them. Just saying 'hi' is all."

"Diego, is that true?" Asked the coach, her eyes narrowing.

"Yeah, yeah, that's right. Just saying 'hi.'"

"Because remember, P.A. has a zero-tolerance policy. All you have to do is …"

"Thanks, Mrs. Raymond. It's cool," said Diego, looking up at her with a neutral expression.

"All right then. Just keep it peaceful, boys. And there won't be any trouble."

Charlie watched her as she walked back down the hill.

"You his little boy toy, kid?" said one of the other guys.

"More like butt toy," said Julio, and they all laughed.

"Or maybe …?" said the other guy, making a gesture with his hand and his mouth that Charlie didn't understand.

"Come on, Charlie, let's get out of here," said Diego, standing up.

"Oh 'Charlie,' is it? Don't you mean 'Charlie Darling'?"

"Dude, come on," Diego insisted, and started walking off.

"Better watch yourself, boy," said the third guy, as Charlie turned to go. "Faggots like you don't last long around here."

CHAPTER 39

Friendly Decisions

DIEGO SQUEEZED THE STEERING WHEEL until the blood faded from his knuckles.

"That Law of Three is hard to follow sometimes. I know I'm just supposed to take a deep breath, listen to the air outside, feel my feet on the ground, all that crap. But I want to smack those guys. They don't have to take deep breaths. They get away with whatever they want."

There was a crack in the boy's voice, and Charlie wondered if Diego was going to start crying.

The two boys sat in the school parking lot in Diego's car, a compact blue Honda stick shift with pamphlets and fliers and other pieces of paper covering the floor and the backseat.

Faggots like you don't last long around here.

Charlie could still hear the threat behind those words. His mind filled with the familiar image of Ted Jones's face. Imagining the football player's high school photo was becoming a habit. He wished he had never seen the news story that day.

Charlie was scared. Were those guys talking about him behind his back, telling everyone that he was Diego's boyfriend? Would they cause him trouble too?

He thought about getting popped. He wanted it to happen fast. If he could do to those boys what his aunt had done ... Well, maybe he wouldn't, since he needed to keep things a secret. But still. He wouldn't be as afraid then. And maybe he could help Diego too.

"Charlie, look," Diego said, "I don't want you to have trouble here at school. You're new and you're just trying to figure everything out. Most of the people here are cool, but there are some idiots, like Julio and Dave Giraldi. They've made it hard for me at times, but always on the side, you know? So no one else really ever sees?

"Anyway, maybe you shouldn't be seen with me. Those guys … they'll just bother you and … I don't want you to have trouble, is all."

Charlie, who saw himself as a shy person, afraid to express his opinion, who always wanted to hide out and not be noticed by anyone, surprised himself by what he said next.

"No way, Diego. I'll be friends with whoever (*whomever*, he heard his mother's voice correcting his English) I want to be, and be seen with anybody I want to. I didn't come all this way to Seattle just to hide out."

He couldn't believe he had said that. He had come to Seattle to hide out.

No, that wasn't exactly true. His mother had brought him here to hide out. It hadn't been his decision.

He thought about how he had always hidden from things—hoping adults wouldn't talk to him or ask him questions, hoping he wouldn't become the center of attention. And then, his mother just continued it by dragging him off to some city where he had never been before and hiding him away like some stupid witness protection program.

Wait. Shouldn't he be more cautious? Look at what happened Tuesday night. Shouldn't he lay low and make sure people couldn't find him?

But trying to hide hadn't worked. The Dog Man found them in California. The witches broke into Beverly and Randall's home. People seemed to know where he was. So he might as well accept the fact that hiding didn't work and figure something else out instead.

Charlie wasn't used to such blunt self talks. It felt strange, and strangely invigorating. They seemed to be happening more often these days, and often times when he was hanging out with Diego.

"I want to be friends with you. That's my decision, not Julio's, not anybody else's," he said, looking at Diego, surprised by the fierceness in his voice.

The other boy stared at him, his mouth open. Then he smiled. "Dude! You are so, like, righteous right now. Wow! I didn't know you were that tough!"

Diego paused, then looked sheepish. "I hope that didn't sound like an insult."

Charlie smiled back. "I didn't know I was that tough either."

Diego's shouts of laughter and dashboard banging could be heard throughout the parking lot.

CHAPTER 40

Malcolm

CHARLIE HEARD VOICES COMING from the living room as he opened the front door and walked inside. He put his house keys in the top drawer of the table in the foyer.

"Hey, Charlie. Come here for a minute. I want you to meet someone."

He walked down the hallway and turned into the living room. Beverly was perched on the edge of the couch next to a middle-aged man with shorn gray-brown hair and a trim beard. Teacups and saucers sat on the coffee table in front of them along with a half-eaten array of fruit and cookies.

"Charlie, I'd like you to meet Malcolm Goedde, historian, teacher, and sneaky wise guy of this community. Malcolm, this is my nephew, Charlie."

The man stood up, laughing. "Thank you, Beverly. Always the kind one."

He stepped around the coffee table, walked over to Charlie, and shook his hand.

"Hello, young man, seems like there's been an awful lot of buzz about you lately."

The man's eyes sparkled, and his hand was large and warm. At the same time, there was an edge to him that Charlie found unnerving.

He turned back to Beverly. "Ah yes, you're right. He's filled to bursting."

"What he means," said his aunt, gesturing for Charlie to sit with them, "is that you are ready to be popped. Quite ready, it would appear."

"Is it too late?" asked Charlie, hoping for all he was worth that it wasn't.

"No, kid, you're fine. But another six to eight months, and it might be."

Beverly went on to explain that there weren't many people in the world who could open up a new witch's ability. Malcolm spent most of his time popping kids and then training them how to use their craft carefully.

"He's a tough teacher. I can speak from personal experience. But his lessons will prepare you better than anything else out there."

Malcolm lived up near Snoqualmie Pass in the Cascades Mountains outside of Seattle. He traveled a lot, mostly in the States and Canada but sometimes South America and Europe.

"Any questions, kid?" Malcolm asked.

"Um, when do we get started?"

The older man laughed. "That's what I like. Lots of gumption."

He turned to Beverly. "Leave us alone for a moment?"

She gathered the teacups together but left the snack tray. "Charlie, make sure you eat something," she said over her shoulder as she headed to the kitchen.

"Just a moment," Malcolm said when they were sitting alone together on the couch. He reached up and pinched his nostrils closed with his fingers, then puffed his cheeks out. Charlie felt pressure against his eardrums much like when he swam toward the bottom of the lake near his house back in Clarkston.

"Okay, just a precaution. No one else can hear us now."

Charlie's eyes grew wide. "Um, okay, well, I'm ready, I guess. Do I have to, you know, do anything, or …"

"What? No, no no no no. I'm not going to pop you now. I need to ask you a few questions and give you some information."

"Oh." Charlie was equally relieved and disappointed.

"First off. Do you understand what popping is? Do you know what it will mean?"

"Yeah, I guess."

"Explain it to me then."

The man's eyes lost their sparkle. He crossed his arms and waited. The intensity in his face increased.

Charlie took a deep breath. "I have witch blood in me, and even though some of it is leaking out, most of it won't, and so I need to be popped so I can, uh, so I can use all the witch blood in me?" he finished with a question.

"Pretty good, pretty good. Though you might want to change your metaphor. You don't have blood that is leaking out of you, like a wound. Your blood is very active right now. Think of it like vapor, or steam, rising from inside you. Your insides are hot, and so steam comes out. It came out in the form of the dream you had that Beverly mentioned to me and what you did to that man down in California. That's the steam. After a few months you'd cool down a bit, and then you might have echoes for the rest of your life, or you might have nothing at all. That's how it works.

"Now," he continued, "I want you to understand what this means, my boy. This is not a decision to be taken lightly. Everyone wants to be popped. But few really take the time to understand the implications of it. Most kids who get popped come from families with a long legacy. They wouldn't dream of not becoming full-fledged witches.

"But it's not all good, okay? You will see the world, you will feel the world, very differently from how you do now. I'm sure they explained to you how disorienting it is right after you're popped. That's true. But it's not like everything goes back to normal. You'll never be normal again. Ever. Even if you try to do what your mother did, forsake her legacy and let her ability mostly dry up, it'll always be there. And a witch who lets his or her abilities get weak is just asking for danger. Witches sense each other. They sniff each other out like dogs.

"Yes, I know, I know, there are wards, and bracelets," he went on, pointing to Charlie's wrist, "but still. We can always smell each other eventually. If you stay unpopped, you might be able to avoid that whole thing. Avoid being on the radar screen. But if you get popped and then decide, 'Oh, I don't want this anymore,' you're in trouble, kid. You might as well paint a big bulls-eye on your face and walk around town yelling 'Shoot me!'

"Now, your mother's a bit of an exception. Even though she isn't a very strong witch and has let most of her abilities atrophy, she can lay low and stay under the radar screen better than most I've seen. And I've met a lot of witches in my day.

"And even she was found, eventually. Well, to her credit, I think they sensed you, not her. But see, she couldn't keep you hidden. And I doubt you'll be able to keep yourself hidden either."

He paused. "Is any of this making sense?"

"Yes," Charlie said. "If I get popped, I won't be able to go back to how I was before, or how I am now. And it'll make me stand out more to other witches, good and bad. If I do it, then I have to learn how to protect myself."

"Well said, kid, well said," Malcolm smiled. He reached over and gave Charlie's shoulder a hard squeeze.

"Okay. On to the next thing. What's her name?"

"Whose name?"

"Don't be shy with me. We gotta put it all out on the table if we're gonna make this work. The girl you're so crazy about."

"Girl? There's no girl ..."

"Oh. Pardon me. What's his name?"

Charlie felt a chill in his heart. Did he mean ...? But they were just friends. Besides ...

"I don't know what you mean."

"Okay, little man. That's your first lie to me. You better make them few and far between, or our relationship isn't going to go so well. Now, I don't know if you're only lying to me or to yourself too. But ..."

Charlie stood up. "I don't think we really need to ..."

Faster than he would have guessed, the man was up and shoving Charlie back down on the couch.

"You think this is a game, kid?"

"No, I ..."

Malcolm stood over him for a moment, arms crossed, then was sitting down next to him before Charlie could register that he wasn't standing anymore. His face was inches from Charlie's, the smell of tea and cookies sweet on his breath. The man's voice dropped low, becoming ominous. Charlie's legs began to shake. "You think this is just something you get to control? You'll just get popped, and you'll be able to do all the neat stuff Auntie Bev Bev does, and everything will be fine? You'll learn hocus-pocus, and fly around at night stopping all the bad guys? Poof, like that?" His mouth had curved into a taunting smile, and his eyebrows arched up toward the top of his head.

Then the smile vanished.

"Now you listen to me, and you listen good. I don't give a rat's ass whom you love or what kind of person floats your boat. It's none of my business. What is my business is training you to use your craft with skill, caution, and most of all, a level head. You're asking me to turn you into a weapon that makes an entire SWAT team look like a bunch of crossing guards. You don't think I have a sense of responsibility here?

"If you lie to yourself, then how do you think you'll do when you learn your first Words? Words that shift and change things. Words that give you power over normal human beings. You gotta be clean with yourself, little man, when you start wielding Words. If not, wouldn't it be easy to push somebody around a little bit? Or a lot? Maybe steal something at school? Just that one time? Maybe force people to do things against their will?"

"No. No, I wouldn't ..."

"Or the flip side. Be so worried about it that you become a recluse, hiding from everyone, living in a little hut somewhere eating tree bark because you can't reconcile what you can do with how the rest of the world works? Like your mother?"

Malcolm's words felt like gravel pelting Charlie's face. "What? No, she ..."

"You think that's what I want to create? You think that's what this community needs? At a time like this? A hermit? Or some kid who lies to himself about what turns his crank and then goes around causing collateral damage?"

Malcolm sat back and glared at the boy for a moment. Then the expression on his face changed, looking more than a little satisfied, like a lion after finishing his kill. Charlie half expected him to lick his lips.

What was Malcolm saying? That Charlie liked Diego? That he was gay? How could that be?

"How did you know?" Charlie whispered. "Is it that obvious?"

Malcolm's face softened. "Kid, this is what I do. I gotta make sure people are very clear what they're getting into before I hand 'em the keys to the car, so to speak. Believe me, I've made mistakes over the years, mistakes that have cost lives, because someone I thought could handle their gifts, couldn't.

"You need to know something. Witches can't read minds. I don't care what anybody tells you. It's one of the nuts we haven't been able to crack. And I'm personally glad we can't. It would be too unfair to normal human beings, and I think it would make us crazy. So, no, I didn't read your mind. You don't need witchcraft to see that everyone on this planet has a secret or two. I just make it my business to see what unpopped kids are hiding. It's always stuff nobody wants to admit to, like you, so I have to 'help' them," he said, making quotes with his fingers in the space between their faces, "to see what secrets they have before I agree to pop them.

"And you'd be surprised how common the secrets are. 'I want so-and-so to love me.' 'I took money from mama's cookie jar.' 'I touch myself at night,'" he finished, his voice high-pitched and mocking. "Make sense?"

Charlie nodded. Only moments before, he had felt the thrill of not hiding anymore, of sitting in Diego's car and tasting the freedom of just being himself. Now it didn't seem thrilling at all. It seemed awful, terrible, the worst of the worst.

Horrified, he realized that fat tears had welled up in his eyes, and his whole body had begun to shake.

"I know I came down on you pretty hard," Malcolm continued. "It's nothing personal. Everyone gets a come-to-Jesus talk with me. I'm sorry it had to be like this, but there's no other way around it. And by the way, you can still decide not to do this. Your secret stays with me. I've heard 'em all, kid. This one doesn't faze me a bit.

"But," he went on, "If you do want to get popped, it can't be a secret anymore. I'm not going to publish it in the newspaper. It's up to you how you handle it. But if you lie to yourself, you're going to have a helluva time learning how to use the craft. It would be like trying to learn to drive with your eyes closed. You might feel the steering wheel and the gas pedal, but you won't know what's coming at you, and eventually you'll crash into something."

Charlie's breathing came in gulps, while more tears fell down his face. He stayed as quiet as he could.

"Kid, can I be honest with you?"

Charlie nodded, thinking bitterly to himself, *Haven't you already been?*

He gripped the arm of the couch, ready for another onslaught of words.

"I'm glad I'm not gay. I don't care how open the world says it is these days. I don't think there's a very big welcome mat out there for people like you. I think it would be rough.

"But you gotta get this, that if you see it as a problem, then you're inviting everyone else to do the same. If not, and if other people still have a problem with it, well then, so what? You have bigger fish to fry." He paused, waiting for a reply from Charlie. When the boy didn't say anything, Malcolm continued.

"I'm sorry it's gotta be this way. But you don't get to have one without the other. You can't pretend to be someone you're not and use what you got. It just won't work. And I won't let you try."

He reached into his pocket and handed Charlie a card.

It read "Malcolm Goedde" and had a phone number and an email address printed on the front.

"The last name's German. Throws everyone off. Just think 'Geddy,' like G-E-D-D-Y." He looked hard at Charlie, as if sizing him up.

"Why don't you think about it? Give me a call or send me a message when you've reached your decision or if you have any questions. But don't wait too long, okay? You already know what you need, and waiting forever will just make things worse.

"Remember, your secret stays with me, whichever way you decide. I won't tell anyone. Not your aunt, not your uncle, not the mayor of Seattle."

Charlie nodded, putting the card in his pocket and wiping his eyes with the back of his arm.

Malcolm pinched his nostrils again and puffed out his cheeks. Just like that, the pressure on Charlie's eardrums released. He opened his mouth and wiggled his jaw, letting his ears pop.

"Okay, little man, enough for today." He stood up. "Let's carry these things into the kitchen, and I'll say goodbye to Beverly."

They walked into the kitchen together. Charlie's feet felt like blocks of cement attached to dead tree-limb legs. He thought he might trip and drop the plates he carried.

Beverly smiled as she stood up from the kitchen table, a magazine laying half open near her hands. Behind the smile, Charlie could see tension and concern in her eyes.

"Come here, gorgeous," Malcolm said, giving her a hug.

She walked him out. Charlie heard her open the front door and say goodbye.

Then she came back into the kitchen and looked at Charlie.

"He can be intense, I know. But it's really for your own good. Whatever the two of you talked about is your business. I'm sure he gave you lots to think about. Anyway, why don't you run up and do some of your homework before dinner?" she suggested. He was grateful for the excuse to go to his bedroom and think about, or try not to think about, everything that Malcolm had said.

CHAPTER 41

Shivering

CHARLIE SAT ON THE DECK off the kitchen watching the wind turn the waves of Puget Sound from gray to white. Beverly was off doing something in the basement. Randall was reading the newspaper in the living room.

"Leave it alone," Charlie scolded Amos, who was pressing his nose up against the glass on the other side of the sliding door and whining. He wanted to come out on the deck where Charlie was. The dog couldn't hear him but wagged his tail anyway, as if he could summon the boy to open the door through sheer animal enthusiasm.

He knew he should get up and go inside, or at least put on a jacket. Goose flesh covered his arms. He continued to shiver. Maybe he could blame his shaking on the cold wind.

His thoughts were loud, as if he stood in a room filled with shouting people. He was having trouble keeping up with it all.

If you want to get popped, it can't be a secret anymore.

Okay, little man. That's your first lie to me.

But you don't get to have one without the other. You can't pretend to be someone you're not and use what you got. It just won't work.

I'm not gay.

You think this is a game, kid?

No, no, he wouldn't let it be true. He didn't …

Boys' faces that he had known over the years floated into his head. Hadn't they just been his friends?

No way. No way would he let this be true. He couldn't ...
More like butt toy.
Don't you mean "Charlie Darling?"
He didn't know what it all meant, and the terror he felt kept him from being able to figure any of it out, making everything stop short in his chest, his throat, cranking the volume in his head so high that the shouting voices blurred together, becoming mind-numbing rants.
Senior high school student, Ted Jones ...
People are nice to me and all, but ...
I'm the president of the GSA.
What was he supposed to do?

* * *

"How long have you been sitting out here?"
Charlie jumped. He hadn't heard his aunt come out onto the deck. "A while."
"It's cold out here. You're shivering. Shouldn't you ...?" She paused, then shook her head, as if her mothering were silly.
"Malcolm doesn't exactly soften his blows, does he?"
Charlie stared at her.
"Becoming a full-fledged witch is a big decision. He wants to make sure that you don't rush headlong into something that will affect you for the rest of your life. I'm sure he gave you the 'once you decide, you can never turn back' speech."
He nodded, then looked out over the water as Beverly continued to talk.
"And the part about how being a witch isn't just broomsticks and parlor games? He wants you to be very clear, because your decision will not only affect you, but countless others, throughout your whole life.
"People like me had a long time to think about all the issues, Charlie. Our parents engrain it in us from the moment we start to learn about our community. All of this has been dumped on you so fast. But that doesn't mean you don't have to face these facts any less

than the rest of us did."

Charlie drew his gaze away from the water and looked directly at his aunt.

"What did Malcolm say to you?"

Beverly looked down at her hands. When she looked up, she attempted a smile but her face showed fresh hurt, as if she too had just been ripped open by Malcolm a few hours earlier, not over three decades ago. She blinked several times before she spoke.

"He said I was too much of a daddy's girl. That my father had huge shortcomings as our community leader. That he was not infallible. I had to either grow up and learn to think for myself, which included seeing my dad as a human being, not as a god, or live the rest of my life as his little hand puppet, brainwashed, just like my mother."

Charlie's mouth fell open.

"He couldn't have been more right. It's even clearer to me now than it was back when he told me."

She wrapped her arms around herself and looked out over the water.

"Okay, it's officially freezing. We're going inside, Charlie. Turning blue isn't going to help you with your decision."

As they stepped into the warmth of the kitchen, he could hear Amos's toenails clicking on the wood floor. The dog rounded a corner and ran to them, pressing into their hands with his back, breathing hard out of his nostrils and quivering as they both bent down and rubbed his fur.

"That's right, buddy, that's right," Beverly said. She slid the door closed behind them, then placed her hand on Charlie's shoulder.

"It's your decision to make, Charlie. I want you to remember that. Don't make it for me, or for your mom, not for Randall, not anybody. You're the one who needs to mull over what Malcolm told you."

Her eyes softened, losing their stern gaze.

"And I trust you to make the right decision."

"What decision?" Randall yelled from the living room. "Does it involve dinner? A guy could starve around here!"

CHAPTER 42

The High Dive

AMOS PULLED AT THE LEASH, trying to inch over to the side of the road to investigate a clump of wild ferns.

"Come on, boy," Charlie grunted as his arm was yanked nearly out of its socket.

"That sure is a big dog," Diego said as they walked farther into the woods.

"Tell me about it." Charlie had to pull hard not to be knocked off balance.

"The first time I came here was in preschool. My mom was the classroom parent for the day, and she and the teacher took us kids for a nature walk here. I remember ... hey, did you hear that?"

"Hear what?"

"It sounded like ..." Diego paused, looking around and trying to pinpoint what he heard.

Chills ran all over Charlie's skin. What if that dog was back? Or what if the witches were following them?

Just then a thrashing sound erupted to their right as a large blue jay flew up from the bushes and into the sky.

"God, that scared me!" Diego exclaimed, laughing. "Anyway, what was I saying? Oh yeah, I remember how big the woods seemed then. And how wet and green everything was."

Charlie inhaled deeply, trying to let the fresh piny air calm him down, relieved that it had only been a bird.

The temperature felt warmer today. Amos stopped yanking on his leash, finally understanding that Charlie wasn't going to let him pull the boy wherever he wanted to go.

"Diego, can I ... can I ask you a question?"

"Sure, amigo, ask away."

"How can you be sure that you're gay? Don't you ever wonder if you're wrong? I mean, how can you really know?"

"Whoa, that came out of left field."

"Sorry."

"No, it's okay. I mean, I'd rather you ask me about it than just ignore it and hope it goes away. Let's see. I've always liked other boys. Just been attracted to them. I paid way more attention to them than to girls growing up. My uncle told me that when I was little and my mom and I would be visiting him in Yakima that I'd always want to go talk to the farmhands that helped him in the orchards, never the pretty girls in town, or even my girl cousins, who are really gorgeous.

"He said he wondered about it when I was little. Even asked my mom about it. She said I was just sensitive. I think she got angry about it all. Didn't want it to be true."

"Your mom didn't want you to be gay? But I thought you said she was cool with it."

"She is now. She wasn't when I told her. It was really hard at first. We fought a lot. I can be a little opinionated when it comes down to it, and I told her she was being stupid and Catholic and mean. She said, 'You don't know what you want. You can't! You're only thirteen,'" Diego said in a high-pitched voice, imitating his mother.

"Well, I just knew, you know? The way you know things? I read stuff about it at the library, and I always had crushes on guy movie stars and stuff. Oh my god, remember Wolverine in *X-Men*? I think I saw it when I was ten years old, and I couldn't stop thinking about him. I told my mom I wanted him to babysit me. What I didn't tell her was that I wanted him to kiss me. A lot!"

Diego laughed as if this was the funniest thing he had ever heard. Charlie frowned. Their conversation wasn't helping things much. He had never talked to his mom about this stuff, let alone fought with her. Maybe it wasn't true. Maybe it was just …

But he felt a chill in his chest, the same one he had felt yesterday, when Malcolm confronted him in the living room. That, and a growing concern that maybe all his life he, too, had thought about boys more than girls.

"I used to play Diego's Kissing Class with the kids in my neighborhood when I was like five or six," Diego continued. "I'd line up the kids in a row in the hallway outside my bedroom, then make them come inside the 'teacher's office' one at a time and 'teach' them how to kiss. I got in trouble because one of the girls told her mom that I kept her in the waiting room too long while her brother got longer 'lessons.' So embarrassing, but it's true. The girl's parents talked to my mom, and my mom tried to explain to me that I shouldn't be teaching kissing to other boys. She said I could kiss girls only after I grew up. I didn't really get it. I thought we were all having a lot of fun."

They came around the corner of the small path, and there in front of them was the bridge, spanning a good forty feet in the air, both ends marked by giant pine trees.

"I forgot about this place!" said Diego. He ran forward, then plopped himself down on the same bench where Charlie and Beverly had sat just before she had leapt across the creek bed. Charlie tied Amos to the bench then sat next to Diego.

Charlie felt some relief. He had never kissed other boys when he was little. Diego had. And he had never really thought about Wolverine before. So maybe he wasn't necessarily …

"When did you and your mom stop fighting about it?" he asked.

"After she talked to her priest. Here I was, telling her she was too Catholic, but it was Father Heneghan who really helped her. She told him she prayed and prayed for me to like girls and wanted him to help her pray harder or to learn a better way to ask God for help. But he just asked her if she thought I was going to change. I guess she started crying and told him she didn't think I would. So he said that it was her job to love me fully, even if she didn't like all of me, and let the rest be between God and me. Can you believe that? Pretty cool for a priest."

"But don't you think you could be wrong? Maybe you just didn't, I don't know, try or something?"

"I did. I totally tried to like girls. I used to pray for the same thing my mom did. I thought I had a crush on Tawny for the longest time because she was nice, and fun, and we really got along so well.

"But I never felt the things for her that I did for other guys. There was this kid in Tawny's and my seventh grade class, Ken Nishimura. He was tall, and quiet, kind of the brainiac type, but good in sports too. I had such a huge crush on him. I couldn't even think straight when he was around. It was Tawny who told me that I should just get over it and admit to myself that I was attracted to guys.

"She said to me, 'It's "Ken" this and "Ken" that. When are you gonna face the fact that you're in love with him?'"

"She did? She just said that?"

"Yeah."

"What did you do?"

"I didn't talk to her for like three days. As you can see, I've really gotten a lot more mature in my old age." Diego laughed. "But then I talked to her about it. I cried, she cried, we both cried, and then well, that was that.

"I told my mom, and she went a little nutty on me. That's when we started fighting. I got in her face about it, like any snotty thirteen-year-old would do, and she pushed back. But a couple of weeks later she talked to Father Heneghan.

"She sat me down one night. At first I was ready for another fight, but instead she told me to be quiet, that she had something important to say. She said that she would love me no matter what, even if she didn't understand it or like it.

"Oh my god! I cried so hard, and then she cried, and then we both cried. You can see the pattern here." He smiled and shook his head. "Anyway, after that it got a lot easier. Well, that's not true. It got easier between my mom and me. I started coming out to people at school, and that's when things started to get really hard. Kids began teasing me. Some of the eighth graders beat me up a few times."

Charlie shivered. It was hard to imagine anyone wanting to beat up Diego, who just seemed so nice and friendly. Who would do that? But he remembered the three upperclassmen taunting him and Diego near the soccer field and how mean they had looked. And of course, there was always Ted Jones

"My mom talked to the school principal. He was a total tool about it. The school didn't have a policy on bullying, and he kept saying that if I just stopped telling everyone, there wouldn't be any trouble.

"She tried to push it at the school, getting all lawyer-like with them, but they got really nasty with her, telling her she would need to document the bullying, she couldn't prove who had beat me up, blah blah blah. So she pulled me outta there. I went to three different private schools that year and the next. But once freshman year rolled around, I started at P.A. and have been there ever since.

"I know what you saw the other day, with Julio and Dave and Randy, was kinda bad. But believe me, it's way better than middle school. Plus, Principal Wang really does enforce the no-tolerance policy. I've never had trouble with any of the teachers. They've all gone through a diversity training program, so it works pretty well."

"I thought you said it was hard at school sometimes. That people treated you special, like being extra positive or something," Charlie said.

"Yeah, but it's still way better than getting beaten up. And really, I was kind of upset yesterday when I told you all of that. I feel like there's good support for me at school, with the GSA and the policies and stuff.

"Besides, we have to start somewhere. Yeah, there are gay talk-show hosts and TV characters. Even movies. But sometimes that doesn't trickle down into the everyday walking-down-the-hall-people-looking-at-you kind of thing. But if I don't do it, then who is going to? If I wait for someone else to be brave and come out to make it safe for me, then it might not ever happen.

"You know that Gandhi quote, 'Be the change you want to see in the world'? I think it's true," Diego said, shrugging his shoulders.

He stopped talking after that, then bent down and grabbed a stick near the bench. He dragged it around in the dirt for a while and threw it into the creek. Amos hopped up from where he was lying on the ground and pulled at his leash.

"Oops, I forgot about you. You wanted to go get that, boy, didn't you? Didn't you?" Diego teased, scratching Amos behind the ears. The dog whined and shivered, caught between Diego's attention and the stick.

"My turn for a question?" Diego said, looking at Charlie, who had been staring down at the water in the creek, lost in thought.

"Yeah. Go ahead."

"Why are you asking me all of this? You seem kind of different about it today than you did Tuesday night. Or even yesterday. I don't know. Like you're trying to figure something out," Diego said, glancing into Charlie's eyes for a brief moment before looking away.

Charlie didn't answer for a long time. He listened to the cars driving across the bridge overhead, sending rumbles into the dirt beneath their feet. He watched a leaf swirl and spin in an eddy near the creek bank.

He thought about what Malcolm had said, about telling lies, about how he couldn't be a witch and hide this part from himself. Or others. He was scared. He wasn't sure what to do.

"I think I might be gay too," Charlie said, his voice abrupt and clear, as if he were announcing something normal, something easy, like a test score in geometry. But he hadn't really meant to say it. Had he?

He began to feel light-headed. He remembered the first time he ever jumped off the high dive at the Clarkston Community Pool. He stood at the end of the board for a long time. He knew it was twelve feet high when he was on the pool deck looking up at it. But from the top of the board, the water's surface looked miles away. He almost jumped off the board in the first thirty seconds or so of standing there. But he stopped at the last minute, grabbed on to the railings and tried to catch his breath. He became light-headed, contemplating that he had almost jumped.

He felt the same now, except that this time he really had jumped, he had opened his mouth and said the thing he was most afraid to say, to himself or to anyone. His face felt fuzzy, as if there were insects crawling all over it. He scratched at his chin.

He could tell Diego was looking at him, but he couldn't turn to face the boy. He looked down at his feet, then up at the sky, wondering if something in the clouds would help him know what to do.

"Whoa. I mean, well ... whoa. Just like that?" he heard Diego ask.

Charlie turned and looked at him. And nodded.

He didn't expect what Diego said next.

"You may be, you may not be. I think it's just important to talk about it." The boy's voice had lost its excitement. He sounded like he was trying to be a serious adult.

"Don't you want me to be gay? Don't you want there to be others? Wouldn't it make it easier for you?" Charlie asked, finally looking into Diego's face.

The boy smiled. "Of course it would make it easier for me. But only if it's true. And making it easier for me isn't the only reason it would be great for me if you were gay. But it's a big deal, Charlie. Can't we just talk about it a bit? I mean really, there's no rush."

"Yes, there is! You don't understand! I have to figure this out before ..."

Charlie stopped himself. He had almost spilled the beans about Malcolm, about the community. What was he doing, flapping his lips like this? If he wasn't careful ...

"No, you don't have to rush it. Not at all. Let's just talk about it."

CHAPTER 43

Me Too

AND SO THEY DID. They sat there on the bench, talking about the boys Diego thought were hot at school. (Charlie didn't know who he thought was hot at school. He never let himself think those thoughts, so he wasn't sure. Or at least he wasn't sure if he was sure.) They also talked about what it was like to tell family members, about the cool programs and groups there were that offered support.

"Really, it's a great time to be gay," Diego said. "So many things have changed in the last five or ten years. And they keep changing. You can now even get married in Washington State. And more states will follow, I just know they will."

They talked about everything ... everything, that is, except the part about them, about their friendship, about how things were ...

Charlie just couldn't bring it up. Diego was too close, too near. He didn't even know what he thought, did he? Or what he wanted? *I want to sit closer to Diego,* his own body seemed to be saying to him. *I want to touch his skin, I want to ...*

What if he did say something? Then what? What if Diego laughed at him? The boy hadn't named Charlie on his list of hot guys at school. Maybe that was a good thing. Maybe Charlie didn't want to be on that list.

But maybe he did.

What if Diego wasn't attracted to Charlie at all?

Or worse: what if he was?

Would he have to do something about it? Would that mean they were going out? Would everyone at school see them together? Would they have to hold hands in between classes? Would Diego try to kiss him? That would be so gross, that would be …

Charlie thought about it. He thought about the other boy's lips, darker than his own, full, the way they moved fast when he talked. He had wondered what it would be like to kiss someone before. But he had always thought about kissing a girl. He mostly worried what her lipstick would taste like. But a boy? This boy, who spoke Spanish and Chinese, who used to teach kissing lessons as a kid, sitting here on the bench next to him. This boy who was handsome and popular and tall and seemed to know everything? What would it be like to kiss him?

I want to know, Charlie heard that same voice say inside of him.

He stood up. This was too much. He started pacing back and forth in front of the park bench.

So that was true too, was it? He, what? Liked Diego? Loved him? He didn't think he loved him. But then again, how did you know if you loved somebody? You let them kiss you? You wanted to listen to them talk all day, even if they talked too much, even if they were silly? You felt shy and excited and worried and ready, each and every time you saw them?

Maybe he was just attracted to the boy. Maybe that was it. He didn't love him. He was just attracted to him.

What did that mean? Did it have to mean anything? Couldn't he be attracted to other boys too? And other girls?

Did it mean he had to tell Diego? It didn't, did it? Didn't Malcolm say that it could stay a secret? Didn't that priest say it was between Diego and God? Couldn't it be between Charlie and God? Did he even believe in God?

Argh! This is too hard! he yelled inside his head. *I mean, Diego isn't telling me that I have to make a decision, and he's not trying to get me to say anything I don't want to. But still. He's just sitting there on that bench, looking at me, watching me walk back and forth like he's at a tennis match. Just waiting for me.*

"I don't know!" Charlie yelled, causing Diego to jump at his sudden outburst. "I don't know! Okay? God, why does this have to be so hard? I don't know what I'm supposed to do, or say, or ..."

"Hey, take it easy, Charlie. No one is telling you to do anything!"

"Yes, you are. You want me to be gay. God, I hate that word. You want me to like boys. Everybody always wants something from me, and I, I'm just, I'm just sick and effing tired of it all!" he screamed into the afternoon air.

"All ... all ... all ... all ... all ..." bounced back and forth across the creek bed.

He stood quietly, his hands at his sides, ashamed at what he had said. Here Diego was trying to help, and all he could do was yell at him. The outburst didn't feel good. It felt dirty on his lips, like he had drunk spoiled milk and couldn't get the taste out of his mouth.

Amos was on his feet, harrumphing into the dirt, tail wagging, looking at Charlie with his tongue hanging out.

Charlie looked over to the bench expecting to see Diego's face crumpled with hurt, or even worse, smiling that fake smile he had done in the car the other night.

Instead, Diego's eyes were wide open, and his mouth hung agape.

"Dude! That was awesome! Awesome! Do it again. Yell it!"

"What? Are you crazy? I don't want to ... . That was, like, totally embarrassing. I shouldn't have ..."

"Shut up! That was amazing. Ms. Barry, the GSA faculty member, says that sometimes we just have to yell stuff out loud. I want to try it!"

And with that, he stood up, threw his head back and yelled, "I am sick and effing tired of it all. I am sick and effing tired of it all!"

Amos began to lurch between the two boys, trapped by the leash. Finally he leaned forward on his front paws and offered up his own "Aroof!" to the sky.

The boys took one look at the dog and erupted in laughter. All the anxiety and confusion in Charlie turned into hard laughter, pouring out of him like soda fizzing from a bottle. Charlie bent over, trying to point at Amos and keep himself from falling over at the same time.

Diego fell back on the bench and howled, drawing his knees up to his stomach and hitting the dirt with his free hand.

"Maybe he's gay too!" Diego choked out between gasps. This made Charlie fall to his knees. As he tumbled forward, he threw his hands out to keep from landing face first on the ground and accidentally blew a rather large bubble of snot out of his nose.

"Gross! Gross!" Diego yelled, pointing at Charlie's face, then dissolving into more laughter and clutching at his stomach.

Charlie was giggling too hard to be embarrassed. Amos yelped a few more times, which set the two boys off again for a good ten minutes, forcing more snot and more tears, more gales of laughter from their tired vigilant bodies.

CHAPTER 44

Hen Weixian

IT SEEMED TO CHARLIE THAT he spent the rest of that Friday, as well as all of Saturday, on the phone. He and Diego talked several more times each day. It wasn't as if they spent the whole time talking about being gay. They talked about school, about California, about Diego being Mexican-American. They spoke of what Diego respected about his mother Lydia: that she was a single parent, that she was a successful lawyer at a downtown law firm. Diego also mentioned what he didn't respect about her: that she was a Republican, a fact that led to endless debates between her and her Democrat son. They talked about Charlie's mother and her quiet capable ways, and Charlie found that it was easy to talk about her as long as he kept to general details. They talked about his aunt and uncle as well as cool things to do in and around town. It was as if, now that Charlie had admitted to himself and Diego that he was (might be? could be?) gay, it gave the boys a chance to talk about everything else.

Maybe it wasn't completely out in the open. It didn't feel that way. But as he stood in his bedroom that Friday night with his cell phone to his ear, hearing the multitude of words spilling from Diego's mouth like bird chatter, he caught himself staring at his reflection in his full-length mirror and wondering if he looked any different.

I'm gay, he would try out in his mind as he looked at himself. Did that feel right? *I'm homose-* ... No, he couldn't say that word yet. It felt weirder, more scientific. More definitive, somehow. *I'm gay ... I'm gay ...*

"And then I was all, 'Whatever, and she was like, 'Yeah.' So I was like, 'You sure, mom? You, sure?' And she was all, 'Diego Alejandro Ramirez,' which totally means I'm in trouble when she uses my full name ...'"

"Uh-huh," Charlie heard himself saying.

It was nice that Diego did most of the talking. He could just add a few words now and then and the boy would keep going.

The one thing Charlie hadn't talked about were his feelings for Diego.

After he had eaten dinner with his aunt and uncle and while they were downstairs watching TV, Charlie went back upstairs and found the card Malcolm had given him. He had never really considered not becoming a witch. Now that he had talked to Diego, though, he was ready to commit. His hands only shook a little as he entered Malcolm's number on his phone screen and hit "call."

"You sure, Charlie?"

"Uh, yeah. Look. I thought about what you said. And I talked to the guy at school who's gay, the one I think I like. I told him I thought I was gay. We, uh, we talked a lot about it."

"Wow, kid, nothing like a little pressure to get the ball rolling, huh?"

Charlie nodded, forgetting that Malcolm couldn't see him on the phone.

"Malcolm?"

"Yeah?"

"Um, I didn't tell that kid, Diego, about, you know, how I feel about him."

"Why not?"

"I don't know."

"Nope. That's not gonna cut it."

"Well, because what if it means I have to do something about it? Like, I don't know, hold his hand at school or something? That would be so weird. And everybody would find out.

"Plus," added Charlie, "what if it changes things? He's my new friend, and I really like it that way. I don't want things to change."

"I see. Any other reason?"

Charlie paused. He didn't want to answer the question. But in a way he felt forced. If he wasn't up front with Malcolm, the man might not let him become a full-fledged witch. Plus, getting all of this off his chest wasn't as bad as he had feared it would be. It actually felt kind of good.

"What if he doesn't like me? In that way, I mean? He's so popular, and everybody at school likes him—well, almost everybody—and he's just so, you know, handsome and smart and can talk to anybody about anything."

"Are you basically wondering why someone like him would be attracted to someone like you?"

"Yes! Yes! That's it. I mean, really, I'm just some stupid kid from some stupid town who doesn't know anything."

"That's how you see yourself?"

"Come on, Malcolm. I know this is where you give me the little pep talk, about how great I am, about how I really can succeed in life. People have been doing that ever since I can remember, 'cause I'm shy and get tongue-tied when I get scared. I hate it! I always feel so stupid."

"I'm sure you're exactly right, Charlie, that people only say those things about how great you are because you are a hopeless charity case and they're only doing their community service to boost you up a notch or two."

"It's true! You don't know. You don't know what it's like to feel so, so clueless all the time, to not understand stuff, to have people expect me to ..."

"Charlie," Malcolm interrupted, "You're right. I don't know what it's like to be you. I came from a witch family who told me all about it when I was very young, about what it would mean to grow up in a community of similar people. I had lots of time to think about it. So that when the time came to get popped, I'd had more time to prepare than you did. It happened in the town where I grew up in New

England. I already knew everybody involved. I didn't have to live in a new house, go to a new school where I didn't know anyone. My parents didn't leave me with strangers. And most of all, I didn't have to come to terms with two big things: that there was witchcraft in the world, because I already knew about it and had seen it growing up, and that I was gay. I liked girls, Charlie, so I fit in. In that respect, all of that stuff was way easier for me. Of course, there were girls who didn't like me the way I liked them, which was hard, but all in all …"

"Why are you saying all of this?"

"Because, kid, you need to go easy on yourself. You keep comparing yourself to people who aren't in a similar situation to you. It's apples and oranges. Give yourself a break, okay?"

"But I'm not being honest about things with Diego. You said that I couldn't lie. And that if I lied, I couldn't be a witch."

"I said you couldn't lie to yourself, Charlie, or it wouldn't work. And you can't lie to me, or I can't teach you what you need to learn. You get to decide what you tell other people. That's your business, not theirs. If you want to talk to Diego about it, great. If you really should, but you chicken out and avoid the whole thing, well, that might cause some problems. But if you aren't ready to do it and you're still being honest with yourself, then I think you're good to go."

"What do you mean, 'good to go'?"

"I mean you're ready to get popped. And I'd be more than happy to do it."

"Really? Honestly?"

"Really. Honestly. You've done your work, young man, and you've shown me how seriously you're taking this. You've got a good head on your shoulders. And you're using it. That's all I ask for."

Charlie held the phone to his ear and looked out the window. Several leaves on the maple tree in the front yard had begun to turn yellow. When had that happened? He thought he had been looking at the tree every day. He had spotted the beginnings of fall colors on the tree at school, but …

Time seemed to be pressing down on him, pushing him forward. Malcolm said he was ready, and Charlie wanted to be popped, but was he ready? Was he ready for all the things coming his way?

"You still there, kid?"

"Yeah, I'm here. Sorry."

"Look, we'll do it this Sunday. Probably Sunday night. Beverly will give you the details."

"This Sunday? Like in two days?"

"Well, yeah. When did you think it would be?"

"I don't know. I thought I'd have to, I don't know, prepare or something."

Malcolm's laugh was loud in his ear.

"This isn't the Eagle Scouts, Charlie. It's not like you have to earn a badge before you advance. All you have to do is show up. Leave the rest to me. The preparation will be afterwards. That's when you'll have to learn everything."

Later, long after he had hung up the phone, Charlie sat in the window seat looking out at the dark night. The trees stood tall, like sentinels, in the yard. An occasional car would drive down the street, its headlights casting a cone of thick yellow directly in front of it. Somewhere out there, a witch and her group were trying to hunt him down. Somewhere out there Grace was planning stuff, stuff that could hurt the people Charlie was getting to know better.

Even though he had been surprised and a bit scared when Malcolm said it would be this Sunday, he knew it had to be soon. Things were coming, and Charlie needed to be ready for them.

"Hen weixian," he heard the girl from his dream say out loud, as if she were standing there in the bedroom next to him, looking out into the darkness.

CHAPTER 45

The Warehouse

AND THAT WAS HOW CHARLIE found himself on Sunday night sitting in the second row on a metal folding chair with ten or so other kids in the middle of a large warehouse in South Seattle. About thirty adults stood along the walls behind him. They sipped at their Starbucks cups, whispering in each other's ears and stamping their feet to stay warm.

The warehouse, near Boeing Field, was as big as an airplane hangar. Apparently it had been used at one point to repair planes. Now it belonged to someone in the community.

The adults were excited, waving to each other and smiling. The kids just seemed scared. Some of them talked to each other. Most sat silently, bouncing their legs or kicking the floor. A few of them looked over their shoulders to check out Charlie, with borderline curiosity, then stared back at their shoes. Or the ceiling. Or their fingernails. They seemed to range in age from about ten to sixteen or seventeen. He didn't recognize any of them from school.

He could barely breathe.

Beverly had driven Charlie to the warehouse that evening. The day had begun bright and sunny, but the sky soon turned gray and filled with thick billowy clouds. Charlie watched the storm clouds in the afternoon approaching across the Sound from the Olympics, and just as they seemed to hit the shore on the Seattle side, fat raindrops began to drop on the deck. It had rained a slow steady downpour for the rest of the day and into the evening.

His aunt drove through their neighborhood and headed down the long hill that led to the West Seattle Bridge.

"I love heated seats when the weather starts to turn," she said, shivering as she patted the leather upholstery with a free hand.

"Beverly, does anyone ever not get popped?"

"What do you mean, honey?"

"I mean, what if someone just can't, you know, get popped? Like maybe Malcolm can't open them?"

"You make it sound like those two or three clams in the bucket that never open, the ones you're supposed to throw away," she had smiled.

"I'm serious. Does it ever happen?"

"Yes, it does. Rarely. And I mean, very rarely, Charlie. Sometimes it's too late for somebody. The window of opportunity closes, and they can't be popped. Or you hear old stories of witches trying to forcefully pop people. Legends of someone resisting being popped. If they resisted hard enough, it wouldn't happen.

"And also," she continued, "sometimes a community is wrong. Sometimes someone just doesn't have the blood legacy in them. No matter how hard people try, they just don't have it.

"But," she continued, a thoughtful look passing over her face as she drove, "does it ever happen that someone who hasn't missed the opportunity, who is open to it, and has the legacy in their blood, still doesn't get popped? I guess it could. But I don't know of anyone."

"But it could happen, right?"

Beverly looked at Charlie, then pulled over to the side of the road at the base of the hill. She turned off the windshield wipers and cut the engine.

"Are you worried that you're going to be a dud? That it won't work on you?"

"Well, no ... well, yeah, I guess so. What if it doesn't work on me?"

"I guess we'll have to deal with it then. But let me put it this way: I would be very surprised, very surprised, if that's what happens. I tell you what. I would even be willing to bet you that it won't. I would even be willing to bet you, oh, say, two hundred dollars that you'll get popped."

His aunt's wager tickled him. He could feel an inch or two of pressure, coming from his worry that he wouldn't become a witch, release from his shoulders, his neck.

"Two hundred dollars? That's not very much. I thought you said you, or we, had a lot of money."

"Okay, Mr. Smarty-Pants, how much should I bet you? A thousand dollars? More?"

"No, something else. Let's see …" he said, enjoying the game. "How about if I win, if I'm not popped, I never have to do dishes again."

"Done!"

"And I never have to weed the garden."

"Done!"

"And I never have to, uh, wash your car, put my clothes away, or ever go grocery shopping."

"Done, done, done! And I'll make you breakfast in bed every morning for the rest of your life," she added

"Done!" They both laughed. Charlie relaxed a bit into his warm leather seat. The silly bet proved to him how much confidence his aunt had in the process much better than if she had just told him not to worry. He knew she wasn't the kind to serve breakfast in bed every morning. Earlier in the day he had called Diego. He needed to tell him that he wouldn't be in school the next day. Or the next. Or maybe even all week. "Yeah, it's stupid, but I have to go back to California to get some stuff. And help my mom." He knew it was the right thing to do, lying like this to Diego. But he didn't like it, especially after so much honesty with the boy in the past two days. "Seriously? You get to miss school? Not fair." "I thought you liked school." "I do. But I like adventures too." *You have no idea what kind of adventure I'm about to take,* Charlie had wanted to say over the phone.

"Anyway, when will you be back?"

"Not sure. Friday at the latest. Maybe Wednesday or Thursday."

"You driving down?"

"Nah. Flying. You know my uncle's a pilot, right? We get to fly really cheap as a family." Was this what it would be like from here on out? That being a witch meant you always had to lie, always had to make sure you kept your stories straight? He didn't like it.

Charlie had never been on a plane in his life. He hoped he sounded legitimate to Diego. If the boy asked him anything about the plane or what airport he was flying to, Charlie knew he would be in trouble.

"Is it weird to say that I'll miss you?" Diego had asked, his voice quiet.

"What? No, no, that's cool. I, uh, I'll miss you too."

"You're just saying that 'cause I said it."

"Come on. I mean it."

"Really?"

"Really," Charlie answered, realizing that telling the truth about how he felt was even harder then lying.

The group of kids sat waiting in the warehouse. Some of them looked over their shoulders and waved to their parents. One boy had to keep getting up to go to the bathroom.

Beverly had explained that there would be a lot of adults there.

"To help out."

"Help out with what?"

"Well, Charlie, when people get popped, everything can get a little weird. It's like taking the lid off of a pressure cooker. There's a lot of heat in there, and you never know what could happen."

"You mean, like bad stuff?"

"No, not bad stuff. More like, it wouldn't be a good idea to have thirty kindergarteners over to your house for a birthday party without other adults around to supervise. One person couldn't be everywhere at once, keeping an eye on things."

"So the adults will be there to keep an eye on us?"

"Something like that. Listen. When someone is popped, a lot of power comes out. There's more power present when you are popped than you'll ever experience as a more mature witch. We just want to make sure everyone stays safe."

"Why isn't Randall coming?"

"What? Oh, Charlie, this event is only for us."

"You mean, like 'us' us?" he asked, pointing his finger at her and then back at himself.

"Yes, just for 'us' us."

Beverly walked in front of the kids and got their attention.

"Listen up, everyone. Malcolm just texted me to say that he should be here in about five minutes. Does anyone want a juice box or water? Or some snacks? We've got plenty of ..."

With that, they all stood up and rushed over to a small table filled with drinks, fruit, and potato chips.

"Hope this isn't a bad idea. Do you think they'll all keep it down? I don't want to have to clean up ..." Charlie heard a man behind him say.

"Ron, will you shut it? Please? Just shut it. You can be so insensitive sometimes," a woman whispered back. Charlie didn't want to think about what the man meant.

"Hi, everybody," a voice called a few moments later from the small doorway at the corner of the building. The larger entrance with a garage-style door and a hydraulic hoist remained closed.

"Sorry I'm late," said Malcolm as he greeted a few of the adults nearest the door. He carried a travel mug and sipped at it as he walked. He came to the front of the chairs and asked the kids to sit down and join him.

"Was everyone able to make it?" he asked the adults standing in the back. They replied with nods and yeses.

"Okay. Now, why don't we begin? Does anyone have any questions?"

"I do," said a thin wispy-haired girl sitting two chairs down from Charlie. She had thick-lensed glasses, a large scab on her chin, and looked to be about twelve or thirteen years old. Charlie hoped she didn't get teased too much. Kids back in Clarkston would have pounced on her nerdy looks.

"Approximately how long do you think this will take?" she said.

Malcolm smiled. "Why, do you have somewhere else to be, Princess? Maybe a club opening?"

The adults laughed. None of the kids did. Charlie couldn't figure out if it was out of a sense of solidarity or just plain nerves that kept the other kids from joining in on the joke.

"No," answered the girl, her neck turning red and blotchy. "I just ... I just want to know what'll it be like, is all," she said, her voice dropping off to a whisper at the end.

"Like nothing you've ever experienced before. Other questions."

"I'm not really sure if I'm ready. What if it isn't time for me yet?" asked a pudgy boy in a navy-blue sweatshirt who looked to be about Charlie's age.

"You are, kid. No worries about that. You are all ripe as late August peaches."

"If there are no other questions ..."

"My daughter Madeleine has to take allergy medication," said a woman in the back. "It's usually before she goes to bed. Should I give it to her now, or ..."

"Yes, now would be fine," said Malcolm, his smile wearing thin.

The woman walked up to the group of kids, rummaging around in her purse.

"Mom, please!" whispered an older girl with red hair tied in a braid. "You're embarrassing me."

"I know, I know, it's what I've been put on this planet to do, apparently. Here," she said, handing her daughter some capsules and a bottle of water.

The girl swallowed the pills, handed the bottle back to her mother, and turned away in a huff. However, soon after swallowing, Charlie saw her turn around and mouth the words "thank you" to the line of adults against the back wall.

"If there are no further interruptions," Malcolm said, "let's begin."

CHAPTER 46

Chicken and Egg

MALCOLM STOOD ABOUT TEN feet in front of them and closed his eyes. His lips began to move. Occasionally he would hold one hand or the other out in front of him, then let it drop. He looked a little like a crazy guy on a street corner talking to the voices in his head.

Or to God, Charlie thought. He had heard those crazy people sometimes thought they were talking to God.

"Could be God," said the girl sitting to his right. "Or he could just be one of those crazy people on the street corner."

Charlie looked at her. Her lips were pursed tightly together, trying to stifle a laugh. Had he spoken aloud? Malcolm had said witches couldn't read minds. Then how …?

He snorted and then laughter bubbled out of his lips before he could hold it back. They giggled together with their hands clamped over their mouths.

Charlie, stop it! he tried to tell himself. *This is not appropriate for the popping ceremony!*

"How did you do that?" the same girl asked him.

"Do what?"

"Make your nose and ears move like that?"

"Like what?"

"Like this," she said. Her ears began to wiggle, and the surface of her nose undulated as if tiny ball bearings were moving back and forth beneath her skin.

"Cool! Gross!" Charlie exclaimed.

One of the boys in the front row stood up and said to no one in particular, "Come on, Lisa, let's blow this taco stand!"

The boy started to walk forward, but as he moved, he flickered like a light bulb about to go out, changing from a young kid to a much older man in a white suit with silver hair, then back to a kid again. Charlie wondered who Lisa was.

"Looks like Steve Martin is the evening's entertainment," said the girl next to him. She was right. The kid kept switching back and forth, between himself and what looked like Steve Martin.

Charlie found himself leaning against the wall, quite far from the rows of folding chairs. The cement felt cool on his face. He didn't know how he had moved across the floor so fast. But he didn't care.

"I really like it here," he said, then looked up to see a few adults nearby, watching him.

"That's great," one of them said.

"I know, huh? It's so great. But not as great as up there," Charlie said, pointing to the ceiling.

He began to crawl up the wall. It was much easier than he would have thought. Not like an insect, or a rock climber. It was like …

"A wall champion!" he said, then wondered why he had never done this before. It was such a nice thing to do and such a useful way to get around. An electric guitar solo exploded in the air as his own personal wall-climbing soundtrack.

When he reached the top of the wall, he saw that the pudgy kid in the navy-blue sweatshirt had climbed up with him. The music had stopped.

"Pretty good view, hey sailor?" the kid said, then winked.

"I'll say," Charlie replied. But he found himself crying, tears streaming down his face in torrents.

"What's wrong? Did someone die?" asked the kid.

Images of a black-skinned family were running through Charlie's head. They were hard-working, dressed in old-fashioned clothes. He saw them building the airplane hangar that he was in. He knew they had built it with a government contract and then had leased it to Boeing Field after the war. It had given them pride, a good income, and status among their community.

"The first Negroes to win a government contract, the Tanner Family built this warehouse in 1938 with determination, commitment, and excellence in design. Seattle is proud to call them citizens," Charlie said, his voice sounding like a narrator from a documentary on public television.

He placed his hand against the blank wall in front of him. A soft orange light began to glow between his hand and the cement. When he pulled his hand away, a gold-plated plaque was embedded in the wall.

It read: *The first Negroes to win a government contract, the Tanner Family built this warehouse in 1938 with determination, commitment, and excellence in design. Seattle is proud to call them citizens.*

"That was the right thing to do," said the kid next to him. He was crying too. "We need to honor all of our heroes, no matter their skin color."

Soon Charlie was floating in midair, suspended high above the folding chairs. A boy and a girl he didn't recognize were in front of him, also floating. They were holding hands and facing each other. He watched as they leaned back and away from each other, bringing their knees up to their chests, and then pushed against each other's feet, executing backwards somersaults while never letting go of each other's hands.

"Looks like I'll have to get in on this little party," Charlie said. Soon he was turning endless somersaults with the boy and the girl, sometimes holding hands with them and sometimes doing them all by himself.

At one point they all held hands with their bodies stretched like skydivers in formation, as a strong wind blew up at them, making their cheeks shake and their eyes water.

Then the wind stopped.

"But what I've always really wanted to do is trick waterskiing," said the girl, as she began to fade away like the Cheshire cat.

Charlie found himself alone in midair, high up near the ceiling. He looked down at the floor. He saw adults running here and there as the thin wispy-haired girl, whom Malcolm had called a princess, shot sizzling bolts of white electricity from her hands. The bolts didn't seem to hit anyone, but small flames erupted wherever they landed.

A sudden sense of heaviness descended on him, and he began floating downward against his will. Below him, several adults stood with arms outstretched as if to catch him.

"Don't you touch me!" he shouted at them. "You're all a bunch of faggots and lesbians! Where's my Aunt Beverly? She's the only one I let catch me. Where is Beverly?"

"I'm right here, Charlie," said a voice that he recognized. He was standing on his hands in the middle of the floor with his legs pointing toward the ceiling, looking up at a woman with long dark hair, wide cheekbones, and large familiar eyes.

"You have the best nostrils in the world," he told her.

Before he could do anything else, he began to hear something. Or sense something. It was as if the sound of everything on the planet began to reverberate in his skin cells. Everything had a smell, a color, a voice, and it all insisted that he pay attention to it. To all of it. He saw an Asian family in a small wooden boat with fishing nets, then a brick-sized container of plastic wrap, followed by blades of grass, the Grand Duke of Luxembourg, a flock of geese in northern Canada, and every single Ford Mustang ever produced. He heard a cacophony of music, like an orchestra warming up. He smelled orange soda, dog manure, dust, and the kind of perfume worn by old ladies.

"It's too much, I can't hear, I can't, it's too much!" he yelled, still standing on his hands, his wonderful Aunt Beverly with the kind and lovely nostrils holding his ankles.

"Breathe, Charlie, you're all right. You're all right," she said.

His gut filled with heat, and before he could stop himself, he vomited the entire contents of his stomach up his throat and out his mouth and nose onto his aunt's shoes. The last thing he saw was a little yellow chick, walking among the contents of his retching. It peeped at him and then winked. In a very human-sounding voice it said, "The chicken does come before the egg."

And then, nothing.

CHAPTER 47

You're Getting Sleepy

IN THE DREAM, CHARLIE SAT with his legs hanging over the back of a pickup truck as it barreled and bounced down a dirt road. On either side of him small children also sat with their legs hanging over the edge. More children were scattered throughout the truck bed behind him. They were all blond fair-skinned kids singing a beautiful kid song, something about trees and the future and blue sky.

The long line of grass and weeds that divided the two small lanes of the dirt road mesmerized Charlie. It appeared as if the line of grass sprang up right between his feet as the truck rolled over it. The sun glared high and hot in the sky. He knew they were somewhere near Clarkston.

"But what about them, mister? What about them?" asked a young voice in his ear. He looked over his shoulder to see a small boy, probably no more than six years old, standing behind him with one hand on his shoulder for balance. He was pointing past Charlie to the road behind them.

Charlie had the sudden urge to take all the kids and cover them up with a large blanket, to protect them somehow, then yell to whoever was driving the truck to drive faster. He didn't know what the kid was pointing to, but he didn't want to find out.

In spite of his fear he finally turned around and looked. Four large German shepherds were running along the dirt lane toward the truck. The distance between them and the truck was quickly vanishing. Behind them, another line of four dogs rounded the bend and gave chase. All eight dogs ran with their tongues hanging from their mouths at the exact same angle. Before Charlie could register what was happening, another line of four dogs appeared behind the second, and then another, making sixteen dogs in total chasing after the truck. They made no noise as they ran, and Charlie couldn't tell if every dog was a simple facsimile or if each one was unique.

"It'll be tonight. After nine o'clock. A heart attack. He might not make it. You'd better tell someone," said the same boy in his ear. He didn't understand what the boy meant.

When Charlie looked back at the road, the German shepherds were now only a few feet from the truck. One of the middle dogs in the first line ran up to the tailgate and opened its mouth.

Unable to stop himself, Charlie stuck his foot out toward the dog's muzzle, until it was a mere inch from the sharp teeth.

"After nine o'clock, mister. A heart attack. Tell someone," said the boy.

The dog clamped down on Charlie's foot. His screams resounded in the thin hot air of the summer day …

… and bounced off the walls of his bedroom.

"Charlie. Charlie, wake up! It's okay. You're okay. Charlie, you're having a bad dream," someone was saying to him. A hand shook his foot.

He yanked his leg up toward his chest, trying to free his foot from the jaws of the German shepherd.

When he opened his eyes, he saw that he wasn't sitting in the back of a pickup truck. He was in his room. In bed. In Beverly and Randall's house (his house, his mind corrected). Raindrops were beating against the windowpane. Beverly stood at the foot of his bed, a cautious smile on her face.

"Hi. It's me, Charlie. Your Aunt Beverly. You're okay."

"Wha- … what happened? How did I …?" he tried to ask. His throat was parched. He reached for the water bottle on his nightstand. He saw his hand shake as his arm brushed up against the bottle and knocked it toward the floor. Beverly was at his side in an instant, catching it and placing it into his hands.

"Thanks," he squeaked. His mouth felt like it was full of sand. He twisted the lid off the bottle and took a sip of the cool water before leaning back against his headboard with a sigh.

"You're popped, honey. You did it. You're home and safe now."

"What? How can ... it worked?"

"It sure did. Sorry, my friend, but no breakfast in bed. Looks like you'll have a long list of chores ahead of you."

Then, with pride and solemnity filling her voice, she said, "You're one of us now, Charlie. Welcome to your legacy."

He tried to recall what happened. All he could remember was sitting in the warehouse, and seeing Malcolm. Some kids asked some questions, and then Malcolm started mumbling stuff. And then what? What happened after that? He remembered feeling nauseous, and a strange floating sensation. That was all.

"Are you sure? I don't really remember anything."

"Positive."

"How long have I been in bed?"

"About eleven hours. It's just past one right now on Monday afternoon. We got home after two this morning. You went straight to sleep."

"I had a dream. A bad dream."

Beverly sat on the end of his bed. "Tell me."

"I was in a truck with all these little blond-haired kids who were singing. One of them pointed, and I saw a bunch of German shepherds running at us. As they got closer, this one kid said ... uh, wait, I can't remember ... what did he say? Oh God, it was important." He closed his eyes.

"Take your time, kiddo. Just try to ..."

"He said something about a heart attack. Tonight after nine o'clock. Somebody, some man, was going to have a heart attack. The kid told me I had to tell someone. Oh God, the kid said the guy might not make it. Who is it?"

"I don't know. Maybe it was just a dream."

"No, I don't think so. It felt different."

A gust of wind blew hard against the trees outside, and a branch struck the side of the house. Charlie jumped as if the limb had hit him. He looked outside. Raindrops spattered against the windowpane. He flinched expecting his face to get wet.

That was strange. It was as if he could feel the drops through the glass. Each one. Wait, he could feel them. Tiny droplets of silver light, round marbles of liquid smacking themselves again and again against the window, against the wooden shingles along the roof. He could feel each wet trajectory, the grain in each shingle as it was struck, the tiny ping every time a drop hit the pane.

He looked away from the window, but the strange sensation didn't leave. It was as if he could see out the window without using his eyes, could sense what was happening out there. Three crows sat perched on the branches of a nearby Douglas fir tree, and they were pecking at needles near their claws. Douglas fir? How did he know it was a Douglas fir? Or that the Latin name for Douglas fir was *Pseudotsuga menziesii*? A woman in a raincoat walked her dog on the sidewalk, and Charlie could feel how each of her toes pressed against the front of her boots, how the dog's paws padded on the wet cement. He knew the woman carried twenty-three dollars in her purse as well as a canister of mace and a pack of cherry-flavored bubblegum. The dog's collar tag said, "My name is Lucy. Please call this number if found."

The tag on the back of Beverly's shirt said Linda, size medium. Her toenails were painted a warm brown-red, and she had a tiny cut on her left shin from gardening.

He began to panic, throwing his arms over his head. "I can, I can hear everything. I can see it all. I can't block it out, I can't ..."

Beverly grabbed his wrists. "Breathe, Charlie, take some deep breaths with me. Come on, breathe."

He opened his eyes and saw her face, inches from his own. Her mouth moved, and while he couldn't make out her whispered Words, he could feel them settling into his skin. Her eyes were calming, their liquid brown pouring outward toward him, their color helping to block out the rest of the sensations trying to invade his mind.

"There you go. Just breathe. Like that. It'll help you relax."

She reached for the bottle of water. "Have a sip," she said. He drank, and the anxiety seemed to melt away even more.

"Are you ... are you making me tired?" he asked, for her eyes seemed large, incredibly large, their soft brown pulling at him, holding his attention.

"I'm helping you sleep. Resting will make it get easier, Charlie. It'll get easier, I promise. In a few days' time, it'll all calm down."

"Do you ... can you hear it like that? All the time?"

"No, nowhere near as strong as you can. It's as loud for you right now as it'll ever be. It's at its worst. It'll only get better from here on out."

"Was it like this for you when you got popped?"

"Yes."

"But I know that that woman on the street has twenty-three dollars in her purse. How could I know that? And the raindrops! What about the guy with the heart attack? What is that?"

"Shh, shh. Lay back. You won't be awake for much longer," she said.

He did as he was told and could feel himself melting back into his bed.

"I'm worried about the guy in the dream. The one who might be having a heart attack tonight." His tongue felt thick and sloppy.

"Honey, you might have to let it go. I don't know if there's much we can do without knowing who, or where ..."

"But, but ..."

"I'll tell you what. I'll make some inquiries, and we'll see if we can't come up with something. Maybe when you go back to sleep you'll have another dream that will help."

He nodded, his head heavy on his pillow.

"Try to get some rest, okay?"

"But I jes slep fer eleven hours. Who sleeps fer that long? I jes don't ..." His words were beginning to slur. He sounded like an actor playing someone drunk on TV. And not a very good actor.

"New witches do, that's who. Your job is to rest now. It is the thing that helps the most."

"Is Randall here?"

"Yes, and he knows to keep a safe distance from you."

"Cuth I'm dangeruth?"

Beverly smiled. "A little, yes. But I am watching out for you. Rita and Jeremy are downstairs, ready to help too. This is what we do. We watch out for you."

Charlie tried hard to keep his eyes open, but they burned and itched too much. He didn't like putting Randall at risk. And he didn't like this sense of utter chaos. And ... how could he be dangerous?

"Anyway, Randall is cheering you on. From a distance, okay?"

"Okay. Will you tell him hi from me?"

"Will do. Goodnight for now."

"Behurly, thankth, uh, for every ..."

He was asleep before he could finish the sentence.

CHAPTER 48

The Best Day Ever

TOM KRULL SHIFTED ON HIS CHAIR. He had been sitting in the booth for nearly four hours, and his butt ached. They were short three agents today, which meant longer lines, grumpier passengers, less breaks. It didn't matter that their contract stated clearly that no agent would be required to perform customs duty longer than two hours straight without a break. He could force the issue and leave his booth for a while, but it would just mean that the passenger line would get longer and his work would be that much more awful. People hated getting off international flights only to stand in long lines. He grew tired of hearing their complaints. Besides, his coworkers would blame him for it. The break room would be intolerable for weeks to come.

So he sat and fidgeted. He looked at face after face, passport after passport, asking the same questions over and over again.

"What brings you to Canada?"

"Where will you be staying?"

"You here for business then?"

"How much money are you carrying?"

Canada. The land of the free, the land of the polite. The land of political correctness. He agreed with it, most of the time. The Canadians who came through his lines were courteous. Respectful. The Americans? Not so much. He hated their entitlement, their indignation at having their very important plans slowed down by a customs agent who wanted to know their business.

It was a common if unspoken practice to pull more Americans out of line than any other nationality. Not to cause real trouble. Just to slow them down a bit. Help them cool their jets while they sat in the immigration office waiting for one of the agents to ask them more questions. He figured he was doing his part to keep Canada friendly by reminding the Americans to be nice. And also reminding them that they weren't in charge up here.

"Next in line!" he called, keeping his voice neutral, commanding.

A tall woman walked toward him. She did not look like most of the other passengers. Fresh-faced, not tired. Quite beautiful, actually. Soft red hair pulled back in a chignon, wearing a smart powder-blue suit, and man, what a pair of legs showing in that skirt. Her smile was sweet and clean, like a bowl of washed apples sitting in sunlight.

That was strange. Since when did he start comparing women's smiles to bowls of fruit?

He cleared his throat and wiggled his head, remembering that he had a job to do. He tried to ignore his sore rear end.

The woman arrived at his booth and stood less than a foot from the counter.

He shifted in his seat again for he felt heat in his chest. He felt it lower in his body too. His face flushed. The woman reminded him of somebody, but he could not place who it was. Someone he had met? Someone in a movie?

She smiled, and he could almost hear the soft skin of her lips expanding. He saw the surprise of her white teeth, strong and feminine. They reminded him of the square mints his grandmother used to keep in a candy dish on the table near her front door.

More heat. His breathing quickened. He shifted again, trying to make more room in his regulation uniform trousers.

"Passport, please," he managed to say, his eight years on the job at Vancouver International Airport helping him to maintain focus.

"Hello, Tom," the tall woman said to him.

His name, just like that, sent to him like a gift, right from her mouth, right into his ears.

For some strange reason, he wanted to cry then, just a little. He wanted to lay his head down in this woman's lap and cry, for his name sounded so beautiful on her lips, like the right kind of homecoming or a welcome he had always wanted. She would stroke his hair, and he would weep, and she would say, "Tom. Hello, Tom," all night until he cried himself empty. Until she bent forward and pressed her mouth to his, until …

He shivered then sat up straight. He found the frown he used when he needed to slow a passenger down. He could feel the crease between his eyebrows grow.

"Stern face," his ex-girlfriend Sheila had called it. "You're doing stern face at me, Tom. Knock it off."

"Tom," the tall woman said again, and her face was smooth, so smooth, the skin fresher than most women's past a certain age. It seemed spreadable to him, a creamy spread of skin reddened at the cheeks. He looked away from her lips to her eyes.

"Hello," his mouth said. His mind began to spin for there were specks of light in her eyes, yellow and white specks against the background of soft green. How did her eyes do that? How did those tiny lights swirl together like that?

He thought of weeping again. He thought of that early evening over ten years ago sitting on a log up at Savary Island. The day had been dry. He had seen two female belted kingfishers perched on the branch of a bigleaf maple earlier in the day and several harbor seals just off the shore. He and his friends had built a campfire before the sun had set. He sat next to Laura, who had lifted her shirt to him a few hours earlier. He had lain nestled between her breasts for some time. Together their fingers had played beneath each other's waistbands. It had been his first time, and it had been gentle and slow, not the fumbled rush he feared it would be. When they kissed later, she told him it had been good.

That day had been his best ever. He didn't like to think about it too much because it reminded him that all the days since then had been less days, worse days, nothing like that weekend on Savary, with beer, and his friends, those female kingfishers flushed with red, brighter than the male of the species, with Laura and her freckled chest, her grape-flavored lip gloss that had gotten all over him. He had licked some of it off his arm later that night when he was alone, knowing that he should taste as much of this day as he could. Because it wouldn't last.

"Tom," repeated the woman, her voice personal, his name like something she was sharing only with him. "I didn't bring my passport today. Isn't that funny?" she said, her smile growing.

His breathing was nearly a rush now. He wanted to stand up, to leave this booth and the intimacy he felt with this woman, because it was too much. But he knew he wouldn't stand. This woman tasted too good in his mind to leave.

He stared at her smile the way he and his brother used to stare at the sun when they were little, seeing how long they could last before their eyes burned.

"Um," he said. Regulations and lists of customs laws fanned through his head, the pages of rules, their printed clutter a noise loud enough to drown out the lushness of Savary Island, threatening to push away the woman before him who was the one kind person he had seen today, maybe even this whole month. He did not want the drone of his responsibilities to block out this sip of honey, the first taste he had had in a long, long time.

"I'm glad that won't be a problem today, Tom. I'm so glad I came to your booth," she said, leaning closer to him. He smelled the fresh apples on her breath, saw the ginger in her hair, heard the delight in her voice from having seen him. Really seen him, maybe even shared a part of his memory of Savary Island, tasting the charred hotdog he had cooked over the fire, felt the pressure of his skin against Laura's, seen the canopy of western hemlock surrounding them as they had held onto each other and pushed on the forest floor.

The thought that this woman could see him was nearly too much, was ...

"That's right," she said to him. "That's right, Tom. Just. Like. That." And he saw the pink tip of her tongue inside the set of her teeth, watched as it poked out, saw it grow brighter as she bit down on it.

He didn't see the frail teenage girl approach the booth from the passenger line and stand next to the woman, her child eyes vacant, her mouth open, looking more like a street urchin than an international traveler.

His heart hammered against his rib cage. There was too much blood coursing through his veins. His head felt dizzy. For a moment, he couldn't breathe. He pressed his hands against his desk to keep himself from pitching forward. He looked away from the woman without a passport, aware that something wonderful and awful had almost just happened, aware that he was in way over his head.

The woman gave him one last smile, like the final glimpse of a red dress before it rounds a corner, then stepped past his booth in a wave of cool air and the unexpected scent of wet wood. Then she was gone. He stared straight ahead, not seeing the dull-looking teenage girl shuffle after her.

Tom felt the brightness of Savary diminishing, the memories of pleasure fading away from him as if down a long dim tunnel, replaced by the dirty backwash of shame and the sight of the long line of impatient passengers with their passports and their self-importance.

He wondered if he should do anything. If he should alert someone.

But he didn't. He sat still for a moment in his booth at Vancouver International Airport as the familiar film of boredom and ambivalence washed down over his eyes and mixed with this new humiliation.

"Welcome to Canada," he said over his shoulder, too quiet for anyone but a witch to hear.

And then, facing forward, he sighed.

"Next in line."

CHAPTER 49

Home Safety

CHARLIE HEARD HIMSELF SIGH. He rolled over in bed aware that he was awake. The bedside clock read 8:49. At first he couldn't tell if it was morning or night. Then he saw the tiny letters reading "a.m." beside the hour.

He counted the numbers in his head. Did that mean that he had slept over seventeen hours? How was that possible? Hadn't Beverly told him that he had already slept for eleven?

He thought about their conversation as he climbed out of bed. His legs were wobbly. He staggered to the bathroom and stood peeing above the toilet for what seemed like a full two minutes.

He looked at his face in the mirror. Lines from the pillow were etched across his cheeks. One of his eyes looked swollen. His hair was even messier than normal, flat against his skull in places, sticking out in others. His mouth tasted like burnt ham and bad fruit. He rinsed it out with water and brushed his teeth.

The fuzziness in his head began to clear as he walked back into his bedroom. He saw his phone on the nightstand. He turned it on, then sat down on the edge of his bed.

Numbers were flashing in his text box and his voicemail box. One, two, three ... eight, nine. He flipped to his voicemail and saw they were all from Diego. He smiled. He would enjoy listening to them.

The text messages started out with simple lines: *Whassup? Hope CA's fun. Thinkin bout u.* But one from this morning read differently:

Call me. And another one: *Call me, Charlie. Bad news.*

He pulled on some shorts and grabbed a sweatshirt, then began to head downstairs. He could hear voices from below. He pressed Diego's number. It was answered after only one ring.

"Charlie! Charlie, is that you?"

"Yeah, what, what's hap- ..."

"Charlie. I hate to bother you. I know you're on your trip, but ..."

And just before he heard the rest of Diego's words, just as his bare foot stepped down onto the floor at the base of the stairs, a sensation like running water flooded over him. It was as if someone had dumped the water, a bucket of it, lukewarm, onto his head just below his scalp. It was pleasant, if not a bit surprising.

Beverly came running toward him down the hallway from the kitchen. Rita and a man he didn't recognize rounded the corner from the living room. They seemed to be moving in slow motion, and the looks on their faces ranged from worry to concern to downright panic.

"Charlie!" his aunt was calling to him, but the running water warped her voice, made it sound warbled, muffled.

"... Principal Wang had a heart attack last night, Charlie. He might not make it," said Diego's voice, clearer because it was on this side of the water, in the phone, close to his face, almost as if Diego were perched on his earlobe.

The water drained from his head and down through his face, a warm cascade on the inside of his chest cavity, past his hipbones, down through the soles of his feet.

He didn't see the three flower vases explode in the living room. Nor did he see the couch upend itself, the magazines catch fire on the coffee table, or the dirty dishes in the kitchen sink fly up and crash against the ceiling.

He couldn't feel the soft blue light descend as his aunt ran at him with her hands outstretched, her lips mumbling fast, didn't know the coolness that the light offered him. He didn't know that the strange man held his hands in front of him, turning the light in the living room dark, spreading a heavy fog throughout the rest of the house, protecting all that was in it.

He didn't see Rita running out the front door, slamming it shut behind her, stopping Charlie's explosions from getting outside. He didn't see Daniel Burman on the deck, doing the same thing from the back of the house.

He sat down on the floor at the foot of the stairs, the phone in his ear, hearing Diego's voice.

"What's that noise, Charlie? Are you okay? Was there a crash?"

"No, I just, I just dropped something … uh, I gotta go."

"Charlie, did you hear me? Principal Wang had a heart attack. He might …" Diego's voice cracked, and he was unable to finish the sentence.

"Yeah, I got it. Diego, I'm sorry, my mom is, uh …"

He hung up the phone, and then looked up to see Beverly and the man he didn't recognize standing over him.

"Did you hear?" he asked his aunt.

"Yes, we heard. We got a call just before you came downstairs." The water was gone. Her voice sounded normal.

"But I knew. I didn't, why didn't …?"

"Honey, you couldn't have. You just couldn't have."

For the first time he saw that the two adults had their hands facing toward him, palms outstretched. There was a buzzing sound in his ears, and the air around him shimmered as if rising from hot pavement.

They were looking at him the way police officers look at someone about to jump from a building. Or the way zookeepers approach a cornered tiger.

"What are you doing?" he asked.

"I'm sorry to have to do this, son, but …" said the man standing to Beverly's right. He was black-skinned and very tall. He wore a fitted shirt unbuttoned down to his sternum, and Charlie could see small black curls of hair on his chest.

The man clenched both hands into fists. They made a cupping sound. For a moment, the air seemed to be sucked from the hallway.

A sharp pain cracked through Charlie's skull, and then all the lights went out.

CHAPTER 50

The Quick Brown Fox

THE NEXT FEW DAYS WERE A BLUR. Charlie slept a lot. There was always someone in his bedroom when he woke up, either standing over the bed and looking down at him or sitting in a nearby chair. At first he wasn't sure why, but he was too tired to ask. Eventually Jeremy, his bedroom guard of the hour, told him that it was to keep him safe and the house in check. When he explained to Charlie what had happened to the vases, the dishes, the couch, and the magazines, Charlie couldn't believe it.

"But I didn't really do all that stuff, did I?"

"Yep, you sure did. You've got a mighty curveball," said Jeremy, as if he admired what Charlie had done.

"But I didn't mean to do that. Why did I do that?"

"You were upset about Mr. Wang, Charlie. All of that emotion boiled out of you. It's normal to have craziness like that happen. That's why we have folks watching over you. It was our fault that we didn't have somebody in your room when you woke up and heard the news.

"He's going to be okay, by the way. He's out of danger. Looks like he had bypass surgery and is now in stable condition."

Charlie breathed a sigh of relief. He didn't know the principal very well but really appreciated the time he took to help Charlie get oriented at Puget Academy.

His thoughts wandered back to being popped and what damage he had caused to Randall and Beverly's home.

"But I can't control it. How will I ever …?"

"You will, you will. You're forgetting everything you've been told—that it dies down after several days, or a week at the most. That once it dies down, it's almost like you haven't been popped. Well, that's not exactly true. It's more like …"

Jeremy paused, stroking his beard with his hand.

"It's more like you can see and feel things differently, but you can't do anything about it. Not right away. You have to learn how. Believe me, there'll come a point in your studies when you'll long for it to be as easy and chaotic as it is for you right now. I remember getting so frustrated when I first started learning. One minute I made stuff happen all around me, and the next minute I couldn't even light a stupid candle!"

"But was it out of control for you too in the beginning?"

"Yeah. Most definitely. It is for everybody, Charlie. I ended up blowing the engine on my dad's Volkswagen GTI, and I somehow managed to singe all the hair off of my little sister's head."

"You what?!" Charlie exclaimed, rolling over on his side, resting his head on his hands and staring at Jeremy in disbelief.

"Yeah, it's true. She was so mad at me for the longest time. It didn't matter how much my parents tried to explain to her that I didn't mean to. She got over it when she was popped though. She completely dissolved the old tree house in our backyard, the one she'd loved since she was a kid."

Charlie tried to understand. It was like new witches were ticking time bombs, and you never knew when they were going to detonate or how big the explosion would be.

"Am I still, uh, in danger? Or, I mean, am I still making things happen?"

"It's died down a lot. Can you hear all that crazy stuff outside?"

He listened. He couldn't hear, or feel, a thing.

"No, not at all."

"That'll come and go. About two hours ago all the pens on your desk shot across the room and stuck in the wall over there."

"Jeez."

"Then one of them pulled out and started writing on a piece of paper on your desk."

Jeremy stood up and showed him the page.

"The quick brown fox jumps over the lazy dog, which is the stupidest sentence in the English language," it said, in perfect cursive penmanship.

"I wrote that?"

"Well, technically the pen did. But, okay, yeah, you wrote it."

"That's embarrassing. And it's not even my own handwriting."

"What's so bad about that? My friend made his dad's dirty movie collection project on the kitchen wall one morning while the family was eating breakfast. His mom didn't know about the secret stash. Ooh, there was fighting in that house for a while after."

Charlie had been listening in dismay to Jeremy's stories, worried about all the things he might do. But this last example struck him funny. He tried to hide his smile.

"Dude, you can totally laugh. It's hilarious!" Jeremy said.

They started to giggle, and then Charlie fell back on his bed and laughed until tears came out of his eyes. Jeremy laughed hard too until Charlie slapped his hand down on his sheets and the comforter rose up off the bed and threw itself over Jeremy, knocking him off his chair.

Jeremy jumped up. He looked like he was trying on a ghost costume for Halloween. His hands moved around under the comforter until it floated off of him and settled back on the bed.

"Sorry! Jeez, I ..."

This set them both off on another riot of laughter. Charlie made sure not to slap the bed again.

After they were able to calm down, Charlie thought about his dream again.

"I should have known it was going to be Principal Wang. I could have helped him."

"Charlie," Jeremy chided, still breathing heavily and wiping his eyes, "there's nothing you could have done. It sucks to have dreamt what you did, but you gotta give yourself a break on this one. Beverly investigated it, by the way, because she knew you would worry. It was a completely natural heart attack. You didn't cause it. And neither did any other witch. Your only involvement was that you picked up a hint of something in a dream. You can't blame yourself for something out of your control. If you do, you'll go nuts."

Charlie nodded, relaxing a little bit. He felt awful about Principal Wang but started to believe that there really hadn't been anything he could have done.

Later that night he told Beverly that he wanted to call Diego. He was worried that his friend would wonder why he hadn't called him back. They decided it was a good idea, but she insisted on standing near him, "just in case." He was beginning to understand what "just in case" meant.

"Tell him you got really sick in California. The flu. That's one we use a lot when kids have to miss school after getting popped."

So he did. The call went through to Diego's voicemail. He explained that he wouldn't be back from California for a few more days, that he was sorry he had had to hang up the phone so fast the other day, that he had gotten a nasty bug while down there and couldn't talk much.

Charlie listened to his message once before sending it. He was surprised to hear how weak and tired his voice sounded, like he really was sick. He hoped Diego would buy it.

On the Thursday after being popped, with nothing else having broken, exploded, or caught on fire for a good twelve hours, Beverly declared that the danger was over.

"You may still feel strange, honey, but it's back under control. We can declare emergency threat level yellow."

Randall came home later that afternoon. He had flown for a few days, then purposefully stayed away, sleeping in a hotel downtown until things died down.

A warm weather front had moved in. He and his uncle sat in the backyard on the lawn furniture, enjoying the summer-like weather and the view of the Sound.

"I tell you, Charlie, I can't imagine what it's like. All that weird stuff happening around you, and how you sense it all? Beverly has tried to explain it to me, but I don't think I'll ever understand it."

Charlie nodded. It wasn't like anything he could have imagined either. He was glad he had stopped breaking things. But his sense, or feeling, of everything around him had come back. It wasn't as overpowering as before. He could control it better, by tuning in to one thing and blocking out something else. But it was still there. He could hear an argument taking place inside a house more than four blocks away.

"Cammie, I'm tired of you complaining all the time. 'You don't love me enough, you don't show me how much you care, you don't ...'" he heard a man's voice saying, fatigue and anger lacing every word.

"Do you think it's fun for me to wait around for your scraps?" a woman's voice yelled back. Embarrassed, Charlie shook his head, hoping Randall wouldn't ask him what he had just heard.

"Um, see that tree over there?" Charlie said, pointing to the maple at the far corner of the yard. "See how it's mostly green?"

"Yeah," said his uncle.

"Well, I can sort of, like, feel the green evaporating. If I focus in on one leaf, there's this feeling, you know? That the green is leaving and that it's going to get a little crinkly and dry. I know, of course, that it'll turn colors soon. Everybody knows that. But I can feel the pull of the green and the, uh, the push of it getting older. The tree is tired and wants to rest. It wants to stop having to feed all of the leaves for a while. But the leaf keeps holding on to the branch, like it doesn't want to lose the green. Something like that."

"You can feel that?"

"Yeah, if I pay attention to it. It's way better than a few days ago, when everything was loud. I thought I was going crazy."

Charlie softened his gaze a moment. "There's a red Saab parked across the street from us. There are envelopes from a ... from a King County credit union shoved on the floor in the backseat. There's a water bottle in the front that says "Yoga for Life" on it. And in the glove compartment, there's an owner's manual and a, let's see, a small plastic bag of something."

"Uh oh. Is it something illegal?"

"I can't quite see it yet. Oh, no, it's little candies wrapped in yellow paper."

"Okay, now you're just showing off."

"No, I'm not. I swear."

"I'm teasing you, nephew. But really," he said, shaking his head, "how amazing. I don't think Beverly can do all that. I mean, not as fast as you're doing it."

"No. She said she can't. She really has to focus. And she said that in a little while I won't be able to do it either. Fine with me.

"I mean, you should feel it. Or hear it. I don't even know what to call it. But this grass back here," Charlie said, indicating the lawn stretching out in front of them. "It's sort of singing or something."

Randall raised one eyebrow. "Singing?"

"Well, not really singing. Humming. Making kind of a green noise. I know that sounds weird, but ..."

He paused, trying to find the words. "It's alive. And I can feel it. You know how you can feel the warmth on someone's skin if they are standing close to you, and you know it's because blood is beating through their veins? I can kind of feel the, the uh, the blood beating through those blades of grass, or the life, or whatever," he paused, frustrated with how hard it was to explain it.

He reached down and touched the lawn. A warm sensation filled his hand, spreading up his arms and across his face. It almost felt like he was going to become the grass. He looked at his arm half expecting the skin to have turned a soft green color. He was relieved to see that it looked normal.

"So you can feel this whole yard and each blade of grass? Just like that?"

"Yes."

"Boy, I tell you," Randall said, shaking his head. Then he added, "I assume asking you to mow the lawn is out of the question?"

OTHER BOOKS BY JEFF JACOBSON

The Boy Who Couldn't Fly Home

BONUS OFFER

Bonus for readers of *The Boy Who Couldn't Fly Straight* ...

Download a free short story about Charlie's witching world with new characters and challenges that will affect the entire planet!

www.jeffjacobsonworld.com/bonus

ACKNOWLEDGMENTS

EVERY ACKNOWLEDGMENTS SECTION worth its salt should begin with two things: a quote and an apology. Because without these two things, all the reader is left with is a long list of thank-yous to people like Aunt Reba.

I'll start this off with the apology: I'm sorry that this section is so long. By nature, I'm as effusive as a cocker spaniel. Add to that the fact that this is my first book, and what you're left with is page after page of acknowledgments. I've done my best to arrange things in categories for an easier read and to leave out too many insider jokes. I'll try to rein it in for the rest of the books in the series. But still. Sorry.

And now for the quote. I'm paraphrasing a bit, since I can't remember who said it, but it goes something like this:

"The only true pain in life comes from love unexpressed."

Here's to expressing some love:

To my teachers: Mrs. Eliason, my second-grade teacher, who enchanted me with her love of Halloween. • Mrs. Smith, who told me in the fifth grade that I had a gift for storytelling. • Mrs. Zozel-Johnson, who without telling me, printed my poem in the program for First Friday Mass at Holy Family Elementary School when I was in the sixth grade, leaving me terrified and secretly thrilled. • Mr. Mangione, Mrs. Westinghouse, Ms. Moffat, my high school Spanish teachers, who introduced me to the fine, fine language of Español. • My sophomore English teacher Sister Judith, who taught me Greek and Latin root words and who led me to the creepy writings of Shirley Jackson. • My junior English teacher Sister Francis, who guided me with gusto through Beowulf, Chaucer, Jane Austen, and Harper Lee. • Lo Sun Perry Laoshi, the best teacher I've ever had for anything, ever, who opened the door to the exciting world of Mandarin my second year in college. • Wu Li Mei Laoshi, at Taiwan Normal University, who taught me to enjoy the poetry of classical Chinese rather than run to the hills.

To my writing teachers: Ms. Parsons, my seventh-grade English teacher, who showed me how to diagram sentences and who made memorizing poems great fun (especially that fantastic poem about cats, "Catalogue," by Rosalie Moore). • My high school freshman English teacher Mr. Danforth, the strictest of grammarians, who drilled into me the correct use of the comma (any mistakes are mine, Mr. Danforth!). • Mr. McBride, my senior English teacher, who introduced me to Judith Guest's extraordinary novel Ordinary People, as well as everything John Steinbeck, and whose compliments about my poetry and free-form writing carried great weight. • Beth Kalikoff, a university writing professor, whose advice to write badly, with enthusiasm and quantity, then poke through the garbage for the diamonds, has paid off in dividends. • Don Matthews and the gang at the Creative Edge in Monterey, who provided the forum where I read my first erotic poetry out loud. • Jen Cross and Carol Queen, who showed me that writing erotica is not only fun, and healing, but also a great way to hone my skills as a writer. • Mary Reynolds Thompson, the intrepid guide of my Kimchees writing group, who somehow manages the perfect balance between information, support, challenge, and compassion. Mary is the patron saint of writers!

To my writing buddies: Francisco Mora, who listened with curiosity and encouragement to early drafts of *The Boy Who Couldn't Fly Straight* even though the writing was so rough at times that I wanted to bite chalk. • My beloved Kimchees: Cat Williford, a truly modern goddess and courageous brazen storyteller, who roped me into joining the group in the first place; Lauren Powers, my fellow Standing Person, incredibly comedic and astute in all that she writes, who published a book before I did, damn it; Kim Fowler, the newest Kimchee member, whose prose is so pretty you could just pull up a kitchen stool and listen to it all day, weeping. The Kimchees' consistency, love, and cheerleading have kept me going when I've wanted to quit. May writers everywhere have such support.

To my champions: Donna Krone, who helped me remember that the LGBTQQ young adult fiction market isn't, actually, fully saturated and that one more book for queer kids so they don't have to switch pronouns when they read is, in fact, a good thing. • Pam Noda, who asked me regularly about the book's progress with sweetness and interest and who shared her own joys of having worked as an editor and bringing a book to market. • Dennis Martin, who listened when I said, at least a hundred times, that I wasn't going to be able to finish the book, that I wasn't really a novelist after all, that I might as well just give up. And who said in reply, at least a hundred times, "Yes you can, yes you can, yes you can." • Sabrina Roblin, who checked in with me on my writing developments, all the while sharing her musical milestones. What a boss!

To my spiritual teachers: Fred Jealous, who showed me that in order to be a strong man I had to be vulnerable. • Janet Thomas, who taught me to love women's innate strength as well as to look for the gold in any conflict (and who knows how to rock a witch costume!). • Karen Kimsey-House, Henry Kimsey-House, and Laura Whitworth, for being friends, colleagues, and top-notch human beings and for helping me to have a passion-filled career. I will be forever grateful. • John Vercelli, who reminded me not to ostracize the majority when taking a stand for the minority. • The Standing People, who pushed me to see that I was funnier than I thought and who gave me lots of opportunities to get over myself. • Jeanine Mancusi, an ardent supporter, friend, and my first coach, who helped me come out of the closet so long ago, who laughed and cried with me over my life's adventures, and who listened to countless early versions of Charlie. • Leza Danly, who encouraged me to breathe life into Charlie, making him as real to me as a nephew, or a neighbor's child, and who championed the entire arc of Charlie's development. • Leza and Jeanine together, two powerful witches in their own right, who guided me to take great interest in, and love, all parts of myself.

To influential authors, books, poems, stories: Keana Davenport's beautiful epic novel *Song of the Exile*. • Patrick Ness's *Chaos Walking* series and his brilliant insights into the adolescent mindset. • Marisha Pessl's *Special Topics in Calamity Physics*. Do you know that was her first book? How intimidating. • Amanda Hocking, who is the folk hero of indie publishing. • Donna Tartt's disturbing, fantastic *The Secret History*. • Suzanne Collins's *Hunger Games* trilogy. I deeply appreciate her work on the impact of violence on children. • Elizabeth Gilbert, for showing the humor in pain and the role of pain in life, as well as for her brilliantly clear stance on that controversial topic: marriage. I am a true Lizbian. • J. K. Rowling, who single-handedly helped magical adults the world over (including me) come out of the closet. • Stephenie Meyer, who swept me up in the romance of Bella's world (this is a minor miracle since I've never liked reading romance novels). • Harper Lee's *To Kill A Mockingbird*, and the way she tackled controversial subjects through the eyes of Scout Finch. • Truman Capote's painful, exceptional short story "The Thanksgiving Visitor." • Barbara Kingsolver's novel *Poisonwood Bible*, and the odd, brilliant relationship between the twins Leah and Adah. • Elizabeth Strout, for the complex relationships she weaves, especially in her books *Olive Kitteridge* and *Amy and Isabelle: A Novel*. • Mary Doria Russell, for her economy of language, her research, and her fine, fine storytelling (her book *The Sparrow* brought me to my knees) and for insisting that I tell the truth as one of her early readers. I feel smarter just by knowing her. • Ursula K. Le Guin's *Earthsea* series, and for the artful way she matured her protagonist over the seasons of his life. • Pablo Neruda's poem "Morning (Love Sonnet XXVII)," or "Desnuda" in Spanish, because it's lush and beautiful and it inspired Tom's interaction with Grace at the Vancouver International Airport. • Ruth Chew, whose urban witch stories enchanted me as a young boy. • Alice Walker, Toni Morrison, and Gloria Steinem, my first official feminist writers. I know they are three different people who write differently and live in different places, but in my mind they all live in a writing enclave together somewhere, which includes both mountain paths and pavement.

To real estate folks: Su Harambe, Sonia and Kendall Baker, and Steve Hughes, for helping me buy my own witchy house in West Seattle.

To my trainers: Rene Bibaud, who not only taught me incredible rope-jumping tricks but is also a wonderful inspiring friend. • Helen Yuan, whose enthusiasm keeps me sweating and punching in the boxing ring in Shanghai. • Priscilla Bell, hands down the toughest trainer on the block. Her workouts push me past my own self-imposed limitations every single time. I am grateful for how this perseverance has carried over into my writing life.

To my fellow readers: Gretchen Batton and Bob Price, early readers of all things Mary. Our teamwork, differing viewpoints, and mutual respect have taught me a great deal about how real readers respond to new material and how to enjoy editorial nitty-gritty.

To food: (A strange topic to acknowledge, I admit. But after the fourth or fifth early reader pointed out how much food was in the book, I stood back and said, "Huh. I hadn't realized." Hence, its own section.) Terry Sweeney, for his delicious gingery mocktails, and for trying to convince me that I'm a closet foodie. I'm not sure it's true, but the prospect is exciting. • Eric Gower at Breakaway Matcha, for his out-of-this-world matcha green tea, my beloved witchy potion for early morning (or afternoon) writing.

To locations: Savary Island, and Jeannie Goodlet who told me all about it. I hope to visit with her and Heather there some day soon. • The Pacific Northwest, especially during the autumn season, which provided much fodder for a young boy's imagination.

To coming out: Shane Ridenour and Jenny Starr. I can't remember which of them I told first, but I know I said something like "I might not be straight" or "There's this guy" or "I could be g-g-g-gay. Promise not to tell. I think I'm gonna barf!" Their support, the way they listened, and simply the fact that they didn't laugh at me or ridicule me have made all the difference to this gay man.

To my early readers: Francisco Mora, Jeanine Mancusi, Kim Fowler, Lauren Powers, Cat Williford, Mary Reynolds Thompson, Margot Page, Rachel Dodd, Tracy LePage, Carla Hamby, Michelle Goedde, Emma Wheat, Donna Krone, Ken Mossman, Leza Danly, Judy Jacobson, Jennifer McMaster, James Von Hendy, Laura Neff, Chong Kee Tan, and Zib Marshall (if I've forgotten anyone, please tell me!). Their questions, comments, and corrections were pivotal in making the book what it is today.

To my editors, book doctors, and business coaches: Anne Connell, for sharing her friendship with me and for introducing me to Liz. One day I might even be lucky enough to pass my work under her Scrutatrix microscope. • Julia McNeal, for her keen editor's eye, no matter how structural or specific, and for believing that what I had was a good story, that with a little tweaking (okay, a lot), could be a great story. • David Shakiban, a talented, fun, and funky website and book cover designer and a delight to work with. • Jason McClain, who just knows so darned much about virtual platforms and building readership and is an all-around swell guy. • Joanna Penn and CJ Lyons, for their ProWriter series without which this book would still be sitting in a Dropbox file. • Dennis Martin, who took the first version of this book that I uploaded on Kindle, replete with typos and horrible formatting, and whipped it into something clean, fresh, and inviting to look at.

To four pivotal comments/conversations: (in chronological order) With my paternal grandmother, Lorraine Geehan, when I was a wee kindergarten lad: "Jeffy, did you know that I happen to be a modern witch, who flies over your house at night on my vacuum cleaner to protect you?" This incredible admission was the genesis for my passionate interest in witches, even though I mostly didn't believe her. • With Martin Donald, while we perused art together at a gallery opening years ago (after I'd mentioned that I didn't find the painter's work particularly interesting and that I probably could have done better myself): "Yes, Jeff, but the difference is she did it and you didn't." This comment has been the singular driver in my creative life, helping me to toss aside excuses and keep writing. • With Susan Moreschi, during a hike on Mt. Tam in 2008 (after I'd told her that, while I enjoyed reading witchy stories, I found that the authors didn't get things right): "Of course they did. Because they're the authors' witches! Why don't you go write about your witches?" It was the perfect bracing face slap I needed. Not even a week later, I began writing about a young teen named Charlie. • With Mary Reynolds Thompson, on May 2, 2011, after having given me just the right amount of compassion in the months following my devastatingly freakish hard-drive crash, where I lost all seven hundred pages of the book after I had discovered that I'd never set up my backup system correctly (word to the wise: check your backup systems, people, I thought mine was fail-proof!): "All right, Jeff, it's time to start all over again and rewrite your novel from scratch. (Insert my whimpering noises here.) I know, I know, it sucks, but it's time to do it. Just start on page one, don't think about it too much, and don't stop writing until you've finished the first draft." As much as I hated to admit it, I knew she was right. I started the next day, and seven and a half weeks later, I finished it!

To family: My family is a lovely mix of original and chosen members. Their support and love are part of the bedrock of my life. • Mom, who saved every little story and Halloween drawing I ever made as a boy and who taught me that there is much laughter and celebration in life if you just know how to look for it. • Dad, a gentle giant, who not only loved me but also liked me a great deal. I miss him and sure wish I could witness him playing with all of the new techie gadgets they keep inventing these days. • My sister Jennifer, who somehow always welcomed me when I begged to hang out with her and her friends as a kid instead of treating me like the bratty little brother I know I was. • My brother-in-law Jack, who shares my love of great Pacific Northwest microbrews and whose addition to my nutty family has brought calm and a smile to our faces. • Jonathan and Justin, my two nephews, who still call me Jiujiu and who have gone from fun little rug rats to fine young men in the blink of an eye. • Nana and Gramma, my two grandmothers, each so different from the other. From them I learned unconditional love, athleticism, the importance of appetizers, and the art of fine conversation. • My mom's partner Wes, who loves her and cares for her like a true gentleman. • Martin, my first life partner, who showed me that creativity is less an inherent skill and more of a developed muscle. His consistent belief that I would one day actually write a book has sustained me through challenging times. • Maren, my second life partner, who has always been game to find new ways to deepen our relationship and whose house, with its fun colors, soft sitting areas, and delicious food, has taught me the importance of creating an inviting home. • Gary, who encouraged me to always ask for what I want at a restaurant and who knows that one crucial ingredient in a really great meal is a deep belly laugh. • Hung and Leng, two lovely men, who to me represent the best attributes of being gay. • And finally, Terry Sweeney, my beloved, my man, my partner. His consistent courage, gentle encouragement, and the beautiful way he lives his life, give me love, joy, and a place to call home.

ABOUT THE AUTHOR

JEFF JACOBSON WAS BORN in Seattle, Washington, in 1968. When he was still in kindergarten, his maternal grandmother told him that she was a modern witch who flew over his house at night on a vacuum cleaner to keep him safe. While he mostly doubted the veracity of her story, he still liked imagining that it was true. This led to a lifelong romance with the idea of witches, and while growing up he read as many witch stories as possible. It only made sense that he would sit down one day and write his own version.

Jeff has also worked as a personal and professional coach since 1997 and has been a faculty member with the Coaches Training Institute since 1999. He recently moved to Southern California after working in Shanghai, China, for three years. He lives in Los Angeles with his partner and their two cats and is busy writing the next book in the Broom Closet Stories. *The Boy Who Couldn't Fly Straight* is his first novel.

Made in the USA
San Bernardino, CA
25 August 2017